CR Sept 5. ⇒ en _____ !

# GONE

Center Point
Large Print

Also by Randy Wayne White and available from Center Point Large Print:

*Night Vision*
*Chasing Midnight*

# GONE

## RANDY WAYNE WHITE

CENTER POINT LARGE PRINT
THORNDIKE, MAINE

This Center Point Large Print edition is published in the year 2012 by arrangement with G. P. Putnam's Sons, a member of Penguin Group (USA), Inc.

The text of this Large Print edition is unabridged. In other aspects, this book may vary from the original edition. Printed in the United States of America on permanent paper. Set in 16-point Times New Roman type.

ISBN: 978-1-61173-579-6

Library of Congress Cataloging-in-Publication Data

White, Randy Wayne.
Gone : a Hannah Smith novel / Randy Wayne White.
pages ; cm.
ISBN 978-1-61173-579-6 (library binding : alk. paper)
1. Fishing guides—Fiction. 2. Women fishers—Fiction.
3. Florida—Fiction. 4. Large type books. I. Title.
PS3573.H47473G66 2012b
813'.54—dc23

2012025916

For Georgia Wilson White, and the
iron-willed Wilson sisters of Rockingham, N.C.:
Johnsie, JoAnn, Judy, Della Sue, Vera,
Authorena, and my dear Aunt Jewel

The Ox Woman (Sarah McLain Smith) had blue eyes and wore her hair in a bun at the back of her neck, as did many women at that time. She was always polite and well-spoken, behaved as a lady, and was grateful for anything that was done for her. There was no record of her ever having misused her great strength to injure anyone, or do harm.

—Phil Philcox and Beverly Boe,
*The Sunshine State Almanac and Book of Florida-Related Stuff*


Pain is an inescapable part of the human experience. Misery, however, is not. Misery is an option.

—S. M. Tomlinson,
*One Fathom Above Sea Level*

# Disclaimer

# Author's Note

As a writer, I still enjoy advantages gained by growing up in rural areas where isolation and boredom were relentless motivators and keys to the limitless worlds that lie between covers, not coasts. Better yet, my isolation was split between bipolar geographies: farms in the Midwest and my maternal home of Richmond County, N.C., a solid place of cotton mills, tobacco, cotton and truck farming (of the vegetable variety), and some of the finest people I've known. The fact that many of these fine people were also my aunts, uncles, and cousins only added to the richness of a Midwestern and Deep South childhood that practically guaranteed that, even if I had failed as a writer, I was bound to succeed at *something*. My Mother, Georgia Wilson White, would not have tolerated anything less, nor would my sweet-natured aunts and charming, tough uncles, most of whom quit school to work in the mills or the field (which only accelerated their love of learning). And my Grandmother Rilla Nay Wilson? The woman did not brook fools, nor the lazy-witted, and she carried a pistol for a reason.

I share this because I feel a great affection for Hannah Smith, the protagonist of this novel, which is rooted in family stories and the music of Southern voices. My mother and her sisters were not only natural-born independent thinkers, they were (and are) *hilarious*. If Hannah's voice has a lyrical, authentic ring, the credit goes to the Wilson sisters of Hamlet and Rockingham, N.C. —most especially my late Aunt Jewel, who was by far the wittiest writer our family has produced.

Special thanks also go to: Ivan Held and Neil Nyren for entrusting Hannah to me; Wendy Webb, my companion, adviser, and friend; Mrs. Iris Tanner, a guardian angel; partners and pals Mark Marinello and Marty and Brenda Harrity; Dr. J. M. Miller, Capt. Mark Futch, Capt. Glenn Pace; my teammates Stu Johnson, Bill Lee, Gary Terwilliger, Don Carman, Victor Candelaria, Dr. Brian Hummel, and all of my Wilson family, especially my cousins Rev. Kearny, Robin, Kay, Tony, Debbie, Jimmy, Brenda, Roxanne, Jean, John, Jeanette, Tommy, Carla, Capt. John, Vickie, Bobby, Butch, Sandy, Dr. Doug, Cindy Sue, Sharon, Christy, John, Crystal, and Angie.

Much of this novel was written at corner tables before and after hours at Doc Ford's Rum Bar and Grille, on Sanibel Island and on San Carlos Island, where staff were tolerant beyond the call of duty. Thanks go to Debbie Bubley, Raynauld Bentley, Dan Howes, Brian Cunningham, Mojito Greg Barker, Liz Harris, Capt. Bryce Randall Harris, Milita Kennedy, Sam Khussan Ismatullaev, Olga

Jearrard, Rachel Songalewski of Michigan, Jean Crenshaw, Amanda Gardana, Rodriguez, Bette Roberts, Amazing Cindy Porter, Ethan Salley, Fernando Garrido, Greg Barker, Jessica Shell, Jim Rainville, Kevin Filowich, Kimberly McGonnell, Laurie Yakubov, Lisa Reynolds, Michelle Boninsegna, Sarah DeGeorge, Shawn Scott and Dale Hempseed, and master chef Chris Zook.

At the Rum Bar on San Carlos Island, Fort Myers Beach, thanks go to Kandice Salvador, Herberto Ramos, Brian Obrien, lovelies Latoya Trotta, Magen Wooley, Meghan Miller, Meredith Mullins, Nicole Hinchcliffe, Nora Billheimer, Ali Pereira, and Andrea Aguayo, Brian Sarfati, Catherine Mawyer, Corey Allen, Crissy McCain, Deon Schoeman, Dusty Rickards, Erin Montgomery, Jacqi Schultz, Justin Dorfman, Keil Fuller, Kerra Pike, Kevin Boyce, Kevin Tully, Kim Aylesworth, Kylie Pryll, Patrick John, Robert Deiss, Sally Couillard, Steve Johnson, Sue Mora, and Tiffany Forehand.

Finally, I would like to thank my two sons, Rogan and Lee White, for helping me finish, yet again, another book.

—*Randy Wayne White*
*Casa de Chico's*
*Sanibel Island, Florida*

# Prologue

When lightning zapped the water a mile from the boat, my fishing client, Lawrence Seasons, looked at me surprised as a child, and the fly rod went sailing from his hands.

"I felt that, Hannah!" he said, meaning the shock. His line had been in the water, connected to a six-foot tarpon that had just jumped, scales bright as ice against purple clouds that held rain.

I told the man, "I bet you did," and lunged after the rod skittering across the deck. Just before it flew overboard, I caught the reel, locked my fingers over the spool, and pulled until the barbless hook I was using set the fish free, which the tarpon confirmed with another greyhound jump. The breeze blowing off the water was suddenly chilly, I noticed, sweet with ozone and electricity.

"We've got to go, folks!" I said for the second time in the last few minutes. "Grab your seats, try to stay low." I was taking fishing rods from their vertical holders, storing them flat on the deck.

"My first tarpon," Mr. Seasons said, sounding dazed and a little sad. He was flexing his fingers to see if they still worked, or maybe to remind me that dropping expensive gear wasn't an everyday occurrence for him.

I told him, "You did a fine job, sir," which seemed to cover all the bases, and then hustled behind the wheel to start the engine. For more than an hour, I'd been watching thermals build over the Florida mainland, which is normal on a June afternoon. But when the breeze suddenly wilted, air dense as lacquer, I knew it was time to move. Trouble was, only minutes before, Mr. Seasons had finally hooked a big tarpon on a fly rod, after years of trying, so I'd waited longer than I should've to make the decision. Now if things didn't go smoothly, my clients and I might get soaked—or worse. From what I could see, hear, and smell, the odds weren't in our favor. The storm was moving fast, towing a mountain of black clouds, and my small boat is as open and flat as an upside-down iron. A "flats skiff," as the design is known by saltwater anglers.

I called, "Hang on!" and pushed the throttle forward, then touched the trim switches, accelerating, and soon we were riding, flat and dry, the storm right on our tail.

For the next several minutes, no one spoke, while I slalomed through a snarl of oyster bars, electricity sizzling behind us. Then I opened the throttle wider as the wind chased us toward the Gulf of Mexico, where, I could now see, a second squall was angling to intercept us.

Mr. Seasons spotted the squall, too. I could tell by the worried look on his face. Having a client who has fished the Gulf Coast for many years is usually a good thing, but there are disadvantages. I tried to reassure him by raising my voice over the noise of the wind. "We'll cut north in a minute or two. That'll put us in the clear."

"On a low tide?" he replied. "I don't know of any channels within a mile—"

"I do," I interrupted, but not in a sharp way. I wanted the man to stay calm, and not upset the woman he'd brought as his guest, Mrs. Calder-Shaun, a New York attorney. She was an attractive woman, even beautiful, although starched and plainspoken, but not used to small boats and big water, which I'd realized right away. She sat to my right, Mr. Seasons to my left, both of them gripping their seats as if on a toboggan that had hit a patch of ice.

"But, Captain," the man said, being formal to show his concern, "risk running aground in a storm? We don't mind getting wet. If it's safer to stay in deep water, why not—"

At that instant, there was a metallic buzz, then *KA-BOOM!*, an explosion so close it seemed to lift the hull off the water and suck the air from around us.

*"Christ A'mighty!"* the woman yelled, "Shut up, Larry, and let Hannah drive the damn boat!"

Beside me, Mr. Seasons sat back, a resigned look on his face, and I knew if I didn't take his advice and got us stuck in shallow water, he

17

would never charter me again. I didn't blame him. Wealthy fishing clients aren't easy to come by, so the temptation was to play safe and do what he'd suggested. But then I reminded myself that playing it safe wasn't safe because the storm behind us was crackling with high voltage, and the storm angling from the southeast was a wall of gray smoke, more lightning and rain.

"Up ahead," I said as if being conversational, "there's a little cut mullet fishermen call 'Hole-in-the-Wall.' Since you've got a boat of your own, I've been wanting to show you—and I can't think of a better time."

I'd been sitting because of the lightning, but now I stood to get a better view and to concentrate on what I was doing. My boat is small, but it's *fast*. I'd bought it used off a local marine biologist who'd rigged the thing with lights, electronics, and an oversized engine you wouldn't expect from a man who is bookish in his ways. The biologist had hinted that the boat would do sixty miles an hour in calf-deep water—power I thought I'd never need unless I was stupid enough to get caught by a storm. Now it had happened.

"Hang tight," I said again, and punched the throttle, which caused my head to jolt back in an unexpected way. Soon my eyes were tearing, vision fluttering because of speed and washboard waves. It took some effort to check engine gauges that confirmed oil and water pressure were just fine, with plenty of throttle left if needed.

Doing forty-plus, we dodged hedges of mangroves where pelicans roosted on leeward branches, then crossed a channel into water so shallow that white herons flushed ahead of us, a flock of spoonbills, too, feathers pink as rose petals in the storm-bruised light. Normally, I would have turned southwest, toward the main channel. But the storm was already there, picking up speed, dragging tentacles of rain across Sanibel Island. So I turned north toward what looked like a shard of mainland, it was so tightly joined by swamp and trees. From Mr. Seasons's expression, I could tell he was spooked and confused.

"Hole-in-the-Wall," I said, pointing. "You won't see it until we're on it." Twice, I had to repeat myself because thunder boomed behind us, a series of trip-mine explosions.

"That's all oysters and sandbars," my client argued, sounding more nervous when he finally understood. "You mean, where those birds are standing?"

It was true, there were hundreds of gulls and terns hunkered together in an inch of water, creating a line that fringed the island.

"No, sir," I replied. "The spot where you don't see birds—that's where we're headed."

The man muttered something and got a fresh grip on his seat. To my right, Mrs. Calder-Shaun sat with eyes closed, then surprised me by wrapping her arm around my leg. Something like that had never happened to me on a fishing charter, but I didn't mind. She was scared, we were the only women on the boat, and I was a little scared myself.

When we were fifty yards from what looked like a wall of mangrove trees, I prepared them for what happened next. "You might feel us bump bottom," I hollered, pleased by how steady my voice sounded. "The engine's gonna scream, but don't let it worry you. We'll make it."

We did make it, skating over two sandbars, my engine geysering water into a cloud of yapping birds before I got the boat trimmed, then steered us through an opening in the trees not much wider than my skiff.

What a change those few seconds made! We exited the storm into a river of glassy water, branches creating a tunnel of silence and shadows that rocked in our wake as we boiled past. I followed the tunnel to the left . . . to the right . . . carving a series of S turns as if on a country road. Then we broke free of the trees, after jumping one last bar, and the sun cleared the towering clouds at the same instant, so it was like the storm had never existed. I knew better, of course. We couldn't dally because the clouds were still chasing us, fast as a freight train. But the tricky part was over.

Beside me, I heard Mrs. Calder-Shaun say,

"How exciting!" to cover her embarrassment and give her an excuse to remove her arm from my leg. Mr. Seasons was staring at me in the way wealthy people sometimes do when appraising an employee, his eyes penetrating and as unemotional as a calculator. Now was not the time to say anything boastful, I decided, but it was tempting.

Instead, I pointed to a ridge of oysters exposed by the low tide. Marking the bar were six plastic milk bottles tied to stakes. "That's the old Mail Boat Channel," I said. "Used to be, there weren't roads or bridges to the islands, so one of the captains delivered mail twice a week. Not many folks use this cut anymore."

"Who maintains it?" the man asked, but I got the impression he was more interested in me than the answer.

"I never figured that one out. Mullet fishermen don't need the markers, so it must be part-timers. Something nice is, every Christmas someone sticks a casuarina pine on that bar and decorates it with seashells and stuff. To me, it doesn't feel like Christmas until I've stopped and hung a shell on that tree."

Mr. Seasons said to Mrs. Calder-Shaun, talking over my lap, "Hannah comes from an old fishing family. Her Uncle Jake guided me for years, before he died—plus that *other* work I told you about."

I wasn't going to ask what that meant, although I had some ideas. More interesting to me was that Mr. Seasons wasn't gripping his chair quite as tight, which gave me a good feeling. We were soon running parallel the oyster bar, following milk jugs, water on both sides not deep enough to cover my ankles. A few minutes later, we were north of Chino Island. Behind us, the storms had joined forces, and rain was gaining on us so fast, a sudden blast of cold air told me we weren't out of danger yet. I had planned on cutting west toward Captiva Island, where Mr. Seasons lives on a five-acre estate, but the odds were against us once again.

I wasn't worried, though. Half a mile away, I could see a tin-roofed cabin built on stilts, standing lonely as a stork in shallow water, a mile from the nearest land. A married man had willed the place to my late aunt—out of guilt, I'd heard—so our family owned it, but how and why, I wasn't exactly sure. The cabin—a "stilthouse," locals called it—was built with thick walls for storing fish back before there was refrigeration, so it was a good safe spot to be, if we could beat the rain.

We did, but only by a minute or two. Throttle backing, I stood with one hand on the wheel, the other holding an anchor, as we approached what would soon be the leeward side of the shack. Not until we were a few boat lengths away did I reduce speed, then dropped the anchor, playing out line, after punching us into idle so we continued toward the dock.

"Nicely done," Mr. Seasons said, but he was watching the squall charging us, only a hundred yards away. Rain was loud as a mountain river and getting louder.

"Stay put until we're tied!" I replied. I had snubbed the anchor to a stern cleat, hoping I'd guessed right about how much scope to use. Sure enough, just before my skiff's nose bumped the dock, I felt the anchor line stiffen and stretch, which is when I stepped up onto the dock and threw a quick clove hitch around a piling.

"Ladies first," I called, offering Mrs. Calder-Shaun my hand, then helped her onto the dock. The woman looked a little woozy but was smiling, and gave my fingers a squeeze that meant something, I wasn't sure what.

Soon, both clients were sitting beneath a waterfall that blurred the world around us, but they were snug and dry inside the stilthouse, where I was lighting a Coleman stove to make coffee. When the coffee was ready, I poured them each a mug, then stood outside beneath the breezeway so they could have their privacy. Some fishing guides try to be entertainers, too, telling jokes and stories during boring times, but that's not my way.

After a while, when the rain had slacked, I returned to check on the two. Mr. Seasons was looking at Mrs. Calder-Shaun, who was staring at me, both with odd expressions on their faces as if they'd just made a surprising discovery.

"I'm right about this, Larry," the woman said, her eyes still studying me. "After today? Goddamn right, I'm convinced—*if* the agency is still licensed."

The first thing that came into my mind was the private investigation agency my uncle had run—obviously the "other work" Mr. Seasons had mentioned before—and where I'd helped out at every once in a while. But I thought it was better to keep my mouth shut, so I pretended to want more coffee.

The man was nodding as I stepped toward the stove, then caught me off guard by including me in the conversation. "Would you be willing to meet for lunch tomorrow, Hannah? Just me, Martha has to fly home for the day. There's something I'd like to discuss with you."

"Fishing?" I said, turning.

The man exchanged looks with Martha, his New York attorney. "Around two would be good," he said. "I'll explain everything then."

"Noon's better," I replied, because it irks me when people dodge simple questions, and also because it was embarrassing to admit I had an open date tomorrow, at the height of tarpon season, when most guides were busy. "Even on days I don't fish, I've got a lot to do," I added, which was mostly true.

"Noon it is," Mr. Seasons replied, then said nothing more about it. Soon enough, though, I would discover that outrunning that storm had meant more to my clients than I ever could've guessed. How I'd handled myself had convinced them a woman fishing guide was a good choice to go in search of a missing girl—although it took some doing on their part to convince me, the woman fishing guide.

Considering all that happened afterward, good and bad, I have no reason to regret beating that storm. But it has made me fretful about how one small event—something as common as lightning and heavy rain—can change a person's life in ways so big, there is no hope of returning. Only hope for what comes next.

# One

My mother says I reopened Uncle Jake's private investigation agency because I'm always losing men, so it's natural for me to search for things that are missing. This would offend some women my age, but she had a stroke two years back and now her damaged brain relies on honesty instead of good manners, so I've got no choice but to take it in stride. One thing I've learned is, don't argue with the truth on those scarce occasions when you're lucky enough to know what the truth is.

Mother was heavy on my mind the next morning. It's because of something that had happened the night before, after the storm. Loretta—that's Mamma's name—got into Uncle Jake's paint shed, then sprayed swearwords all over the walls of a house being built next door. Not a house, really. It's more of a concrete box the size of a Walmart, and just about as tasteful—which is only one of the reasons Loretta hates the building so. Some of the words she wrote were so foul, they had never even passed my lips—not louder than a whisper, anyway—let alone would I use Day-Glo orange to write them in cursive, exclamation points dotted, *t*'s neatly crossed, for all the world to see.

Well . . . as much of the world that ventures down the road to York Island and our little fishing village, which is on the Gulf Coast of Florida, just across the bay from Sanibel Island.

Thank goodness, it was only an hour after sunrise when I discovered what that addled woman had done. I was on the dock, making sure my skiff had enough fuel for the trip to Mr. Seasons's place, when Arlis Futch whistled and waved to me from the throttle of his mullet boat.

I waited for the man to kill his engine and drift closer before calling, "How you, Arlis?"

"My Lordy, Hannah, you lookin' more and more like your dead aunt every day—God rest her soul."

Old Arlis loves to talk, and I had things to do, but it peeves me when men confuse lying with flirting. "Aunt Hannah's been in the grave ten years, Arlis, so that's not much of a compliment. Except to her, maybe, but you might be right. Hannah Three in her coffin is probably prettier than me and all the rest of us put together. Don't you have some work to do?"

There have been four Hannah Smiths in our family, which Arlis knows better than most, so there was no need to explain. My aunt was a pretty woman, and more than a tad wild, which is common knowledge. Along with the stilthouse, which a guilty husband had left her, I had inherited Hannah Three's name, height, and crow-black hair. Unfortunately, that was about it—until a few years ago, anyway, when my body began showing some of her other assets as well.

The old man started to apologize, saying, "Dang it, I wasn't comparing you to a dead person—though you are lookin' pasty since you moved across the bay. Tell the truth, now. You been eatin' too much that damn hippie food and not enough fried mullet. Ain't I right?"

Hippie food, I guessed, was anything that didn't produce grease for gravy or a good old-fashioned heart attack. I was about to suggest this to Arlis by inquiring about his recent double bypass, but the man slipped the hook by staring over my shoulder, with a weird expression on his face, like an image of Jesus had just materialized in the sunrise clouds behind me.

"I wouldn't've missed this for nothing," he said to himself, chuckling, then began to laugh. "Loretta and me learned cursive from the same schoolteacher, so I recognize her hand. But her spelling used to be better. Tell your mamma the word *truckers* starts with a *t*—same *t* that don't belong in the word *ship*."

That's when I turned and saw it.

"Oh dear," I said, jumping up onto the dock. "My Lord! Maybe if I get her to apologize, they won't call the law." Even before her stroke, no one would have described my mother as "sweet," but neither had she, or anyone else in our family, behaved like trailer park drunks. I didn't want to believe what I was seeing.

Arlis was still laughing. "Tell 'em it's modern art and send 'em an invoice. Don't apologize. Folks who'd dig up an Indian mound to build a big-ass dog kennel might be trashy enough to believe it."

The old man was right about what Loretta's neighbors had done. Our village sits on a paw of waterfront that is dotted with the remains of shell temples built three thousand years ago by Florida's first people. "Indian mounds," some call them, but they're more than that. When tourists think of the Sunshine State, they picture Mickey Mouse, not pyramids, but that's what the mounds were, and a few dozen still remain between Tampa Bay and Key West.

There was one less pyramid now, which was the main reason Loretta was mad enough to combine her painting skills with her knowledge of profanity —neither top-notch, which her only daughter was now ready to confess in a court of law.

"You're gonna need some help," Arlis said, rubbing his bad leg before swinging his boat alongside the dock. Arlis had been bitten by an animal of some sort a while back—a giant reptile, he claimed—and never missed a chance to rub his wound to remind people he had survived.

I was still gaping at the stuff Loretta had written. The sentences were neatly spaced, I had to admit, and easy to read even from a long distance because Day-Glo orange is like a magnet to the eye.

"Some of those words, you don't hear every day," I remarked, keeping my voice low. "Where in the world you think she learned them?" It wasn't that I really wanted to know, but it was important to make clear she hadn't learned the words from me.

Arlis replied, "Hannah One chopped wood for a living, and I suppose they'd come natural to a lumberjack who also hunted wild hogs. Could be your mamma learned them in the cradle. I was jest reading something about that: parents got this computer program, recites foreign words to

29

their sleeping babies. By the time they're off the teat, those babies are talking whole sentences in French, Italian, you name it."

I turned and started toward the house because the old man would have stood there jabbering all day if I'd let him.

Arlis couldn't let it go, though. By the time I was off the dock, stepping through mangroves, he was still offering possibilities, calling, "Lock up her computer at night, that's my advice to you. And check with the cable company—make sure Loretta ain't watching HBO!"

Two hours and a gallon of turpentine later, Arlis and I were just getting the last of the mess off the stucco when the brain-damaged artist appeared. A daughter doesn't need eyes to know when her mother is charging up from behind. Loretta pushed a wall of tension ahead of her that had a brittleness like glass. It made my stomach knot and set off an alarm in my ears.

"Hannah! What you and Arlis think you're doing? That paint cost your Uncle Jake four dollars a can, and I was up writing past midnight! Not that you care. Or that I hurt my ankle real bad when I slipped off that damn ladder."

The last part, she said in a self-pitying way as if she'd broken a bone and would soon die.

"Loretta," I replied, wiping my hands on a rag, "I've got an appointment with Mr. Seasons at noon, as I've told you more than once. That gives me less than two hours to clean up, which is not much time for a woman who smells like a pine tree and has orange fingernails—" I turned and looked at Arlis. "Is it in my hair, too? Please tell me my hair isn't orange."

The old man appeared nervous, and was backing away, as Loretta informed me, "I'd of used lavender, if we'd had it. Aquamarine can be nice, too—so blame your uncle for his poor taste in paint, not me."

Then her tone suddenly became suspicious.

"As for Lawrence Seasons, that man has been coming here to catch tarpon and snook for twenty years, but I don't trust him. Never did. Never will."

My mother and I had been over the subject umpteen times the previous night, and I didn't want to cycle through it again. Her brother, Jake, had died the year before, and I'd been taking out his fishing clients for almost two years, which is when my sweet, funny uncle first got sick. Now Mr. Seasons was *my* fishing client, along with about twenty of Jake's regulars. Combined, it brought in enough money for me to rent my own place, and also pay for the nurses Loretta needs— one of whom would soon be explaining why she'd let a crazy woman escape with a can of spray paint and a head full of swearwords.

Actually, fishing came up a little short in the

money department. It almost always does for people who depend on saltwater for a living. It was now late June, and tarpon season was about over. Soon, we'd be in the dead months when tourists avoided the heat of hurricane season. By Thanksgiving, my savings account would be drained, and I'd have to find a part-time job, as I'd done for the last two years, to see us through until Christmas.

I turned and headed up the shell mound, toward the old tin-roofed house where'd I'd grown up. Loretta had to hustle to keep up, still fuming.

"Why's that old snob want to see you? Is it about fishing?"

I shook my head, and reminded her, "It's unprofessional to speak badly of clients—Jake warned you more than once. Mr. Seasons brings interesting people on the boat, he's polite, and he tips nice. That's all I care about."

"Sure, sure, but why's he want to see you if it's not about fishing?"

I shook my head again, meaning it was none of her business. Truth was, I still didn't know, only that I was to meet him at his estate on Captiva Island, which was a ninety-minute drive by truck but only fifteen minutes across the bay in my fast little boat.

"That man's got as much personality as a bucket of ripe mullet," Loretta said. "Did I mention he made a pass at your Aunt Hannah?"

"Yes, I believe you did," I replied, staying calm. *Mention it?* My God, she'd told me a hundred times.

"And Hannah Three, well . . . I'll bet the old snob got more than he bargained for *if* he made it past that girl's front gates. Right to your face, Hannah would admit she liked men as much as some men like women. And she had an eye for the rich ones especially. Not that your aunt ever took money—that I *know* of."

I said, "Don't start, Mamma."

" 'Course, most men were scared of Hannah Three—but those were the ones she'd hop into bed with, once she had 'em buffaloed. There was a term she used to excuse her raw behavior"—Loretta had to think about it as she clumped up the hill—" 'Womanly hormone something,' as if a naked man was a type of vitamin pill. She was sort of like a spider that way. You know about female black widows, don't you?"

I was on the porch, holding the screen door open, saying, "Yes, Loretta. Now, go on inside where it's cool, and let Mrs. Terwilliger bring you some sweet tea. I need to shower and wash this paint out of my hair. Tonight, I'll give you a call and make sure you're okay."

Loretta didn't move, though. She stood there staring up into my face. "He just wants inside your panties, I hope you realize."

"I've got no interest in Mr. Seasons, so just quit."

33

"Darling, that's not what I'm saying. There hasn't been a man in your life for years. And that one was only around for a day after you was married, so it hardly counts."

I knew I shouldn't bring up my friend Nathan Pace, but I did because he was all I had as a defense. "What about Nate? I have dinner with him two or three times a week, and he's a man."

"In the looks department, maybe!" my mother countered, a wicked grin on her face. "I used to think the same thing about Liberace. Only difference between him and that butterfly Nathan is, one of them had nice hair and played the piano." Loretta's eyes started to drift. "Nathan don't play the piano, does he?"

"Violin," I said, feeling tired. It was how Nathan and I had met—in high school band, two outsiders thrown together less by mutual interests than a mutual fear of not measuring up.

Her eyes snapped back.

"Keeping company with a muscle-bound homosexual is no way to attract a man, Hannah. Not the ones who got no interest in *wearing* your panties, anyway."

I tried again, even though it was pointless, by mentioning our good-looking UPS driver, whom I enjoyed seeing in his brown uniform, particularly when he wore shorts. "Christian Rhoades is getting friendly," I argued. "I suppose you haven't noticed how often he stops even when he doesn't have a package."

"Men in uniforms!" Mamma snapped as if that meant something. "A handsome boy young as Christian, with a good-paying job to boot, he won't let hisself get trapped by a woman your age. You're bad as Hannah Three sometimes. I swear you are."

I looked at my toes, which is something I'd promised myself I'd stop doing—acting ashamed when Loretta got that scolding tone in her voice.

"That Seasons man still married?"

"I don't know," I replied, which was not the first lie I had told this woman who had carried me in the womb but was slowly becoming a stranger.

"A wife don't matter to rich men," Loretta countered with a sniff. "They collect lonely spinsters like bottle caps. Especially spinsters with mileage as low as yours." I shook my head and sighed while she added, "It's a poor hunter who waits for the game to come to him, Hannah Smith. You did the same in high school—sat around moping instead of getting out, meeting boys. How you expect to catch fish if you don't dangle some bait? You need to stop being so prudish!"

I said, *"What?"*

"Dress pretty for a change, honey—that's all I'm saying. Something without too many buttons and straps. Lawrence Seasons is a snob, but he'd probably treat you good for a couple of months just to prove he can afford it. And he might have a workman on the payroll who's younger and got some money. And less morals than our good-looking UPS driver!"

Finally, it was all too clear what my befuddled mother was suggesting. I stood taller and pointed to the kitchen door. "Go inside right now! I'll be in after I've thanked Arlis."

"Darling, I'm only saying it's the rusty hinges that snap first. As wrong as your Aunt Hannah was about *her* morals, she was right when it comes to a woman's hormone tensions being dangerous. At the grocery, I read in a magazine that's why Lizzie Borden did what she did with that axe. And she was a girl in her twenties just like you!"

Actually, I'd turned thirty-one earlier that June, which I was about to point out, but then Loretta became secretive and wagged a finger for me to lean closer. "It's not like I don't know what you do to calm your frustrations. But using a plastic gadget can't be healthy, child."

My ears were suddenly warm. I said, "Pardon me?"

Loretta lowered her voice. "I found the electric candle you kept hidden in your dresser. That's not what God had in mind when he gave us hormones, honey."

My face feeling hot, I turned my back and

was reaching for the door but could still hear my mother saying, "First time I plugged it in, the thing went shooting across the floor like a snake on a griddle. I'm surprised you didn't hear me scream . . ."

The woman was still talking as I walked, then jogged down the Indian mound toward the dock. I still had almost two hours before my meeting. Time enough to get to my makeshift apartment, shower, change, and then make my appointment —if I hurried.

I did hurry, cowboying my skiff fast across the flats, running backcountry through the secret cuts and tidal riffs that I had learned as a girl, and was still learning, in truth, because currents can change shallow bottom as fast as wind can change the shape of sand and snow. I was mad at Loretta for invading my privacy with her sneaky ways and her tainted suspicions, so I drove harder than usual, eager to put some distance between the house where I'd grown up and the future that lay ahead. It's not that I felt bitter about my past. I didn't—not on a daily basis, anyway. I was just weary of the life I'd lived with my mother, eager to shed the past as cleanly as some creatures can shed their skins. It's not that easy, of course, but it is doable—or so I've convinced myself. All I know for sure is, the only way to leave something behind is to keep moving ahead.

That was easier said than done, though, after some of the things Loretta had said to me. Especially galling was her claim that I'd done nothing in high school but sit around and mope. Had the woman lost her memory along with the best half of her mind? I had gotten good grades, played clarinet in the band, swum on the varsity team, and always had a paying job of some sort, often working for my Uncle Jake—although, as even I had to admit, my teen years weren't the happiest of times.

I still think of high school as the three long years I spent trying to recover from the upset of acne and middle school. I was the gawky, silent girl in the back of the room who slouched because I was too tall and who used whatever I could to hide my face when someone tried to strike up a conversation. In all that time, I'd had only one date and kissed only one boy—my childhood neighbor, Delbert Fowler—whom I married six years after graduation because he joined the Army and believed he was going off to war where he might be killed by *Malls-lums*. From the way Delbert pronounced the word, I always suspected he pictured himself plinking away at a bunch of charging Nordstrom hoodlums wearing towels on their heads.

I was in my mid-twenties before another man gave me a second look, and almost thirty before men actually stopped and stared—even then I worried it was because of the few faint acne scars hidden by my hair. Only lately have I begun to suspect the truth. Men look at me now because they *like* what they see. Not that I'm sure it's true—I'll never feel the sort of confidence some have when it comes to being comfortable with their looks. But when I go striding by a group of men wearing jeans and a nice summer blouse, or stockings and a crisp skirt, what I see on their faces is a look of slow surprise. It's as if they don't expect to be interested, but then their brain gives them a kick to remind them of what their eyes are actually seeing.

I hope it's because I'm a big woman, too big for a quick snapshot, so it takes men a while to put all the parts together. I'm beginning to believe it's true because what I see next on their faces is usually a confused smile, like they're boys who've been caught at something they enjoy but shouldn't be doing.

Not that I spend my hours worrying about what men think. The last few years have been a happy, comfortable time for me, and I'm content enough not to rush. Some of us mature and blaze early in life. Others take longer to grow into the person they are meant to be. I bloomed very late, which, in truth, has surprised no one more than me. Maybe my brain will never fully replace the person I used to be with the woman I've become because, like a lot of people, I grew up feeling lonely and unattractive and that's the person I wake up with every morning. It's the same girl who sometimes still bawls herself to sleep at night. But when I get into one of those moods, feeling down, just a stubbed toe away from an hour-long crying jag, I go to my closet, lay out my best clothes, turn the lights down real low, and stand myself in front of the mirror.

The lighting is important, so I take some time and get it just right. Then I feel a lonely girl's delight as I watch a grown woman change moods as she changes and rechanges her outer skin. That woman is a whole lot different from the homely child she once was. That woman has long, long legs. Her thighs might be a tad heavy, her ankles definitely too thick—but not too thick to wear elegant stiletto heels with peep toes. Or a pair of crystal pumps that the woman found for ten bucks at a Palm Beach thrift shop. *Ten bucks!* The woman has decent hips, too, and a waist that appears skinny enough, but only because her shoulders are so darn wide from swimming laps. Things get better, though, as the lonely girl's eyes move up the mirror where the woman spills out of her favorite 34D bra just enough to cause the girl to get teary-eyed and smile, because she, in her own mind, is as about as shapely as an ironing board balancing two peas.

Sometimes it takes a while to convince myself that the woman in the mirror is me. Not a fashion model, nope. That'll never happen—unless God drops everything else to lend a hand. Or unless shower curtains become some kind of fashion craze. But my body is pretty darn good, thank you very much. And my face is strong and sometimes handsome—even pretty—when the light is right. Good high cheeks, glossy hair, and eyes that are sharp and perceptive when they aren't focusing on those few old scars that even the little girl realizes helped create the strong woman she has become.

Just being alone on a fast boat improved my mood, feeling the sunlight and smelling the wind. By the time I'd showered and changed, I felt a lot better, even though I had only thirty minutes to get to Captiva Island for my appointment. By car, the drive would take an hour and a half an hour even in the light summer traffic. So I did what I often do when in a hurry: I got in my boat and flew.

# Two

Mr. Lawrence Seasons placed a napkin beneath his glass, scowled at the ring on the table, then summoned the maid, before telling me, "I invited you because we have a problem and a woman's insight might be helpful. It has to do with my niece. She hasn't disappeared, exactly. But we

41

don't know where she is and she won't return our calls. Every two weeks, though, as required by the trust, she telephones the executor's office—that's my office. But then hangs up before my secretary can ask any questions."

I said, "Hmmm," as if I understood, but, of course, I did not. "How can your secretary be sure it's your niece calling?"

"We gave her a list of test questions that only Olivia could answer. It's the first thing she does when Olivia checks in."

"Olivia . . . ?"

"Olivia Tatum Seasons. My late brother's only child."

I asked, "Any close friends you could get to talk to her?"

"We've tried," Mr. Seasons said. "Olivia doesn't have many friends—not that she trusts, anyway."

"What about Mrs. Calder-Shaun? She seems like a nice lady. Or her mother? Sometimes a minister can talk to people when no one else can."

He shook his head. "Her mother moved to Europe long ago. And Olivia's stepmother is only ten years older than Olivia. She was an actress. Still is, I suppose. And, well"—Mr. Seasons swirled the ice in his glass—"she and the stepmother have never gotten along. You can see why it's become a problem."

"What about Olivia's cell?" I offered. "Most phones have a GPS signal."

The man attempted to cloak his impatience at what I realized was an obvious suggestion but was still polite enough to reply, "Yes, actually, we did think of it. She's turned off the GPS service. Or gotten a different phone."

To my left, outside the ballroom-sized enclosure that screened the swimming pool, a cabana, and an outdoor gas kitchen, I could see a dock through the foliage, and the shiny transom of Mr. Seasons's expensive yacht. The vessel dwarfed my little skiff, which was tied in the shallows like a waiting pony. I was beginning to wish I was on my boat, and gone. But I tried again by asking the niece's age and what she was like.

"As a person, I mean," I said.

"Olivia just turned thirty—about the same age as you, I would guess. But her behavior is not as . . . *solid?*" The man thought about it for a moment, his silver hair catching the light. "No, that's not the right word. Olivia has lived a privileged life, I'll put it that way. It's like mothers who use antibacterial soap. Their children don't build up the necessary immunities—you know, out there wrestling in the mud, swapping germs on the playground. The same with Olivia. Her father's wealth protected her, so now she doesn't possess the immunities—street savvy, you might say—that a woman needs to function in the real world." He paused when we heard the click of shoes on Mexican tile.

43

I had been doing my best not to gawk but the maid was marching toward us and I couldn't help glancing beyond her into the library beyond. Through doors framed with pecky cypress, I saw a room that was a museum of artwork and antiques. A chandelier sprinkled light across a marble floor, then spilled over onto sculptures, Renaissance-looking paintings, an oriental carpet, and the largest fireplace I'd ever seen in Florida, or anywhere else.

I said to the maid, "Thank you, ma'am," as she poured tea over ice, then returned my attention to Mr. Seasons. "I can't imagine how I can help. But I'd be pleased to try."

The man waited with exaggerated patience while the maid wiped the table and didn't respond until she was out of earshot. The interruption prompted him to say, "Everything we say here is confidential—I'm sure I don't need to tell you that."

"Sure—of course," I said, and tried the tea. It was unsweetened instant tea, weak as tap water. I was reminded that by boating five miles across the bay, I had entered a different world. I'd left behind what remains of Old Florida and was now in one of the wealthiest enclaves of the North's southernmost state.

"You know, I've been very impressed by your competence as a fishing guide," he continued. "I hope I didn't offend by mentioning confidentiality. It's not that I'm sharing some terrible family secret, it's just—"

"First thing I learned," I said, trying to help the man, "is my clients have a right to their privacy, whether they're on my boat or a thousand miles away at home. What they say when I'm around leaves when they leave the dock. Fishing guides who aren't respectful don't last very long."

*"Exactly,"* Mr. Seasons said, then sat up straighter and smiled as if a pleasing thought had just come into his mind. "I bet Captain Jake taught you that. Professionalism. He took a lot of pride in what he did."

"My uncle knew his business," I agreed.

"My God, I fished with Jake for almost twenty years before he got sick. All kinds of weather. I've always said you can learn more about a man's character in eight hours fishing than you can in eight years at some damn office pretending to be something you're not. That applies to women, too, of course. You are a very impressive young woman, Captain Smith."

I smiled my appreciation, although I don't particularly like being called captain. In my mind, a real captain stands at the wheel of a ship, not a twenty-one-foot skiff.

Mr. Seasons's mind was still on the subject of fishing. "March and April were my favorite months because we'd hunt those big female tarpon at the mouth of the river. But we'd go

45

holidays, too. Christmas was always fun, if the bay wasn't too rough. I remember one afternoon—this was around Thanksgiving, I think—it was glassy calm, like summer, and Jake took me offshore looking for tripletail. Now, the tripletail is a very strange fish, isn't it? Floats on the surface like a giant leaf. So convinced it's invisible, you can scoop it up in a net, don't even need bait. Some people are like that. Unaware of their vulnerability, secure in their own illusions. I'm afraid my niece, Olivia, might be one of them."

I nodded, aware he didn't expect an answer.

"Tell me, Hannah, have you done much fishing in the Ten Thousand Islands area?"

He was asking about a wilderness region forty miles south, a jigsaw puzzle of uninhabited islands, black water, and swamp that abutted the Everglades. I could picture the mangrove shadows and smell the brackish air as he continued, "I've fished there twice. Liked it, but found it a little spooky, too. For an outsider, I mean. All that unmarked water . . . all those little backcountry towns where people're still suspicious of strangers. Everglades City, Caxambas, Goodland, Chokoloskee—do you know the waters down there at all?"

For some reason, I got the strong impression the question had more to do with his missing niece than fishing. I said, "Vacations, Jake would take me camping on Panther Key, just off the channel into Everglades. There's a little strand of beach, and we'd fish the whole area. Refuel and sometimes eat at Chokoloskee, there's a couple of nice places. You knew Mary, before they split up?"

"Jake's wife, of course. A, uhh. . . a lovely lady."

There was nothing lovely or nice about my uncle's poisonous ex-wife, but I said, "She didn't care much for being outdoors, so I filled in."

Mr. Seasons liked something about the way I said it. It caused him to grin, and remember, "Jake always told me his niece was the son he'd never had. And he was the—"

*The father you never had,* is what the man meant to say but caught himself in time. Instead, without fumbling too badly, he finished, "—he was the best uncle he could be to his favorite niece."

In that instant, I liked Mr. Seasons better than I had during the five or six times he'd chartered my boat. Thought it was sweet of him to worry about hurting my feelings as I watched his smile turn inward, aware he was thinking about the days he'd spent on the water with my uncle. Mr. Seasons had a nice face, tan and smooth with angles. Still handsome for a man in his fifties, which may seem strange for a woman my age to notice, but Loretta is right when she accuses me of liking older men. Particularly the strong ones, and Mr. Seasons certainly qualified. His was the sort of regal face you see at charity functions, framed neatly by a starched tuxedo collar, or at tennis clubs where people dress in white and talk about the heat.

Because of mother's gossiping, it was a battle not to imagine this fit-looking rich man when he was fifteen years younger, trying to seduce my aunt who was wild in her ways and who loved men—something I knew for a fact because I've read Hannah Three's journals many times. But then the man saved me by launching into a story about landing a hundred-pound bull shark, which required that I pretend to be interested.

Mr. Season went on for several minutes about catching that shark, which clients tend to do when they've enjoyed themselves. My tea was gone when he finally changed the subject, saying, "Over the years, a man's fishing guide becomes an extended member of the family. That's how close Jake and I were." His eyes focused tight on my face. "He did some other work for me, too."

Now we were coming to it. He said, "It was my understanding you worked for Jake at the little investigation agency we started. Office work, but you also took the state test and got your license—what, about three or four years ago?"

Part of what he'd said surprised me. "I knew my uncle had a financial backer, but I didn't know it was you, Mr. Seasons. You're the one put up the money for the office?" Now I was worried, think-ing maybe Jake had died owing the man money.

Seasons didn't respond. Instead, he sipped his drink, eyes still on me, waiting for the rest of my answer.

I said, "Well . . . I worked part-time at the agency while I was going to community college. I was after an associate degree in criminal law, so it was a good fit. And Jake needed the help. But we were never that busy, you know—Jake mostly fished. Four, maybe five years, I worked a few afternoons a week, or at night, at the agency. Depending on how much free time I had from my studies. Sometimes, I even got class credit for what I did."

Because it was true, I had to add, "Jake never took the business that seriously, in my opinion. It was just something to bring in a little extra money. And because I think he sometimes missed being a police officer after he got hurt and was put on disability."

I didn't like the way Mr. Seasons was staring at me now. It made me uncomfortable, and gave the impression this wealthy man in the creased slacks and white Ralph Lauren shirt knew things about my own uncle that I didn't know myself.

Turned out, he did.

Lawrence Seasons looked down, seeming to be perturbed that the ice had melted in his drink.

"I forget," he began, which told me I was being tested, "when was your uncle shot? Was it when he was working undercover in Tampa? Or when he was in South America, working for that federal agency?"

Sometimes I dislike myself for not being able to hide my reactions better, particularly when I'm embarrassed, or—in this case—blindsided. My uncle had worked for a federal agency? It was news to me.

I replied, "Mr. Seasons, we agreed your family's business is personal and private. Just because my family lives across the bay doesn't mean I don't expect the same courtesy. If you want to discuss your niece, I'll listen. If not, I've got work that needs doing."

Instead of being offended, the man nodded his approval. "Made you mad, didn't I?"

I shrugged, the way people do when they're lying.

He set his glass on the table as if he'd just made a decision. "You've got backbone, Hannah. And you don't rattle easily. I like that. I've always suspected it, but you proved it yesterday, the way you took charge when that storm chased us. Other times, too—remember last year when I told you to gaff that tarpon? A seven-foot fish, had to weigh close to two hundred pounds. Biggest I've ever landed. Wanted to have it mounted, but you refused. There was nothing I could say to change your mind. You are one stubborn lady."

What the man had wanted was to hang a dead

fish for his friends to admire and to snap pictures. By refusing him, I'd made him so angry he'd only tipped me five bucks, then booked two different guides later in the week before deciding he had better luck on my boat.

Even so, I reminded him, "Fish mounts are made from Styrofoam and plastic. All the taxidermist needs is the measurements. There was no reason to kill that fish, Mr. Seasons, or I would have done what you told me. I'm not stubborn when it comes to taking orders—unless I know I'm right."

The man laughed as if I'd said something funny, then turned serious. "You still haven't answered my question. The reason I fronted money to your uncle is because I needed someone I could trust to do certain jobs for me. Background checks, mostly, on staff I hired to take care of our properties in Florida, or people who came to me with business proposals. Your uncle had an incredible amount of local knowledge when it came to fishing—but also about people, too. In an area like this, where almost everyone's from somewhere else, that's more valuable than you probably realize. Local knowledge and integrity —that's a rare combination these days. What I'm getting at is—" The man paused, then changed his approach. "There's a legal term—'due diligence.' Do you know what it means?"

I did, but I let him talk.

"It has to do with taking responsible steps to gather information in an accountable way. If for some reason I had to go to court or to my insurance agency, I couldn't just tell them, 'Well, I hired my old buddy Captain Jake to do the background check because he's an ex-cop and a great guy.' It would be meaningless. But if I hired a licensed, bonded professional by the name of Jake Smith, I would have fulfilled my responsibilities regarding due diligence. Same person, same talents, but entirely different in a legal sense. We could then pursue the matter through whatever legal avenues available. Opening that little agency was my idea, not your uncle's. I suspect you didn't know that either. Understand now why I'm asking personal questions?"

Mr. Seasons was looking at me in a kindly way, but there was also an underlying bedrock seriousness that is not uncommon in my successful clients.

I decided to open up a little. "Jake was always after me to better myself any way I could. I got my captain's license because of him. Never thought I'd need it, but he gave me the books and helped me study. Same with the private investigator thing. In Florida, a person with two years' experience at an agency can apply for a Class C license, which my uncle insisted I do. Then when Jake got sick, he had me upgrade to a Class M license so I could sign paperwork that needed taking care of."

"Have you kept your license current?"

"No need," I replied. "It hasn't expired."

Mr. Seasons was pleased, I could see it. Because I didn't want to mislead him, though, I felt obligated to add, "But I won't renew it when the time comes. There's a fee, and I have no interest in doing that sort of work. For one thing, I quit college before I got my degree, so I'm not qualified—aside from doing the computer stuff. I'm sorry your niece is missing, but if that's why you asked me to lunch, I've got enough charters booked to last me through the first week of—"

Lawrence Seasons was searching around for the maid, still perturbed about his melted ice. As he stood, not looking at me, he interrupted, "Just a few seconds ago, didn't you say you never thought you'd need your captain's license either?"

"That's different," I told him. "Finding fish is something that comes natural. And I *like* my clients. It always irks me when I hear some guide talking about his anglers like they're idiots. Why in the world would someone go into the business if that's the way they feel? The main thing, though, is—and I don't mean to be blunt—agency work, the investigating part, is *boring*. Hunched over a computer for hours, calling strangers on the phone. Jake offered me the business, maybe you know that, too. But we were only billing about two or three hours a month, which didn't even pay utilities. So we closed it officially a few weeks before he went into Hope Hospice. Now I've converted the space into a sort of apartment, and that's where—" I hesitated because it was embarrassing to admit I was living in a parking lot next to a 7-Eleven and a fitness club. So I left that part out, saying, "—and that's what happened to the little building you helped Jake buy."

Maybe Mr. Seasons heard me, maybe he didn't. I got the impression what I was saying didn't matter much, anyway, because the man had already made up his mind. I found that irritating. He had invited me to his home, the least he could do is listen respectfully.

Instead, though, he said, "Excuse me," turned on his heels, and carried his empty glass into the house before I could finish what I was saying.

Loretta accuses me of having a temper, which might be true, but only when someone is unfair or treating others like they're not worth the time of day. That's the way I felt now, so I got up, exited the pool area, and walked toward the dock, telling myself I should hop in my skiff and go home—although I knew I wouldn't do it. Then, a moment later, I heard Mr. Seasons calling, "Hannah—hold on there!" then turned to watch him maneuver through the lanai door, trying not to spill his fresh drink in one hand and carrying what looked like an old leather briefcase in his other.

"Needed to check on my boat," I told him, then waited for him to join me on the dock.

"Here," he said, handing me the briefcase. "These are some things Jake asked me to hang on to but I kept forgetting to return. You can look at them later. Let's get our business settled first, okay?"

Too late. I had unsnapped the case, which was heavier than expected, and saw that it contained two oversized books, one of them on Florida history that I remembered seeing as a girl. As I stowed the briefcase beneath my skiff's steering console, I couldn't help but stare up at the yacht moored a few yards away, which he noticed. His expression suddenly warmed as if he'd just had a good idea.

"A beauty, isn't she?" His eyes were tracing the vessel's clean lines, all teak, tempered glass, and stainless steel. "I had her built in Palmetto almost . . . my God, more than fifteen years ago. It's a shame, really. Sits here at the dock like a yard decoration. Only used the thing once in the last two years. My wife hates Florida—I've probably mentioned that. So I have one of the Jensen brothers stop every week or so, when I'm traveling or in New York, just to start the engines. She's a real work of art, don't you think?"

Actually, I'd been thinking what a pain in the backside it would be to maintain a vessel that size, but I complimented the craft anyway by saying, "I've always favored boats with midnight blue hulls and white upper decks. Yacht-sized boats, anyway." I gestured to my skiff, which is twenty-one feet long, flat as an iron, and overmuscled at the stern with a 220-horsepower outboard. "In a fishing skiff, though, I like light blue. Or gray. Makes it harder for other fishermen to see me and steal my spots."

Mr. Seasons enjoyed that kind of talk and it showed. He asked a few questions about my boat, then about how chartering was going—a money question, which I dodged—then got back to business.

"Let me ask you something. You helped with Jake's P.I. work, so you know I was one of his few clients. Maybe his only client. Which means you probably did some of the background checks I ordered. You and I have fished together for, what, almost two years? Yet you've never mentioned it. And a few minutes ago when I asked about my dealings with Jake, you avoided telling me. Why?"

I started to answer, but he stopped me, holding up a hand like a traffic cop. "You have character, Hannah Smith, that's why. Character and local knowledge. You don't gossip and you don't risk compromising your clients by opening your mouth. Same with people you care about. Am I right? Plus, you know how to handle a boat, which I think is a must in this case."

I could feel my ears warming, but not because of what Mr. Seasons was saying. It was the way he was looking at me suddenly, his eyes liquid blue in the sun, moving over my jeans and blouse as if I were a freshly framed canvas. There was a pleased expression on his face that showed a hint of surprise.

I asked, "What's wrong? Is . . . something on my—?" My fingers automatically confirmed my blouse hadn't come open, then wiped at my cheek, expecting to find a streak of that damn orange paint.

Mr. Seasons made a dismissive motion with his hand, his expression now telling me *Relax.* "Sorry if I was staring. It was something the sun did for a moment . . . the way the light hit your face just now."

I cleared my throat, and said, "I should be wearing a hat, I guess. I usually do." As I spoke, my eyes sought the safety of the bay and found it, focusing on a hedge of mangroves where pelicans roosted heavy as bricks on guano-streaked limbs.

"That's not what I meant, dear. It's an odd sort of experience, maybe it's happened to you. You meet a man, or a woman, and that first impression sticks in your brain for years. Then you run into them at some unexpected place—an airport, maybe . . . or the light changes, like it did just now—and you're surprised to find out the person looks nothing like the picture that's stuck in your brain. Especially if you don't see the person very often."

"Why don't you tell me about your niece, Mr. Seasons," I said to ease the awkwardness we were both feeling. Then I glanced at the sun to remind him the temperature was already in the eighties on this June afternoon.

He got the hint. "Let me show you around the boat. Would you like that? It's not really big enough to call a yacht, but it's a damn fine day cruiser. Or at least it was."

"It runs twin Yanmar diesels?" I asked. "The lines sort of remind me of a Hinckley."

The man interpreted my interest as assent.

He said, "Come aboard. If I can get the air to work, and if the mildew's not too bad, we'll talk business inside. Someone with local knowledge, that's exactly who I need to track down my niece. Martha agrees—it was her idea, in fact. Martha's not easily impressed, but she's sold on you. The woman kept me on the phone half an hour last night, which is a marathon session for someone like her."

I didn't know how to reply to such a compliment, so I didn't, which must have caused Mr. Seasons to think I was being stubborn again. "I know, I know, talk is cheap. So give me a few minutes to outline what we think is a very solid proposition. For you, possibly even career changing. Then we'll have lunch—and I'll even book another charter as thanks no matter what you decide."

"There's no need for that," I said, watching him undo the chain to the boarding ramp. "I've got no interest in changing careers. And . . . well, I'm just going to come out and say it. What if your niece doesn't *want* you to find her?"

Mr. Seasons glanced over his shoulder at me, his eyes suddenly hard. "If ninety million dollars were transferred into your account the instant you signed a legal document, would you want to stay missing, Hannah? Or would you want to be found?"

# Three

The next morning, idling my skiff along the back side of Captiva Island, I was telling my body-builder friend Nathan Pace, "Olivia's uncle thinks she's living on a boat somewhere on the west coast of Florida. Olivia didn't date much. She was practically a recluse, he says. But then she got involved with a guy the estate hired to build a stone seawall. Big guy with an attitude, Texas accent and a belt buckle—that type. For three weeks, he lived behind her house in some kind of cabin cruiser. I'm not sure of the make, but the guy knows boats, I was told.

"Three weeks ago, he finished the seawall, took his pay, and pulled out. Olivia left a note and disappeared a couple days later. But not actually disappeared because she stays in touch by phone, which is why her family can't get law enforcement involved—she's not actually a missing person. Plus, I don't think they would anyway. They're real private. People with money don't like seeing their names in the paper."

"What do you mean, 'the estate' hired him?" Nathan asked, shifting his weight from one leg to the other, which caused my boat to tilt. The man is two hundred fifty pounds of muscle, kindness, and childhood scars.

I said, "Olivia lived in Naples—her father's house before he died. A gated community called Port Royal. Mr. Seasons is executor of the trust, but his attorney—Martha Calder-Shaun, the one I told you about—is the one who actually looks after things."

My friend was nodding. "I know who she is; seen her around the island. She's so freakin' beautiful—drives a white Bentley convertible. All business and style."

"That's her," I agreed. "She hires managers to take care of the family properties, so it was one of the managers who had the seawall built. She didn't hire the guy. She's mad as can be because the manager didn't run a background check. In Port Royal, that's required of workers."

Nathan made a whistling sound. "Bavarian castles on the sea. I made a delivery to Port Royal once when I was working at the furniture store. Properties start at around five mil."

I filed the information away before adding, "There's a chance you might know the guy who built the seawall, too, Nate. Or know someone who knows him. He's a gym rat like you. Lots of muscles. And he supposedly lived in this area for a while."

"On Captiva or near Fort Myers? Half a million people live in this county, for cripes' sake."

I was about to explain, but then we rounded a bend in Roosevelt Channel, and I said, "There it is"—meaning Mr. Seasons's dock, where his yacht floated blue and solid on a turquoise slate that was speckled with mangrove shadows and sunlight.

Nathan was with me because I needed his help and also because, coincidentally, he'd just finished at the fitness center as I was leaving my apartment early that morning. He wanted to pick up some things from a friend's house, which was easier by boat, and it didn't take me out of my way much. There's a famous photographer who lives on Captiva, and he and Nathan had been close for a year or so. How close, I'd never asked, because I suspected my oversized friend would've had fun providing more details than I wanted to know.

Nathan is considered shy by most. Some even wonder if the man can speak English, that's how quiet he is. Around me, though, he jabbers and jokes, and tries his best to embarrass me whenever he can. Always privately, though. Never in front of others, which makes it okay. As Nate says, "People didn't include us when they had the chance. Why include them now that we're old enough to relax a little and have fun?"

If you're thinking neither one of us enjoyed high school, you are right.

Nathan wasn't joking now, though, as he gazed at Mr. Seasons's thirty-seven-foot yacht and said, "He's going to let you live aboard *that* for a year? It's too small, for one thing. And you can't dock on Captiva because of zoning. My God, Hannah, you'd have to live in some crappy backwater marina full of mullet fishermen and crabbers."

It wasn't like my friend to be so negative, and I was a little hurt, which the man noticed, so became instantly remorseful. "That was a bitchy thing to say, I'm sorry. Truth is, Four, I'm worried I won't see you as much if you move away from the gym."

"Four" was his pet name for me, as in Hannah Four, which made me feel better. I said, "I've got an SUV and a road map, so don't worry about me finding you. And it is a *pretty* boat, isn't it?"

The big man grinned, which was something he didn't often do because of a crooked front tooth. "Pretty? Are you kidding? It's drop-dead gorgeous! So I guess I'm jealous, too. Does it have a galley and a full shower?"

I was happy to have a chance to talk about the boat's appointments, especially the kitchen area. "It's got two burners, even a little oven and a stainless Sub-Zero mini-fridge. Originally, the stove was propane, but Mr. Seasons had it replaced with electric."

Nathan liked that. "Propane's dangerous. Remember the sailboat that blew up a few years back?" He took another look at the yacht, nodding. "A freakin' awesome place to live—especially for a *single* woman who doesn't date."

I ignored the barb by reminding him, "It's not a done deal yet. And I'd have to do all the maintenance work, of course. The boat needs a bottom job and a good cleaning. The bilge is a mess. It's a Marlow Prowler, built in Palmetto, which is near Tampa, I think. If I owned a boat like that, there'd never be a drop of oil on it. Or a spot of mildew."

I couldn't pull my eyes off the Marlow even when Nathan asked me, "No strings attached? You can't be serious."

"Not the sort of strings you're talking about," I replied, giving him a look.

"Gezzus, even if it's true, the least you can do is surprise the man with something special. He'll expect it no matter what he says."

I replied, "He's not the type to appreciate a thank-you card. And I couldn't afford much of a present."

"No! I'm thinking more along the lines of giving him a peek. Just a quick look—that's a hell of a lot better than a card."

I didn't understand what Nathan was talking about, which he could tell from my expression.

"A *peek,*" he repeated. "You know, as in flashing the man—but in a tasteful way, of course. A quick look at your breasts at the very least. You have an incredible body, Hannah—not that anyone suspects, the way you dress."

"Quit," I told him, but I was smiling. Probably a hundred times I had idled past that midnight blue boat on my way to South Seas Plantation or the Green Flash Restaurant, carrying clients, and I'd never given the vessel a second glance. Now, though, looking at the Marlow's lean, old-timey lines, her sparkling stainless work, gave me the pleasantest feeling in my chest. Like Mr. Seasons had said, even though a thing is right in front of our eyes we sometimes don't see the truth of it until the light shifts in just the right way or the unexpected happens.

In this case, the unexpected was that I had agreed to search for Olivia Tatum Seasons. In return, I would be paid expenses, a flat fee that was more than I made in two months of fishing, a bonus if I found her, and I would also be allowed to live aboard the Marlow for a year—but only after I had delivered a sheaf of legal documents into Olivia's hands. Whether or not she also had to sign the documents, I was still unsure and, frankly, was afraid to ask. I'd never experienced such a sudden change in fortunes and I was reluctant to risk the happiness I felt.

Accepting the job meant canceling my fishing charters for the next two weeks and e-mailing the necessary documents to Ms. Calder-Shaun to confirm my uncle's investigation agency was still licensed and state-bonded. All of which I'd accomplished before midnight, but I'd still found it hard to sleep.

Mr. Seasons had given me an incomplete dossier on his niece, Olivia. A leather-bound scrapbook sort of thing that I'd stayed up until two reading. Then I stayed awake another hour, sitting at the computer, researching everything from stone seawalls to steroids. I was being honest when I told Mr. Seasons I wasn't qualified for the job. Now that I had accepted, though, I was by God going to do everything I could to fulfill my end of the bargain.

Probably because the memory of the way Mr. Seasons had stared at me was still fresh, my ears warmed a tad as Nathan continued to chide me, saying, "Seriously, Hannah. Don't be obvious about it, but you owe the guy something special. The man's an art lover, you said."

"Lots of paintings in his house," I agreed. "The classic-looking kind you see in museums and books."

"There you go. And your body is as classic as any Hollywood actress. All the right curves, just taller—although you're too stubborn to believe it. I've never opened a *Playboy* magazine in my life, but, I swear, Hannah, even *I* love your tits."

I shot back, "You've never seen me that way and you know it," trying my best not to sound flattered. Nathan has no interest in women in a physical way, but compliments of that sort have been scarce in my life, so I wanted him to stop exaggerating—but not drop the subject entirely.

"Have too seen 'em. The day you took me snook fishing and you had to go overboard to cut a crab line off the propeller. You were wearing a white T-shirt and a lacy bra. Same thing."

The man grinned and leaned to look shoreward, which caused me to hold the steering wheel so as not to lose my balance. "Is that his house through the trees?"

Both of our heads were turned as far as they could go, so I clicked the throttle lever into neutral so we could take our time. From the channel, forty yards away, Mr. Seasons's estate was five acres of tropic foliage and vines, landscaped neatly as a pineapple plantation. You couldn't see much of the house. Just a wedge of gray wood and a chunk of chimney framed by hibiscus and coconut palms with leaves as green as parrots' wings.

I'd already told Nathan that Mr. Seasons said I could hire a part-time researcher, so I decided to get back to business. "You haven't said you'd take the job. It would mostly be computer stuff, just a few hours in the morning when I'm traveling. Mr. Seasons thinks it would be smart for me to work my way down the coast by boat, talking to people at marinas. It wouldn't interfere with your job at Sanibel Rum Bar, but you'd have to sign a contract of confidentiality. I found blank contracts in my uncle's files and brought one along just in case."

"Why down the coast?" Nathan asked. "If his niece is on a boat, they could have headed north just as easy. Or taken the river to Lake Okeechobee, across to Lauderdale. She could be anywhere."

I replied, "A friend thinks he saw Olivia on Marco Island, getting into a boat," while I opened the console locker and brought out a computer bag, aware my skiff was drifting toward Mr. Seasons's dock. Nathan was still looking toward the house, standing on tiptoes to get a better view. "Is there a pool?"

"Big one with a black tile bottom," I answered. "I like black tile in a pool a lot better than blue. You don't see that many. If I had the money, that's what I'd pick."

Nathan looked at me, using his hands like a filmmaker, wanting me to imagine something. "Okay, here's how you do it. You're out lounging by his swimming pool, getting a tan. No . . . it's

67

dark, with a big full moon. Which is when you notice the great man standing at the window. But a very lonely man because his wife's a bitch and she doesn't like Florida. Or sex, or fishing—or anything else that's fun. Poor bastard hasn't seen a fine pair of young breasts in years. With me so far?"

I said, "My God, you're something," which didn't stop Nathan, of course.

"That's when you and the great man make eye contact. When he's at the window—only for a second, though. It's an electric moment—for him, at least—then you turn so you're in profile. That's when you let your bikini top drop to your feet. Don't even look at it—your top, I mean. Like it's all accidental, but he *knows* it's your private way of thanking him. A personal gift to a lonely old man who has too much money to count."

Nathan was grinning again, but then the grin faded because of what he saw in my face. "Oh, now you're *mad*. What'd I say? Usually, you like it when I talk dirty. Lord knows, it's the only sex thrills either one of us gets."

"I am not mad," I replied, my tone formal, pretending to concentrate on what was inside the computer bag. "It's not professional to speak ill of clients, that's all."

"Speak ill? Christ, Hannah, all I said was you should let the old guy have a peek at your goodies. There's nothing bad about that—unless you think it might give him a heart attack or something."

I was tempted to point out that Nathan was thirty years younger than his famous photographer friend but didn't. "That's not the way you talk about a person who's paying for your livelihood," I told him sternly. "Besides, Mr. Seasons can't be much more than forty-five or . . . or so. A lot of people consider that middle-aged."

Nathan was looking at me like I was nuts. "Sure—if we lived to a hundred. I wait on Mr. Seasons sometimes when he comes into the bar. That's how I know he's unhappy and his wife's a bitch. Trust me, the man's closer to sixty than forty."

"He is not."

"You can't be serious. I know grandfathers younger than him. And a lot happier, too."

I snapped, "Lawrence Seasons is not a *sad old man!*" raising my voice and turning—which is when I noticed that Mr. Seasons was inside the cabin of the Marlow, door open now, looking at us from only thirty yards away.

I whispered, *"Shit,"* a word I seldom use. It was because I know how sound carries across water, so the man had definitely heard me. I shoved the computer bag into Nathan's hands, then slammed my boat into gear, eyes locked straight ahead. Because I'd surprised Nathan, though, the bag dropped to the deck, which caused the sheaf of papers to spill around our feet.

I didn't care. Putting distance between us, that beautiful boat, and Mr. Seasons was all I could think about. Even when Nathan knelt to gather the papers, asking me over and over, "What's wrong? Hey, what's the problem?" I ignored him and drove.

A couple of minutes later, though, when he said, "Does this guy have anything to do with the missing girl?" I had calmed enough to stop behaving like a statue, so I turned and gave him my attention. Nathan had gathered the papers Mr. Seasons had given me and was looking at a photo. I recognized the photo easily enough. I had spent time memorizing it the night before.

"He's the man they hired to build the seawall," I said. "They can't be sure Olivia went off with him, but it's what they suspect. His name's Ricky Meeks."

Nathan was still examining the picture but was now pursing his lips. "His name's not Ricky. Or maybe it is, but Mrs. Whitney called him something else. Mike . . . Matt . . . it began with an *M*."

"You *know* him?" I said, startled but also pleased because Mr. Seasons put a lot of stock in the value of local knowledge. Maybe I was already earning my money.

*"Mick,"* Nathan said. "Yeah . . . Mick, I'm pretty sure that's it. A woman named Mrs. Whitney used to bring him to the restaurant

sometimes. This was back around New Year's. For a week or so, those two came almost every night, usually just drinks. She always paid, of course, because she's a lot older—and she's rich." Nathan looked at the photo again. "Or Mickey, maybe. Which at least rhymes with Ricky, so it's the sort of fake name a guy would use."

I said, "You can't be sure from just looking at one picture," which I didn't believe but, suddenly, I felt uneasy because so much good luck was piling on me all at once.

"Nope, it's him all right." Nathan turned to me. "You're doing some kind of reverse jinx thing, right? Hannah, how can someone smart as you be so damn superstitious?"

I replied, "I just want you to be sure, that's all. Plus, you have to sign that confidentiality form before I can even let you see those papers."

Captiva Island, less than five miles long, isn't much more than an ancient sandbar built up over centuries, shaped by current and waves. Now it's rooted to the Gulf of Mexico by multimillion-dollar properties, sea oats, palms, and a couple of bayside marinas. We were approaching Jensen's Marina now. Nathan's photographer friend, Darren, lived to my right in a house with a pool and studio so beautifully designed, they blended into the island's foliage like elegant, storm-tossed shells.

Darren had gotten famous in New York,

photographing rock stars and actors, but now he mostly lived and worked on the island. He was a handsome man, willowy as a fashion model, and always had a whiskey in one hand, a cigarette in the other. We'd spoken only a few times, but Nathan liked Darren a lot, and his self-confidence had improved a bunch since they'd met. My friend seemed happy, and that's all I cared about. When we were close enough to Darren's dock, I reversed my engine . . . popped it into forward, spinning the wheel . . . then I switched off the key, and let my skiff drift itself to a stop, nudging the pilings as if it belonged there.

That's when Nathan, his shyness showing, patted my shoulder and assured me, "I might be wrong about the guy's name. But not about him and Mrs. Whitney. I remember 'cause the dude's so mean-looking. He, uhh . . . it made my hands shake sometimes when I waited on their table. Nervous, you know?"

Nate is the size of a pro wrestler, but he's timid as a bird, so I tried not to smile as I stepped out and tied the boat.

Ricky Meeks—the name I associated with the photo after studying it—was indeed a scary-looking man. The photo had been taken outdoors at a place where there was snow and a parking lot, possibly backdropped by a bar or strip club. Nothing in the picture to prove it, just a feeling I got. The man's sleeves were rolled tight, biker's tats and muscles on display like trophies, a deliberate spit curl calling attention to a face that leered at the camera as if he'd just insulted the photographer and knew the guy was too scared to fight.

"He has kind of a dirty redneck look," Nathan said, handing me the photo. "You think? And smelled bad, too. Sweat and cigarettes, but mostly this terrible, cheap aftershave. The dollar-a-gallon stuff you buy at Walgreens. Like limes mixed with cough syrup."

I asked, "What in the world was Mrs. Whitney doing with a man like him? I've never met her, but I know she's wealthy. It's the same family that started the cereal company, right? That's what I've heard, anyway . . . and they own a place—"

"Right there," Nathan said, pointing toward a screen of hedges a hundred yards down the seawall where there was a dock that was boatless, some busted planks hanging in the water. "I haven't seen Mrs. Whitney for a while. Months, probably. A lot of the owners are seasonal, so maybe she went north for the summer. I can ask Darren."

In my head, my courage was having an argument with my brain, saying it was too early to begin questioning people and that I hadn't done the proper research. But then my eyes swiveled toward Mr. Seasons's dock, a quarter mile away, where the Marlow Prowler was a pretty black blossom that glittered in the heat.

"Don't bother Darren yet," I told Nathan.

"Still intimidated because he's famous?" my friend chided. "Darren likes you, Four. His feelings are hurt because you never come up for a drink. My God, a few weeks ago the man practically begged to photograph you! That doesn't tell you something?"

It was all true, but that wasn't the reason I didn't want to ask Darren. I said, "Later, I'll stop and say hello, sure. But first I'm going to walk down to Mrs. Whitney's place. You know, find out for myself if she recognizes the photo."

"If she's still on the island," Nathan replied, sounding like he hoped she wasn't. Even so, he fell into step. We followed the bike path toward Blind Pass, past three driveways to a wrought-iron gate the size of a mall entrance. A bronze plaque read *Battle Creek Bay-N-Beach*, which was the sort of clever name owners call their estates on Captiva Island. I guessed it referred to the cereal town in Michigan.

"Gate's locked," Nathan said, rattling the bars, "unless you know the code."

"That's for people with cars," I replied. I paused to check for traffic, then slid between the gate and a hedge, onto Mrs. Whitney's property. "You going to let me trespass all by myself?" I asked. "Or you coming along?"

74

# Four

By the way Mrs. Whitney reacted to the photo of Ricky Meeks, I knew the man scared her and had somehow hurt her, too, even though she denied knowing him at first. Maybe not physically hurt her, but hurt her in the way a certain type of rough man can damage a woman who is twice his age and has lost everything that's solid about herself including her looks and self-respect.

"I really don't see the point in discussing some handyman I paid minimum wage to . . . well, I can't even remember what I hired him to do. Staff come and go, even on a property as small as this." Mrs. Whitney skated Ricky's photo onto the table, but I noticed that her eyes lingered on the man even as she reached for an ebony cigarette case.

I said, "Small?" We were in what felt like a Spanish palace with twenty-foot ceilings where arched hallways opened into more rooms and hallways, floors of pale marble, and a sound system that played Johnny Mathis, volume low.

"It's a winter house," Mrs. Whitney replied, exhaling and giving me a sharp look through the smoke. "But let's back up. Are you sure you're not here because this person"—she gestured at the photo—"is trying to get in touch with me? Two or three months ago, I had my contact information changed. Phone, e-mail, everything—my attorneys insisted, for security reasons. But if the man wants to come back . . . I suppose there's a possibility."

"He's not trying to contact you," I interrupted, and watched the woman's expression waver between relief and disappointment. "Your name didn't come up until today, Mrs. Whitney. Someone said they'd seen you two at a Sanibel restaurant. They thought the man's name is Mick, or Nick, but he also calls himself Ricky Meeks." I kept it vague because the woman had yet to recognize Nathan, who was standing behind me, or even look at him, which I found strange.

*"Ricky?"* the woman said like she'd just tasted something bitter. "I can't keep track of every minimum wage drifter we hire. But 'Mickey' sounds more familiar." When she tapped her cigarette on an ashtray and added, "As in Mickey Mouse—that's the only reason I remember," I knew she'd had feelings for the man, and maybe still did.

I watched her flick the photo toward the middle of the table as if to create some distance. No . . . that wasn't the reason. Mrs. Whitney *was* disappointed, I realized, which told me a part of her, at least, had hoped Meeks wanted to see her again. Her pride was hurt, and now the anger inside was starting to build. "Then I'm confused," the woman said, her tone sharper. "You're a fishing guide on the island?"

"I'm Hannah Smith," I repeated for the third time. "I pick up some clients at South Seas. Sometimes Jensen's Marina. Mostly, though, I work out of my house."

"Then why the questions like some kind of cop?"

Before I could explain, the woman shushed me with a wave of her cigarette. "Let me guess. You're carrying his photo because the guy knocked you up, then dumped you. Which fits from the little I remember about that bum. Or you lost a bar napkin with his phone number." The woman blew smoke toward the ceiling. "God spare me the trailer park dramas of the island locals. It's one of the blessings of money."

I don't have much experience with jealous women insulting me, but that's what was happening now. Mrs. Whitney had refused to unlock the door until I'd held up Ricky Meeks's photo for her to see. After that, she'd hurried us inside to find out the connection—or because she was ashamed someone would make the association. That's why I wasn't offended by the woman's mean words. She was revealing more about her relationship with Meeks than she realized.

"Admit it," Mrs. Whitney pressed. "You've got what we used to call a 'wet crush' on the man—

figure out for yourself what it means. Now you're trying to find him. Am I right?"

In my chest, I felt regret because I knew she was talking about herself, not me. So I tried to reassure her by saying, "I've never met him, ma'am," then immediately regretted using *ma'am*. It's something an older woman doesn't like, especially if that woman has invested in a face-lift, breast implants, and injections to make her lips so full that she had to feel to confirm her cigarette was in place before taking another long, aggressive drag.

"Sorry, kitten, don't believe you. Besides, I don't get involved with my employees' personal problems."

I replied, "I don't work for you, Mrs. Whitney," but the woman talked over me, saying, "If I hadn't been expecting my shopper, I'd have never let you two through the door. Where in the hell is that absurd little fool?" Suddenly, the woman got to her feet, pulled her white silk robe tight around her neck, and crossed the room to the front window, apparently hoping her groceries had arrived.

Silhouetted by the window, Mrs. Whitney's coil of orange hair had a chemical tint. Sunlight pierced the sheer robe so I could see that she was naked beneath it, her skeletal legs too frail to support the unhappiness I sensed inside her, let alone her melon-sized implants.

Nathan looked at me and mouthed the words *She's drunk,* which was something I knew from the whiskey stink of the room and the glass of melting ice on the table. Maybe drunk for days or weeks, judging from the woman's gray skin and shaky hands.

That wasn't the only evidence that Mrs. Whitney didn't have someone to look after her. Not even a maid. There were empty glasses piled atop magazines, volcanic ashtrays everywhere, clothing strewn on floors, and what might have been a Chantelle bra, raspberry lace and glitter, draped over a velvet divan. Seeing the bra caused me to feel even sadder because it was a pretty thing that Mrs. Whitney had probably had fun buying back in happier days. Near the door was a gorgeous mahogany secretary with feet sheathed in ornate copper. A month's worth of mail had been stacked there until a landslide had scattered envelopes onto logs of sodden newspapers below.

Something I expected to see, but didn't, were dirty dishes. If the woman had been eating, there would have been dishes, or takeout boxes, scattered among the litter. And she wouldn't have looked so sickly skinny. The realization replaced the sadness I was feeling with a chill. Why didn't a woman who lived in a ten-million-dollar palace have employees looking after her? That's when Mrs. Whitney hinted at the reason by flinging the curtains closed and calling across the room to us, "That lazy son of a bitch! And my attorney wonders why I fire every goddamn person I hire!"

Nathan and I looked at each other before I said, "The Island Store's close enough, we can be back in five minutes if there's something you need—" Just in time, I caught myself before calling her ma'am again, but the woman wasn't listening anyway. She was concentrating on her balance as she returned to the table, legs so wobbly that she zigzagged until she was close enough to reach out and grab a chair.

"Can I get you something to drink?" I asked, worried because Mrs. Whitney appeared woozy, tilting the glass of melting ice to her lips.

"A drink?" she said. "That's a laugh! There's nothing to drink in the whole goddamn house. The idiots I hire, they want my money, sure. But they don't want to do a damn thing to earn it. This little man who calls himself a 'personal shopper,' he's just another example. On the phone yesterday, he promised he'd be here no later than two. Three times, I made him promise! He's got a five-hundred-dollar order, groceries and liquor. That's worth how much to some out-of-work fool? A fifty-buck gratuity, just for starters. So where the hell is he?"

I noticed Nathan check his wristwatch, same as me, even though we both knew it wasn't even noon yet. The person doing her shopping wasn't late. Truth was, Mrs. Whitney didn't know what time it was. There wasn't much we could do, though, but sit and listen as the woman took off on a talking jag, ranting about undependable workers, then switched to the maid she'd fired a few weeks back for stealing.

Despite his size and all those muscles, Nate is sensitive. Loud voices make him wince. Angry voices cause him to retreat inside his head, often rocking where he sits, hands cradling his knees, even when he's not in a rocker. Nathan was rocking now, I noticed, but then he did something that showed his improved confidence. He got to his feet, saying, "Maybe the maid didn't put things where they're supposed to be, Mrs. Whitney. Mind if I take a look in your kitchen?"

The woman looked at him for the first time, her eyes struggling to focus. "I know you," she said finally. "I've seen you before."

"You usually drink Johnnie Walker Black, easy on the soda," Nate replied. "But sometimes you'll do a daiquiri, no sugar. Or Bloody Marys, if it's early. How about I see what I can find?" My friend had a soft look on his face that told me he was worried about the woman, too.

"Good luck!" Mrs. Whitney laughed, sounding more cheerful, but it was scary the way she said it. Way too loud, with a warble of hysteria. As Nate disappeared into a hallway, she hollered, "I've been through every goddamn cupboard and cranny in this house. In fact"—she gripped the arms of her chair, ready to stand—"I'll help you look."

Because her balance was so poor, I was already on my feet and prepared when the chair went over backward. I threw my arms around the woman and lifted her clear, startled by the way loose skin moved over her bones and the birdlike lightness of her body. It was like catching something warm but barely alive in a plastic sack.

"Get your goddamn hands off me! What do you think you're doing?"

If the woman was trying to wrestle free, she was so weak I didn't notice. I held her by the shoulders until she seemed steady, then pulled the chair I'd been using under her. "Have a seat, Mrs. Whitney. Are you okay?"

"And what the hell is that supposed to mean?"

I tried to calm her, saying, "Sometimes, when I get a head cold, it settles in my ears, and I can barely cross the room without stumbling. Have you felt some congestion lately? There's something going around, that's what everyone says."

"If you hadn't grabbed me, I'd have been just fine, you dope!" the woman hollered, but the anger was draining out of her, along with her confidence. She sounded frail, exhausted. Embarrassed, too, because she added, "Lately, I *have* had a sort of cough, which I figured was because of the cigarettes. But I would have

82

managed perfectly well without you crushing the wind out of me!" That was as close as she could come to apologizing, I figured.

"I'm sorry," I said, looking toward what must have been the kitchen. I could hear Nate opening and closing doors, then the suction sound that an expensive refrigerator makes when the freezer is opened. "Is your shoulder hurting?" Mrs. Whitney was using her fingers to explore an area near her neck, then her right arm.

"You're as strong as a damn man," she snapped. "Maybe you are—I don't see how anyone could tell for sure." The woman glanced at me, hoping she'd hurt my feelings or made me mad. She'd done both, but I wasn't going to show it, especially when she added, "Baggy denim shirt and shorts, my God—you look like a damn housepainter. Or some dyke who works at Goodwill. Have you ever heard of something called 'a hairstylist'?"

Loretta's damaged brain, rather than hardening me to insults, has taught me that mean words are the only way a person in pain has of striking out and warning others to keep their distance. Not that Loretta doesn't sometimes make me so mad I want to hurl a cup across the room. And not that all people can use that excuse. I've met men and women who've got so much poison in them, it'll seep into everyone around them if you give it the chance. But Mrs. Whitney had the cloudy, glittering eyes of a wounded dog that didn't want

83

to be touched. She had secluded herself inside this house and inside herself. Now she was warning me not to come any closer.

There was no knowing what events had dragged this woman so low, but Ricky Meeks had done at least some of the damage, I would have bet on it. From the way Mrs. Whitney looked, from the amount of trash that had piled up around her, she'd been sinking for months, which fit with the time line I was piecing together in my head. Meeks had worked for the woman in February, March, and part of April, too, from what Nathan had told me. According to the folder on Olivia Seasons, Meeks had moved his boat to Naples during the first week of May to work on the seawall, spending his nights at the dock behind Olivia's house.

I couldn't be absolutely sure the man had something to do with her poor condition, of course, unless Mrs. Whitney was willing to open up. Yet, I felt certain enough to risk taking the woman's hand in mine and saying, "After I've said what I came to say, I'd welcome advice on how to dress better. Thing is, Mrs. Whitney"—the woman was struggling to free her hand, so I released it and slid the photo of Ricky Meeks in front of her—"this man ran off with the niece of somebody I know. That's what they think, anyway. She's about my age but not a strong girl. Her family's got money, and it's made her sort of trusting and naïve. What I need to know is, is this man dangerous? If he's dangerous, if you think he'll hurt the girl, the family needs to do something."

That got the woman's attention but also might have wilted what little spirit was left in her. "My God," she said softly. She'd turned her head as if not trusting herself to make eye contact with Ricky Meeks, whose careful spit curl formed a hook, I noticed for the first time, above his small black eyes. "My God," she said again, then added, "he's doing it to someone else now."

The temptation was to ask, *Doing what?* but I decided it was better not to push. The woman was hurting inside and it showed—which had to be even more embarrassing for someone like Mrs. Whitney because she was revealing it to me, a stranger, who had nothing in common with her. That wasn't true of her and Olivia Seasons, though.

"The girl's father left her a lot of money when he died," I continued. "To inherit the money, she has to sign a legal document. That's why the family asked me to find her. I'm being paid, but that's not the only reason I'm doing it. I don't like rough men who hurt women. More than anything, the family's worried about him." I tapped a finger on the photo, thinking it might cause Mrs. Whitney to look.

She didn't. The woman had her face in her hands, so still and quiet it took me a moment to realize she was crying. She was sobbing harder when, a minute later, Nathan reappeared, carrying three miniature-sized bottles of liquor he'd found somewhere, the kind they serve on airplanes. He was proud of himself, all smiles, but then figured out why I had my arm around Mrs. Whitney, letting her rest her head on my shoulder. He stood there for a moment, probably fighting the urge to sprint for the door, then shot me an accusing look that asked *What the hell did you say to her?*

I told him, "Nate, why don't you walk over and visit with Darren for a while. I'll be there soon enough." Then, because he was flustered, I had to remind him, "Leave those little bottles. Mrs. Whitney would appreciate a nice cold drink, I think."

# Five

It took a while for it to come out, but what Ricky Meeks had done to Mrs. Whitney was rape her over and over during the weeks he'd worked for her, although not in a legal sense. At least, the woman wouldn't admit he'd forced her more than a little, at first, before she joined in and did things that still shamed her too much to talk about.

Not that I wanted details. Talking about such things has always made me uneasy, and feel sort of sneaky, even when the person is eager to share. What's private in a person's head isn't like seeing them step out of a shower. It's the sort of nakedness that can't ever be covered once it has been revealed.

Within fifteen minutes of Nathan leaving, the woman had downed the three airplane whiskeys, and her tears had turned into spitting anger. Instead of making her more wobbly, the liquor had steadied her enough so that she got up and paced while she raged about Ricky Meeks.

"That sick white trash con artist! He's only after her money, of course. Doesn't the stupid little bitch realize that? He's a predator. A two-timing predator—no more class than a wild dog."

I was still sitting at the table but ready to move in case the woman lost her balance again. Meeks had robbed money from her in some way, that much was clear. And I'd guessed they'd had a sexual relationship long before she'd finally admitted it. But calling him a two-timing predator stuck in my head as even more important because it had a double meaning. It told me Mrs. Whitney hated Ricky Meeks for what he'd done to her, but she hated him more for taking up with another woman. That was as troubling as it was confusing. How could she still feel jealousy for someone who'd hurt her so badly? It was so far beyond my understanding that I picked up Meeks's photograph, still listening to Mrs. Whitney, and gave it another close look, thinking maybe I'd missed something.

No . . . the man wasn't handsome. It was the same surly-looking face I'd studied before. Round dark eyes, and a leering expression that had a dirtiness about it. The same gaunt cheeks of a man who worked too hard with his hands and muscles to accumulate fat, but an otherwise ordinary face. Not good-looking, not even the oddball attractiveness that some plain-looking men have. I couldn't understand how someone who worked for hourly wages, and wasn't handsome, could have buried a hook so deeply into Mrs. Whitney's heart. But he had.

"What's the family's name?" The woman had her hands on the table, leaning toward me. She was asking about Olivia Seasons, I realized.

"Like a lot of people on the islands," I replied, "they're real private."

"I don't really care what their damn name is!" the woman said, getting madder. "I'm trying to find out if they're actually wealthy or just have a lot of money. There's a difference."

The way Mrs. Whitney said it told me the difference had to do not only with snobbery but also something that ran deeper. "You'd recognize the name," I replied. "I imagine you and your friends go to the same parties, if—" I stopped myself before saying *if you still go to parties.* Instead, I finished "—which might help you sympathize with the girl's situation. Knowing you have more in common than just him." I tapped the photograph again, but she still wouldn't look at it.

"What would you know about the people I socialize with? Outsiders and real estate bums crash parties all the time on Captiva. Tell me her goddamn name or you can waltz your big ass out of here!" The woman was being mean again, but not in the same way. This was more like a test, with some jealousy thrown in. Mrs. Whitney was dying to know who Ricky Meeks was with, which gave me hope she'd open up if I could win her confidence.

I stayed calm, just as I did with Loretta when she's being stubborn, and named fund-raising parties in Palm Beach and Sarasota I'd heard about from some of my fishing clients, including Lawrence Seasons. Then I took a chance and added, "They're part of the same group that goes to house parties and fund-raisers in Naples. A wealthy section called Port Royal—you know the place?"

The woman didn't say anything for a couple of seconds. "How could someone like you know about parties in Port Royal?"

Thanks to what I'd overheard on my boat, I added other convincing details. "The girl's family attends the big Valentine's fund-raiser every year.

The Wine Fest, too—which is bigger than the polo thing in Palm Beach. And why they don't bother with it anymore."

Until that instant, Mrs. Whitney hadn't looked at me, not really. I'd been a faceless female who might have been hired to trim bushes or clean floors but who, instead, had invaded her privacy with pestering questions and some bad memories, too. Now the woman was assessing me, concentrating in a way that seemed to sober her. "You understand more than I gave you credit for," she said finally.

I looked the woman in the eye but didn't offer a comment.

After a few more moments, she said, "Okay. So you might possibly know the difference between wealth and flashy money. You know people in our circle, anyway. But, bottom line, you're not going to tell me the family's name. *Are* you?"

"If we decide to trust each other, I will—but only if I get their permission first. I won't say I've never broken a promise, but it's not something that comes easy."

I learned something new about Mrs. Whitney from the way she misunderstood me. "Comes easily or comes cheaply?" she asked, pretending not to care much either way. "You expect me to pay for the name of a girl you want me to help? Just for laughs, name a figure. A thousand? Five thousand?"

The woman would have paid that and more to find out what she wanted to know. I could read it in her eyes. That's how desperate being with Ricky Meeks had made her, which for the first time, caused me to feel spooked and wonder what I was getting into. But I stayed calm, and told her, "You took what I said wrong. No point in discussing it."

"Honest and trustworthy," Mrs. Whitney shot back with a sneer. "I suppose you're brave and reverent, too."

I had to smile at that. Mrs. Whitney didn't have any psychic powers, that was for sure, or she'd have seen I was not the virtuous woman she'd just described. "Dependable," I responded. "That's about all I can claim. So you might as well drop the subject of money or the girl's name."

When the woman was angry, her nostrils flared. They flared now, spouting cigarette smoke. "You're a stubborn little bitch. Know that?"

"If it was your privacy I was protecting," I replied, feeling my face redden, "maybe you'd see it differently. I know you're mad. If it helps you feel better talking that way, I don't mind—as long as there's a chance of helping the girl we're discussing."

The woman leaned closer, and I realized she had spotted the faint scars that had made life miserable in high school. My abdomen went tense, but it didn't last. I've gotten over that embarrassment—

more or less. Instead of providing another target for her meanness, though, my dabble of scars—mostly hidden by the way I wear my hair—caused the woman to soften for some reason.

"Pass that here, would you?" Mrs. Whitney was stabbing an ashtray with her cigarette but also looking at the photograph of Ricky Meeks. There was a shakiness in her voice that told me she was done being mad and giving in to something else. Plain weary of being mean was a possibility. Or maybe she'd been reminded of scars she had carried into adulthood, as all people must.

She took a breath, reached for the photo, hesitated, then finally held the face of Ricky Meeks an arm's length from her own. "You son of a bitch," she whispered. What felt like a minute later she said, "You filthy animal."

After that, I didn't watch. The woman was battling her emotions so hard I got up and went to the kitchen out of respect for her privacy. In the cupboard, I found Tetley tea bags and a can of Campbell's chicken noodle, which I heated in a pan without adding water. Strong soup would be good for someone in Mrs. Whitney's condition. Aside from some canned milk and stale crackers, there wasn't much else in the cupboards but stacks of tinned capers, cocktail onions, rolled anchovies, and other stuff no one uses unless they're making a pizza or having a party.

On the counter, there were also three more little bottles of whiskey, part of a six-pack Nathan had managed to find. I knew it would be wrong of me to get the woman drunker in hopes she'd talk about Ricky Meeks. The last thing a fragile little thing like her needed was more alcohol. So I wrestled with my conscience until I found just the right lie to excuse my sneakiness, then carried the soup, a cup of milky tea, and the whiskey into the main room.

Mrs. Whitney was old enough to make her own decisions—to ease my guilt, that's what I'd told myself. But the lie didn't help when I saw the state she was in. The woman's face was so pale and makeup-streaked from crying, I didn't think I could feel any worse than I did when I put that tray on the table.

I was wrong. Without hesitating, the woman moved the cup and soup bowl out of her way and went straight for the whiskey as I knew she would.

"You asked if he's dangerous," she coughed, the first miniature bottle down her. "*Yes*. He's dangerous. And what he does—the goddamn pervert, he's a thief, too—he does it without breaking the law. He's not smart, but he can smell weakness. It's like an animal thing. And that's a hell of a lot more dangerous than being smart."

More concerned with the guilt I felt than with what she'd just told me, I said, "Mrs. Whitney, at least try the soup. It's good and strong—"

"And stop calling me Mrs. Whitney!" the woman snapped, sounding more sober and in control. She was holding out the second bottle, wanting me to crack it open, the wounded-dog look in her eyes gone. "It makes me feel even older. My name's Elka. And I'm not as old and washed-up as I might look." She waved vaguely at the chair next to her, then reached for her cigarette case. "Have a seat."

I did.

"There was a shrink I started seeing after Mickey took off"—she turned her head away from me to exhale smoke, the first show of politeness since I'd arrived—"and this shrink kept preaching to me about forgiveness. Forgive the man who'd totally screwed up my life, forgive myself. Yatta-yatta-yatta. Know what I told her, our last session?"

I shook my head.

"I told her forgiveness is for women who don't have the balls for revenge. I haven't shown any balls for a while, but that shit's about to change." Mrs. Whitney glanced at the photo, which she'd crumpled, then had tried to smooth out so I wouldn't know. "You're sure Mickey's with this girl you mentioned. Somebody's niece?"

"The family thinks so."

The woman smoked, disappearing inside her thoughts for a while. Finally, a bitter smile appeared on her face. "I guess I don't have to ask if you can keep a secret, do I? . . . Uhh—"

"Hannah Smith," I told her for the fourth time. Then, because it was the professional thing to do, I added, "We can sign a contract of confidentiality, if you want. I've got some forms on my boat. But first, eat some of that soup . . . Elka. *Please.*"

# Six

Darren, the famous photographer, was holding open an old *Life* magazine he'd taken from a stack and was saying to Nathan, "You don't see the resemblance? *Tell* me you don't see a resemblance."

Darren was smiling, having fun, eyes moving from the magazine to me, then to Nate, whose shaved head looked flushed like he'd worked out, gone for a swim, and maybe had a shower during the five hours I'd spent with Mrs. Whitney. We were in the photographer's studio, floors of blond wood, high white walls that were silken with sunlight from windows spaced along a beamed ceiling. The room, furniture, pastel colors meshed so cleanly, it was hard not to be jealous of the man's good taste. On the other hand, the thought that places such as Darren's cost more than my mother, Loretta, made in her lifetime didn't enter my head—but only because I'd reflected on that fact so many times while idling my boat along the back side of Captiva Island, or fishing with clients off the beach. On the west coast of Florida, it's something you get used to.

"Hannah . . . *Hannah,* at least have a look." Darren was feeling talkative after a few whiskeys. Not drunk, not disrespectful—the man was always so sweet and caring, it was sometimes hard to believe he was who he was. I knew he was working hard to make Nathan's friend his friend, too, so I let him see me smile and showed some interest in what he said next.

"I've obsessed about shooting you ever since you refused to sit . . . two weeks ago? No, three, because I'd just gotten back from L.A. But that's not the reason, dear. Ask Nate. Nate . . . tell her! I see you as a gawky American colt who's turning into a swan but doesn't realize it. Your heart's too . . . something. . . . Solid? Yes, too *solid* to know or even care. Said it from the start, didn't I?" Smiling wider as Nathan nodded shyly, Darren held up the magazine as if it were a prize. "Then I find this!"

Before I knew what I was saying, I replied, "A colt's a male horse, Darren. And shooting swans has nothing to do with taking pictures, in my experience. But I am flattered you think I look like a woman in an old magazine."

Nate turned to me, his expression stricken, and said, *"Hannah,"* which I felt in my chest because

I realized I'd been rude and I hadn't intended to be rude. Truth was, I still felt numb from some of the things Mrs. Whitney had told me regarding Ricky Meeks. Most especially were the embarrassing acts Meeks had forced upon the woman and other bad things he'd manipulated her into doing. Never in my life had I heard such stories and I'm not a naïve person. Like everyone else, I spend more time on the Internet than I should, sometimes peeking at videos and reading about subjects I know I shouldn't.

There was something else bothering me, too, which is probably why I'd snapped at the man without thinking. It was something nasty that Mrs. Whitney had said about Darren an hour or so after I'd made the mistake of mentioning his name to Nathan. The woman had been in one of her mean moods at the time. I wasn't ready to accept the meanness of what she'd said about Darren—and Nathan's stupidity—as truth, but I was feeling tense and on my guard more than usual.

I stared at my hands, which were folded on my knees, and said, "Darren, that didn't come out right. I don't know why but I'm still nervous around you. It's not you, and please don't fault Nate. It's my problem. You're always so kind to me, but then I end up opening my mouth and saying something stupid."

"The camera will see that quality in her—that *exact* quality," Darren said to Nate, which confused me but didn't stump my friend for a moment.

"Hannah's always had a gift for pissing off people," Nate agreed yet sounded defensive. "Especially when it comes to putting men in their place. But I'll always take her side, Darre. It's the way it's always been with us and that's not going to change."

Nathan's warning tone startled me, but Darren appeared to like it. "Her *honesty,* that's what I meant, you goose. Match the right camera, the right glass and light, and the lens doesn't lie. A person's soul is a robe worn on the outside. Like skin . . . or an aura."

"The outside," Nathan echoed, thinking it over while trying to hide his relief.

"A camera in the right hands, of course," Darren added, reaching for ice tongs, then a bottle with a label that read *Laphroaig,* which was scotch whiskey. "The soul on the other side of the camera has to commit total energy to the moment. All of his . . . well, it's a childlike quality. Spontaneous. An openhearted love of whatever the lens discovers. I don't let myself explore why or how it all works, it just does. Photography— art, not Photoshop tripe—has more in common with sorcery than engineering. Spirituality . . . passion . . ."

The man paused, looking toward the hall gallery where photos of actors and rock stars were hung, individually lighted, one of the most famous, an AC/DC guitarist, shirtless, mouth open wide in the spotlight, his long hair dark with sweat. Then Darren said, "No! *Sensuality*—that's the real key. Never underestimate the power of raw sensuality and sexuality. Those two elements, they fire every passion in us. Love, devotion, courage. And also all that's evil and ugly and weak. Scratch the surface of either, and those two elements come pouring out like blood."

Darren had clanked cubes into a rocks glass, poured it half full, now lifted the glass in salute. "The sun's almost below the yardarm, mateys. Sure neither of you will join me?"

He and Nathan were on barstools, a lead-sheathed counter supporting an ice bucket, crystal ashtray, plus Nate's elbow along with a quart of grape Gatorade, most of it gone. Opposite them was a restaurant-quality kitchen, stainless gas burners, a butcher's block, pans and pots suspended above, polished and orderly as church bells. I'd been sitting off in a corner by myself on one of the sleekest Manhattan-looking chairs I'd ever seen, drinking a bottle of water and texting an update to Lawrence Seasons on what I had learned. I still regretted my stupid words to Darren, but my brain immediately locked onto what he had just said, aware that it might be important. Sex, passion, weakness, and evil. I didn't understand his meaning—not in my head, anyway—but it did offer some hope that I might yet understand why Mrs. Whitney had behaved as she had with a man half her age who had no solid job or education. I knew I'd have to spend time on the water, or in my bed, to think it through, but the connection alone was enough to give me faith.

"I'd like to see that magazine," I said, storing my cell phone and getting to my feet. "Sorry about my rudeness. I should be thanking you instead of interrupting your cocktail hour."

Darren sat straighter, watching me cross the room, then said, "Sensuous," as if the word had reappeared inside his head. As an aside to Nathan, he added, "Pure motion . . . physically at ease . . . no wasted effort. I can see why they called your great-aunt 'Big Six.'"

It was meant as a compliment, of course, but his words reminded me of Arlis's exaggerations, which that rough old man considered a smooth way of flirting. It also caused me to once again recall what Mrs. Whitney had said about a young, handsome boy like Nathan being a fool to trust a celebrated homosexual photographer.

I took the magazine, which was folded open. After several seconds, I pulled out the barstool that separated the two men, straddled it, then placed the magazine on the counter.

"A cowgirl?" I said, perplexed by what I saw, which might have sounded sharp, so I added in a rush, "She's real pretty, of course. Long-legged, and I like her boots. She's . . . well, handsome, I guess."

"I'll be damned," Darren said. He was chuckling in a way that told me I'd noticed something he'd missed, which apparently pleased him. "Let me see that."

Instead of giving me time to slide the magazine over, the photographer leaned his shoulder against mine so he could see better. Just as unexpectedly, Nathan, on my right, did the same thing. For an instant, I stiffened, a claustrophobic reaction . . . but then I took a breath and stopped trying to shrink myself. It was pleasant, I realized, to be sandwiched between two nice men. I could feel the warmth of their shoulders clear through to my ribs, something I'd seldom experienced, which was enjoyable in a mild way and made me feel more at ease.

"Actress Barbara Stanwyck, in costume, on the set of *The Big Valley*." Nathan read the caption aloud as if he'd never seen the picture before. Which made no sense until Darren said, "My God, she's a classic example of female masculinity. Of course . . . Barbara Stanwyck—perfect. This isn't the image I wanted you to see, Hannah pet, but it has a wonderful duality that fits. How in hell did I miss it?"

Darren leaned in front of me to say to Nathan, "Didn't I tell you? Serendipity—if your heart's open, if it's free of meanness, destiny takes us by the hand and leads us to wonderful places. We'll compare the two shots in a minute, but"— he took the magazine, flipped it over, and squared it in front of me—"here's the image I wanted you to see. It's the image that told me I must get you in front of the lens."

I said, *"Her?"*

Darren's expression read *Don't be so surprised*. Whatever success he had earned could have had something to do with the look he was giving me, a private signal that connected his eyes with mine. It offered reassurance and told me what happened next was safe no matter what I decided.

Then he explained the picture, saying, "This image was taken in nineteen forty-two by Otto Schmidt, a master of black-and-white. A true craftsman with the old large format Leica cameras. A near genius, of course, when it came to lighting, as you can see."

Now, instead of looking at a handsome woman wearing jeans, boots, and a cowboy hat, I was looking at a woman the caption said was *Marlissa Dorn, Hollywood Siren*. The actress was standing, eyes tilted upward at the camera, hip canted against a concert piano, wearing a black gown, low-cut, and balancing a freshly lit cigarette between her fingers at ear level.

"Beautiful," I said softly. "I've never seen any of her films, but the name's familiar. And I love old movies. She reminds me of Rita Hayworth."

Darren waited for Nathan to tell me that Marlissa Dorn's family had once owned a vacation home on Sanibel Island before agreeing, "Rita Hayworth, another one. The camera loved them both. They had a sensuality that was visceral . . . subliminal, very, very private. But they couldn't hide it from the lens. My God, they practically melted the lens. And a physical fluidness, perfectly at ease with their bodies."

I felt my ears warm, recalling what Darren had said about me—*physically at ease . . . no wasted effort.* But it was silly to think I looked anything like this glamorous woman who'd been about my age eighty years ago.

Darren was on his feet. I watched him cross the room, slim and elegant in the way he moved, then my eyes returned to the magazine.

Nate said in a low voice, "He's dying to have you sit for him." Then, about Marlissa Dorn, "She has a smoky look. Sort of smolders and she's not even trying. That's what Darre likes about the shot."

The woman was staring at the camera through a luminous frame of cigarette smoke. Her hair was combed full and glossy to her shoulders, head tilted in a way that had an attitude but was attractive, not superior-acting or off-putting. For an instant, Mrs. Whitney came into my mind and I found myself hoping that she, too, had once looked as glamorous and confident. A pleasant memory might help the poor woman finally get some sleep—that, plus the soup I'd reheated and forced her to eat before leaving.

"Thanks to Nate, I've been reading about your family," Darren called from across the room. He was returning, carrying a newer version of the Florida history book that was still in the old briefcase stored on my boat. "I'll be honest. I love the historical connection. It gives the project . . . fabric. Makes shooting you part of a larger canvas."

I've heard my family's stories so many times, I only pretended to be interested when Darren opened the book, still talking about photography, then switched to the subject of history. My great-great-grandmother Hannah Smith was called Big Six by early Floridians. She was well known because of her height and unusual strength, which was required of a woman who chopped wood and hunted hogs for a living. Not hogs natural to Florida but feral hogs that had escaped the Spaniards and still ran wild on the islands. The first Hannah Smith—like my late aunt, Hannah Three—had fallen in with rough men, and both Hannahs had died violent deaths due to their bad judgment. It was an error that I have probably been overly careful not to repeat.

Hannah One's sister, Sarah Smith, was called Ox Woman because Sarah was the first person—

maybe the only person—to drive an oxcart across the Everglades before roads were built. Having hiked part of the Glades with my Uncle Jake, who was a crack shot and expert hunter, I knew better than most what my relative, Sarah, had done was near impossible by my own weaker standards. I admired her for that more than I've ever admitted publicly, but the last remaining photo of Sarah—which Darren and Nate were looking at now—still makes me wince. Sarah was anything but a handsome woman, unlike Hannah One. And certainly not beautiful like Hannah Three. Secretly, I feared early Floridians had nicknamed Sarah for her looks, not her gift for driving oxen through swamps and sawgrass.

Out of politeness, though, Darren was disagreeing with the thoughts in my head, telling Nathan, "See the high cheekbones? Might be a touch of American Indian in the family. And an incredibly strong jaw . . . those piercing eyes, Sarah Smith is still alive on this page, see what I mean? It's a woman's inner strength, her physical presence, that makes for a timeless image. Like this." Darren tapped the picture of Marlissa Dorn I was still studying, which was easier for me than suffering yet another look at my great-great-aunt, the Ox Woman.

"Hannah?"

Darren's friend wanted my attention again, but I was becoming uncomfortable. Plus, I was still thinking about Mrs. Whitney and what Ricky Meeks had done to her—and what at this very moment he might be doing to Olivia Seasons, who was a younger woman and not nearly so toughened by life as Elka, who had survived four husbands, three of them wealthy.

Returning to the chair where I'd been sitting, I said, "While we're on the subject of pictures, you mind taking a quick look at this?" I opened the grocery bag I'd placed on the floor beside me.

Nate said quickly, "I don't think Darre would be interested," sounding nervous, and then waited through several seconds of silence before asking me, "Where'd you get that?" The bag, he meant.

Aside from a manila envelope with the photo of Ricky Meeks, the grocery bag, which read *Bailey's Store,* contained a few things Mrs. Whitney had given me, including the Chantelle bra, and a beautiful blouse that I'd hand-washed in Woolite while waiting for a load of wash to finish and after putting away bags of groceries and liquor that had been delivered. The woman had behaved almost fondly toward me at the end when she saw I was willing to work to help clean up the mess her life had become. That work included phoning her attorney and her doctor, alerting both that the woman needed some assistance. The fact that Mrs. Whitney and I wore the same bra size—34D—had helped, too. It created a sisterly feeling that is often the reward when women share private matters they wouldn't entrust to a man.

Closing the bag, I said to Nate, "Just some things," then walked the manila envelope across the room and placed the photo in front of Darren. "You mind? Maybe the camera lens sees something my eyes don't."

Darren had some snobbery in him when it came to photos but appeared to relax when he realized the wrinkled eight-by-ten was just a picture, not someone's attempt at art.

"A snapshot," he shrugged after a glance. "What do you want me to say? Is this a relative of yours?" Darren patted the pockets of a white guayabera he'd bought on a trip to Cuba. "Where'd I leave my glasses, Nate? Damn it, in the bedroom, I bet. Would you be a dear?"

Nathan stood, face reddening, and it was still red when he returned.

The famous photographer's reaction was much different, once he had his glasses fixed low on his nose. I watched him take another fast glance and do a double take. After several seconds of scrutiny, he looked at Nate and asked, "How do you know this person?" which sounded like an accusation, and also contained a hint of distaste.

"We don't," I said. "Nate saw him a few times at the Rum Bar, that's all. There's something about the picture that upsets you, I can tell. Is it what the camera shows? Or maybe you've seen that man before."

Darren knew something about Ricky Meeks, I felt sure of it. Maybe even met him. Either way, it wasn't surprising. Darren wasn't wealthy by Mrs. Whitney's standards, just rich with money he'd earned on his own. Even so, he moved in the same social circles—when he wanted. At parties and fund-raisers, being famous is better than being wealthy as far as a guest list is concerned. This was something else I'd learned from fishing clients.

Darren picked up the photo, thought for a moment, then placed Ricky Meeks's face down on the counter. "He was my neighbor's boy toy for a while. I saw him around a few times." The man used his glass to indicate the photo and then lit a cigarette. "She gave this to you? I wouldn't be surprised, the sad, pathetic old bitch. She probably still has the hots for him."

I felt a tightening in my head that was anger, but showing it wouldn't keep Darren talking, so I asked, "Does the picture tell you anything different from what your eyes saw?"

"No . . . and yes." He touched the photo as if to take another look, then decided it wasn't necessary. "The guy's white trash. A vicious little animal who isolates rich, lonely women, then screws them into submission. That's my guess. Even a cheap camera tells part of the story. The rest I know because I have incredible instincts for people. Human sexual drive is the ultimate power—weren't we just talking about that?"

I started to dig for useful details, but Darren interrupted, saying, "Why the questions? More important—if we expect to have any fun tonight —who's going to join me?" The man raised his empty glass, his face masked with another smile, but suspicious. From Darren's tone and the way he eyed me, I could tell he expected drinking company—if I expected him to confide what he knew.

I replied, "My uncle found a good mojito recipe in Havana. Otherwise, I stick to red wine."

The photographer, not listening, was already lining two fresh rocks glasses on the bar, the bottle of scotch nearby.

# Seven

Walking me to the dock through shadows, Nathan took my elbow and said, "Are you sure you're okay to drive? I hate you crossing that bay by yourself. It's so damn dark."

He was right about that. Through an opening in the foliage, I could see my skiff, the dock, then a horizon of water so black that a heaven of stars did not brighten it, nor a crescent moon, new and waxing, that was drifting west over palm trees toward Mexico.

"You've got to make Darren quit smoking," I replied, sniffing a strand of my hair, then my shirt. "It stinks even worse than his whiskey. I'll have to wash everything and take two showers. Where else can I do it but home?"

"*Here* . . . please? Seriously, Four. You can't see a goddamn thing out there. When Darre drives me home later, he'll drop you off. He already said so."

Later? In my opinion, Darren had no intention of taking Nathan home. No matter what the man pretended, his patient manipulation and gentle words only made his intentions more obvious. Nate might be shy, but he isn't dumb, and I suspected he knew the truth, too.

It was already 9:45, an hour after sunset. Amazing how fast time had passed after I'd sipped down a glass of liquor that, at first, tasted like peat moss soaked in vodka. After that, it had tasted smoother, but I'd been too focused on what Darren was saying to risk getting drunk. So I'd dumped most of the next two glasses into a potted palm, determined to remember details about the life Mrs. Whitney had lived while she was under the spell of Ricky Meeks.

After I'd explained to Darren about Olivia Seasons—without naming names, of course—he was eager to help and knew more than I could have hoped. It wasn't because he was chummy with Mrs. Whitney. It was because he was fond of booking a cabin on an overnight luxury yacht that sailed four times a month to Key West, then back again the next day. Twice, he'd seen Meeks and Elka Whitney aboard that vessel, which is how he'd learned so much without even exchanging a word. Or so he claimed.

The boat, named *Sybarite*, was moored at Fishermans Wharf, near Fort Myers Beach, and was unlike any luxury cruiser I'd ever heard about. For one thing, the price of a one-night cabin cost more than I make during a month of fishing, even at peak season. Another oddity was that a regular person couldn't buy passage, even if he offered twice the fare. New passengers had to be recommended by established clients or invited aboard by the owners. Or they had to be someone obviously special in a rock star sort of way.

It had taken Darren an hour of hinting around, and several more whiskeys, before he'd finally described those cruises in plain words—but only after reading the definition of *sybarite* to us from the dictionary.

"Hedonist . . . sensualist. Voluptuary, libertine . . . pleasure seeker!" Darren had spoken each word in an alluring way as if reciting a list of fine wines, each delicious. The dictionary did nothing for me, but I will admit that I began to feel my body changing when his low voice detailed some of the scenes he'd witnessed. Not at first, of course. It was a slow feeling that came over me—a heated restlessness made more intense because of the whiskey I was sipping.

Dinners aboard *Sybarite* were formal, tuxes and evening gowns, he'd told us, for those who chose not to eat in their cabins. There was gambling once the boat was outside the twelve-mile limit, and dancing, too, but the codes of dress and behavior remained strict. After midnight, though, everything changed. Lights were turned low in the vessel's main salon, and private areas sectioned off with nothing more than cushions or beaded curtains, so there was no real privacy, and it was easy to view what others were doing—something Darren's tone said he enjoyed.

Couples or small groups sometimes stayed to themselves, while others roamed, almost everyone naked except for Mardi Gras–type masks that, upon boarding, passengers pulled from a box blindfolded. It was a tradition aboard *Sybarite*, and part of the fun, Darren explained. My impression was, people sometimes traded masks, a behavior I'd found weirdly enticing for some reason, but I didn't want to reveal that by asking questions, of course. Fact was, I disliked even admitting it to myself.

"A sex orgy boat, that's what it sounds like," I'd finally interrupted, which was actually an attempt to stop my body from reacting to behavior that my mind, at least, knew was wrong. "You're saying the man forced Mrs. Whitney to go on the cruise?"

That had amused Darren. "Is that what the old bitch claims? Gabby—she's the one who books *Sybarite*—she'd never allow trash like him aboard. Elka had to've set it up. Or through someone she knew."

He had already said so many nasty things about the woman, I lost patience and asked him to speak with politeness, at least, if he couldn't manage to speak of her with respect.

That had amused him, too. I could tell by his laughing apology and the patient way he then explained the boat wasn't just about orgies. There was a gourmet chef, fine wine, Cuban cigars, all sorts of expensive niceties. A cruise aboard *Sybarite* was an escape for people sick of what Darren called "puritanical bullshit" and over-whelmed with rules, pressure, and boring social obligations that apparently were the price of being rich.

"That's why I think the guy banged her into submission," Darren had added, softening his language. "I can't be sure, just the impression I got. It's the way Elka responded when the punk told her to do something—like a pet too eager to please. And rather nervous, too, as if he might scold her. No . . . it was a flinching reaction"—Darren demonstrated by swinging his head away—"so he'd probably slapped her around a few times. That's another guess."

I didn't comment, but he was right on both

points. Mrs. Whitney had told me she'd been hit by Meeks more than once, but always in a careful way so as not to break a bone or leave a bruise that couldn't be hidden. The hitting didn't start, though, until Meeks had taken her body so many times during the first four days and nights that she'd become "dazed," in her words, her thoughts so focused on sex that what the man was doing to her changed from nightmarish to "dreamlike."

"Do you think he'd try to book a cruise with the girl I'm trying to find?" I'd asked Darren.

"Does she have money? Lots of money, that's important."

I had nodded, then waited for him to light another cigarette.

"Of course he will—if they're still in the area. Punks like him, they don't stop once they get a taste of the swinger's life. It's cool, hip, to the blue-collar types, somehow makes them feel like an equal. And I think he gets his rocks off by humiliating women. That's the bottom line. Wealthy ones especially, maybe because they represent everything he's not. He likes three-somes, foursomes. All sorts of combinations, I would think. If you want, I'll call Gabby tomorrow and check the schedule."

Darren had written a note to himself on a pad of paper, then paused for a moment to think, his expression turning serious. "Please, Hannah, please, please, *please* don't get any ideas about booking the same cruise this freak books. You're a smart girl, very competent in most ways I'm sure. But my guess is, you don't have a lot of . . . Well, Nate told me you married a local boy who left for the Army the day after your wedding. And haven't dated much since. A true male predator like the one we're talking about—are you listening to me, Hannah pet?—if he ever got his hands on you, you'd never be the same girl again. And it would positively kill me—Nate, too, I'm sure—to see that happen to you. Understand my concern?"

Giving Nathan a sharp look, I nodded, not pleased that he had no doubt also told Darren the truth about how my late husband, Delbert Fowler, had died—hit by a car his first night of Army leave in Berlin, Germany. Delbert's death is one of the few things I've given myself permission to lie about out of respect for that skinny little mullet fisherman who I'd felt pity for, not love, when he'd gotten down on his knee and proposed. That had been six years ago, and I'd long since given up trying to think of him as my husband, dead or otherwise.

But Darren's warning about Ricky Meeks had been so sincere, it was heavy on my mind as Nathan followed me onto the dock, still pleading for me to stay because I'd had some whiskey and it was so damn dark. As I listened to him, I checked the sky for squalls and distant lightning. Next, I checked the pilings beneath us to see what the tide was doing, then I moved around and studied the bay, deciding on the best route.

Home for my boat was five miles to the east, invisible from where I stood. Once I crossed the Intracoastal Waterway, where a lonely span of markers sparked in the blackness, I knew I'd raise a cluster of lights among the far mangroves. Those lights marked Gulf Cooperative, where Uncle Jake had bought thirty feet of dockage before the Florida net ban had put fishermen out of business. The cove was in a pocket of trees, no houses or lights or people on either side, everything isolated by government wetlands and swamp.

"At least stay long enough to tell me what you found out from Mrs. Whitney," Nate said after I'd stepped onto my skiff and was getting ready to go. What he actually wanted was for us to sit there talking until I was too tired to leave.

I reached under the steering console, found a flashlight, a contract of confidentiality, and a pen before replying, "Until you sign this, I can't tell you anything. Even after you sign it, I can't share anything Elka wants kept private. That's just the way it is."

"So it's 'Elka' now," Nathan said while I held the flashlight and watched him sign. "Only you could make friends with a dragon like her. That's

116

what's in that sack, isn't it? A present. I bet she gave you something expensive."

"Most people are nicer than expected if you give them a chance," I replied, taking the contract, then opening a ziplock bag to keep it dry. Wind was out of the southwest, not strong, but I guessed I'd take some spray when I crossed the Intracoastal. "Give me a hug, Nathan. I'll call you in the morning."

We hugged—something we always did when parting—but the man held me longer than usual, then stepped away, saying, "There's something I want to tell you. It's about Darren and me. We're not . . . we're not what you might think. It's not the way it looks, I mean." He was still embarrassed about being sent to the bedroom to fetch Darren's glasses, I realized.

"To me, it looks like you two have fun," I said. "What else matters?"

Nate didn't want to drop it so easily. "I'm not sleeping with him, that's what I want you to know. Not in the way you probably think, anyway. Darre's a nice man. Gentle and understanding. He doesn't push—not me, anyway. I know he got a little pushy about doing a photo session, but that's different."

It made me feel good hearing Nate speak kindly about a man I'd been suspicious of, especially after what Elka Whitney had said. Because of Nate's words, and maybe because the whiskey was still warm in my cheeks, I reached for my skiff's ignition key and said, "Tell him yes."

Sounding hopeful but confused, Nathan asked, "Yes? About what? Me tell Darren yes, you mean?"

I couldn't help smiling as I reached to start my engine. "That's up to you. I was talking about Darren taking my picture. Tell him I'll do it—but only if I can wear a nice dress like the one in the magazine. And keep all my clothes on, of course."

# Eight

Idling my boat through darkness, along the back side of Captiva, my cell phone flashed in its waterproof case. Lawrence Seasons had replied to my text. When I took a look, I discovered he'd actually sent the text more than half an hour ago.

Call soon as possible, even after midnight.

The man used punctuation and spelled-out words, unlike most. It struck me as classy and solid, a person who took time to do even small things right.

I touched a button on my rubber watch and saw that it was a little after ten. The Seasonses' estate was ahead; to my left dock lights glowed in pools

118

of green water, showing the Marlow's starboard side, cabin windows silver but dark inside. The temptation was to pull up to his dock and call from there in hope we could speak face-to-face. I was troubled by what I'd learned tonight but also rather proud I'd uncovered important information in such a short time. It might be enjoyable to watch how the man reacted, possibly see some sign he was impressed.

I shifted the engine to neutral and let the wind drift my skiff until soon I could see the lighted windows of Mr. Seasons's house through trees, and the blue undersides of palm fronds told me swimming pool lights were on near the guest-house and the screened area. It was tempting to dock, yes, until I lost my nerve and told myself it was too bold a move to surprise a new employer without an invitation. Not at this hour, even though it was a Friday night and the island appeared lively. From the tiki hut at Jensen's Marina, a local band, the Trouble Starters, were doing "Old Captiva," electric guitars and vocals crooning a laid-back Grateful Dead sound. A mile north, a sixty-five-foot party cruiser, *Lady Chadwick*, was a village of yellow windows, steel drums and laughter reaching my ears even from that distance.

Hearing that laughter filled my chest with an unexpected hollow sensation. I was alone, on a small boat, on a weekend night, when so many others were having fun. It caused me to take another look east, where I saw sparking channel markers, wind, and miles of darkness that was made cavelike by stars and radio towers in the far, far distance. They were miniature towers from where I stood, but so tall they flashed red or white strobes to warn planes.

I had made that crossing at night, alone, many times. Usually—especially if seas are rough—I get a giddy, wild feeling about midway that causes me to laugh aloud and sometimes sing. It is a powerful feeling to have the confidence to thread a boat through so much shallow water in darkness, relying only on memory and range markers, a thing not many watermen would risk. But I wasn't looking forward to it now.

Fact was, my whiskey glow was fading, and I suddenly felt as alone as Elka Whitney in her Spanish palace. When I imagined what she might be doing, the stories she'd told returned like a weight, bringing back the hurt and anger we'd shared, the two of us sitting, talking about events so ugly they had brought even me close to tears, and I don't cry easily. Not among strangers, anyway. So I'd spared the woman the embarrassment by concentrating on my anger while I listened to her talk.

Ricky Meeks was a mean man, smart and sneaky enough to bleed the self-respect out of a woman while also denting her banking account in legal ways the police couldn't touch. In my mind, he'd become a monster who didn't actually scare me—not much, anyway—but it was frightening to imagine what he now might be doing to another woman. Olivia Seasons, for one, if she was with him.

To shake myself out of my low mood, I whispered, "Find Olivia, stick to business," which brought back some of my spirit. Then told myself, *Stop pitying yourself, she's the one in trouble,* which raised my spirits a little more, as it always does when I focus on other people's problems rather than my own gloomy thoughts.

My client had told me to call and that's what I decided to do. Just as I reached for my cell, though, it rang, flashing *Lawrence Seasons,* whose number I'd stored the previous afternoon. When I answered, I heard the man ask, "Did you just pull away from the Ottofurd dock? Maybe you don't understand how anxious we are to hear the new information."

Ottofurd was Darren's last name. I shouldn't have been surprised Seasons had kept an eye on my boat since the properties were so close, and it certainly explained why the man sounded peeved.

"I was going to make some notes first to keep the information straight," I lied, which is the sort of silly lie I use too often even when I've done nothing wrong.

"Look toward my house. You've got your

running lights on, I'm sure that's you." Then he said, "See this?"

From an area near where the swimming pool turned palm trees blue, Mr. Seasons was blinking a flashlight at me. I reached to grab my boat's spotlight to return the signal but realized in time how stupid that would have been.

I replied, "You're on the patio?"

"Pool courtyard," the man corrected. "Martha's down listening to the band—she flew in late this afternoon—and I came back to make another batch of drinks. Can you stop by?"

It took a moment to remember that Martha was Mrs. Calder-Shaun and that she was at the marina, where the Trouble Starters were playing. I said, "Sure," feeling better already. But then I remembered that my hair smelled of Darren's cigarettes, and I'd been wearing the same clothes since early that morning, so I added, "Give me ten minutes or so because I need to—"

"You can freshen up here," the man said. "Martha uses the in-law suite, so the pool cottage is yours. I'll have Carlotta lay out towels and things."

Carlotta must have been evening shift because I remembered the maid's name as something different. The man's tone was so flat and sure, it was clear he didn't expect an answer, but I didn't want him to see me even for a minute the way I looked and smelled.

"I appreciate that, Mr. Seasons, but it'll still take me about ten minutes. I need to check something on my boat, then I'll be right there." Which contained enough truth that I didn't consider it an actual lie. What I wanted to check was the change of clothes I always carry in a waterproof bag in the anchor locker. Since I almost always stern-anchor when fishing, that little locker beneath the bow is neatly packed with extra clothes, a well-equipped first-aid kit, mosquito repellent and netting, bottled water, flares, a headlamp for reading, a sleeping bag, and enough military surplus food for two days.

Not many watermen will admit they've run aground after sunset and had to spend the night waiting for the tide. But it has happened to me, as I suspect it has to most everyone who makes their living on the water. Twelve hours on an open boat, stranded miles from nowhere, can be a cold, buggy, boring, and thirsty space of time, so I always carry extra provisions.

After I'd hung up the phone, I idled away from the channel toward sandbars that lie north off Jensen's Marina, where the band was playing a different song now, something cheerful I didn't recognize. A derelict sailboat, long ago demasted in a storm, was anchored off the channel and has served me as a bathing screen on more than one occasion. When I was east of the sailboat, shielded from anyone on shore who might be watching through binoculars, I dropped anchor, stood and opened the anchor locker, hoping I'd packed something decent to wear.

I had, but the selection could have been better. I chose jeans instead of green linen cargo shorts because it was night and jeans seemed more formal. There was a clean bra, plain beige, unpadded, and cotton panties that were more like boy's briefs, but they were burgundy with white stripes. The mismatched colors told me I should pay more attention in the future when packing for emergencies. But they would work okay, barring a ride in an ambulance.

I wasn't as lucky when it came to a blouse. There were two T-shirts, one long-sleeved, and also a button-down blouse of gray chambray I'd bought at Target. It was soft and nice but had paint stains on the collar—the only reason it wasn't still hanging in my closet. I didn't want to walk into a millionaire's house wearing a T-shirt or a blouse stained the same color as the bottom paint on my boat.

I whispered, *"Shit,"* for the second time in a single day, feeling harried because ten minutes isn't a lot of time. That's when I remembered what was in the bag I had carried from Mrs. Whitney's house: the Chantelle demi-bra, and a sheer black blouse made by Dolce & Gabbana, a label I'd never heard of, but the material felt and looked expensive. It was new, too, tags still on it, but didn't fit her, Mrs. Whitney had said, a present from someone in Paris who was unfamiliar with American sizes. She was all for me washing it and trying it on.

I took the garments from the sack and held them up to the stars. They smelled clean and fresh from the dryer I'd used, and the blouse was folded so carefully it wasn't wrinkled badly. But would it look odd wearing jeans with such a fancy top? I decided it was better than paint stains on a shirt from Target and that I'd wasted enough time worrying about it.

I took a quick look around. I'm not modest, but neither do I like people watching me undress. I removed my blouse and shorts and stored them in the sack. After another quick look, my underwear came off, then I went naked over the side into waist-deep water that sparkled like green fire, sparks clinging to my arms and body when I submerged. The bay often glows on moonless nights when stirred by a propeller or a streaking fish. Fishing guides call it phosphorus, but it's actually caused by billions of tiny sea creatures that throb like fireflies when disturbed, as the Sanibel biologist had explained when we'd negotiated for my skiff.

It was a delicious feeling to be in warm seawater that sparkled when I moved my arms. It was as if I held a magic wand. On my skiff's gunwale, I'd placed a bar of Kirk's Castile soap and a bottle of Prell shampoo, which are best for sudsing in saltwater. I washed, rinsed, washed and rinsed again, then spent five minutes with a heavy cotton towel before trying on my new clothes.

Once I got the straps adjusted, the bra was such a soft pleasure, the way it held me, I experimented with the new blouse by using one less button near the neck, then two. If I'd had a mirror, I might have risked three—but this was a business meeting, I reminded myself. Not one of my rare Friday-night dates.

I tucked the blouse into my jeans and liked the way it sculpted a sharp angle chest to hips. After listening to a phone message from Loretta, asking, "Has the rich man from Captiva tried to get the pants off you yet?" I sat and texted Nathan that business required me to speak with Mr. Seasons. I'd be just down the road if needed.

Starting my engine, I steered toward shore.

# Nine

Sitting next to the swimming pool, sipping a frozen margarita, I listened to Mr. Seasons ask, "Is your hair wet? Please tell me you weren't out there swimming. For Christ's sake, you know sharks feed in that channel at night. Big hammerheads sometimes—I've seen them."

After explaining I'd spent the day with people who smoke cigarettes, a smell I hate, the man started to tell me the guest cottage had a full bath, for Christ's sake, I should have used that. But then he shook his head in an *I give up* sort of way and told me, "You're a stubborn one. Can you at least call me Larry? Or even Lawrence? We're in business together now, so let's drop the formalities."

Mr. Seasons wasn't drunk, but he'd had a few. It made him seem less dignified but also less intimidating, and I relaxed a little. Not completely, though. I still felt some tension because of what he'd said the previous afternoon about seeing people in a different light and also because he was paying me money to do an important job. The margarita seemed to help. I took a longer sip, then another, before trying his name aloud, saying, "Lawrence feels more comfortable than . . . than the other. Should I wait for Mrs. Calder-Shaun or tell you now?"

The man was going through a folder he'd brought on a tray with glasses, a pitcher of margaritas, and a bottle of what might have been brandy. He placed the folder in front of me, then the thinnest laptop computer I'd ever seen. "Take a look at this while I text her. Martha will want to hear. Plus, she has documents for you to sign."

More documents? Mrs. Calder-Shaun had already sent two attachments by e-mail, a fee agreement and a contract of confidentiality that consisted of five pages, not one, like the contracts I'd found in Uncle Jake's office. Instead of wondering about it, though, I opened the folder, which contained a second folder and a single sheet of paper. It was a copy of Olivia's American Express credit card statement for the previous four weeks. I looked at the statement, then looked at Mr. Seasons, who nodded, meaning I should start with it.

There wasn't much to see—at first, anyway. Olivia had used her card only three times. In late May, there were charges at two Naples restaurants, one for more than eight hundred dollars, so it must have been an extravagant place. She hadn't used the card again until June 9th, paying $5,753.97 to a company called Monkey Business '12 LLC. Today was Friday, June 17th, so that had been more than a week ago, near the end of her billing cycle, but there was no hint as to what she'd bought.

I couldn't ask Mr. Seasons about it because he was busy texting, so I noted Olivia's personal details on the statement to pass the time, not expecting to find anything interesting. But I did. The credit card Olivia carried was nothing like the card I keep in my wallet. It was an American Express Centurion, which meant nothing to me until I saw the spending limit. At first, I thought I'd misread the numbers, the limit was so high, more than a million dollars. The statement also informed me that Olivia had an annual spending *obligation* of a quarter million dollars—a minimum she had already satisfied, according to the figures.

Because I'd helped my uncle with his businesses, I knew that the fiscal year, for most, begins and ends in February. It was now June, midway through the calendar. How had a thirty-year-old woman who lived in her father's home managed to spend more than $250,000 in only six months? And why in the world would she use a credit card that *required* her to charge at least that much annually?

"What do you think?" Mr. Seasons had finished texting Mrs. Calder-Shaun and now placed his hands on the back of my chair to look over my shoulder. He stood so close I could smell what might have been soap or a hint of aftershave. The tension I was feeling peaked momentarily, then began to ebb when he became more businesslike, saying, "We finally managed to freeze the card, but it took Martha's people a week to do it. Thank God, Olivia didn't use the thing more than she did after she met the guy."

I said, "Maybe I'm reading this wrong. Your niece spent this much"—I placed my finger beneath the figure—"since February or January?"

Mr. Seasons said, "Hannah, you're missing the point. That particular card requires substantial yearly expenditures, so everything gets billed. Taxes, investments, everything. So don't worry your head about numbers. What's interesting is, Olivia used the card twice just before that man finished the seawall—three days before she took off. But she's only used it once since. What's that tell you?"

I couldn't yet feel the tequila in my drink, so I was honestly irked at Mr. Seasons for telling me not to worry my head about numbers like I was some stupid girl.

"It doesn't mean anything," I replied, "until I know more. Does she have any other credit cards?"

"Of course, but she hasn't used them. We'd know because all statements are billed to my office. I have no idea how much cash Olivia had on hand before she left, but I'm sure it would have been a substantial amount. The point is, the statement suggests a certain intent—"

Maybe I was wrong about feeling the tequila because I interrupted, "I understand what you're saying, Mr. Seasons. Your niece didn't use the credit card because you could have tracked her. The places she's been staying, buying gas, food. That's obvious. What I'm asking is, could she have a credit card you don't know about? And, if she does, would it have had a credit limit lower than this?" I touched my finger to the charge of $5,753.97 to Monkey Business '12 LLC posted two weeks ago.

I felt the man remove his hands from my chair and stand. "I've never heard of a limit lower than ten or fifteen thousand. What are you getting at?"

There was no reason to tell him my card maxed at eight thousand because I'd found out what I needed to know. I wasn't happy about what I had learned, though. In fact, I felt a chill that was partly suspicion, partly because I felt sure I was right.

"The last time Olivia used this card, she did it for a reason," I said. "If she has a card you don't know about, she could have used it if the limit was over six thousand. Or maybe even paid cash. But she didn't." I took another look at the statement. "American Express Centurion. Is this card well known in circles where people have money?"

Mr. Seasons was giving me that look again like he was inspecting me, trying to gauge my intelligence. "I suppose so," he said, then made a sound of exasperation. "*Of course* it's well known. A Centurion card is the most prestigious card in the world. Only a few thousand people qualify. It's called the Black Card."

"A business owner would be impressed if a new client or customer pulled it out?" I asked. "Or said, 'I've got a Centurion card,' over the phone?" I was thinking about what Darren had said about booking a cabin aboard *Sybarite*. You had to be invited, recommended, or prove you were someone very, very special.

131

The man was paying attention now. "Why does it matter?"

I answered, "It might be important or I wouldn't bother. Would a Centurion card impress even someone who dealt with wealthy people on a regular basis? That's what I'm asking."

"You have no idea. Salesclerks get shaky in the knees. Maître d's at restaurants. I've seen it. The reason I wanted you to look at the statement, though, is what you figured out very quickly—the pattern of avoiding a money trail. It suggests that Olivia was with that man for three weeks at least. What I'd hoped you'd also see is that she started using the card again. Or was until Martha had it frozen. We think Olivia got rid of the guy somehow, Hannah. We think it's good news."

I pushed the margarita away, deciding I'd had enough alcohol for one night—until we were done with business, at least. "Mr. Seasons, hate to say it, but I think you're wrong. Her using that card isn't the worst news in the world, but it's not good news. You still think we should wait for Mrs. Calder-Shaun?"

He bent over the table. "What can you possibly see here that I don't?" meaning the credit card statement. At the same instant, his cell phone made an old-fashioned ringing sound. "Wait—it's Martha. Let me find out what's keeping her."

The man put the phone to his ear but then covered it with his hand long enough to tell me,

"More photos on the computer, and here's more stuff on Olivia." He nodded at the file and laptop next to the bottle of what might have been brandy. "Have a look while I take this."

Mr. Seasons turned and walked into the shadows, wanting privacy, so I busied myself by opening the file. In it were a few photos, a curriculum vitae Olivia had compiled after graduating college six years ago, and a spiral notebook that, I realized after opening it, was what amounted to her daily diary. It gave me a start to be looking at something so personal, so I immediately closed the thing . . . thought for a few moments . . . then opened it again so I could at least check the dates.

Olivia had started the journal in January the previous year, entering drawings and notes about an orchid house she was having built, but the notebook had gradually turned into something more personal. Or so it seemed as I leafed through the pages and saw that some of the longest passages were written in a sort of shorthand code that wasn't easy to read but doable if I took my time. Shorthand or petite cursive—there weren't a lot of entries. The girl had skipped whole months, sometimes offering explanations such as one from the previous year: *August/September —felt awful, four doctors apts.* But the notebook did more or less record what the woman was thinking and some things she had experienced over a period of fifteen months.

The last entries were dated May 3rd and May 5th, both written on the same page. There were simple notations about a book on Catholicism she was reading, then another about a church charity she planned to attend.

Church? I don't know why it surprised me that a wealthy, single woman attended church, but it did. After that, the notebook contained only blank pages, more than a dozen.

Mr. Seasons had told me Ricky Meeks had moved his boat behind Olivia's house the first week of May, but an exact date hadn't been mentioned. He had lived there, on his boat, until May 24th, the day after he'd finished the seawall. Olivia had disappeared two or three days later. That meant Meeks and the girl had had at least three weeks living in the same space, no house staff around after five p.m., just them alone. Yet, during those three weeks Olivia hadn't bothered to write anything about the new seawall, or the man who'd been hired to build it. To me, the fact she'd written nothing, not a single word, meant a lot more than a few dry entries. The emptiness of those dozen pages shouted out that something had changed in her life.

I took a look toward the shadows where Mr. Seasons was still on the phone, his voice too low to hear but sounding perturbed by something Mrs. Calder-Shaun had said. Out of politeness, I turned my chair to face the bay as if the light was better for looking at photographs I had pulled from the folder. Older photos that had been taken with a camera and printed on glossy paper. They were of Olivia when she was a girl.

There were only six. I shuffled through them a few times but kept coming back to one that meant more to me than the others. No telling why—or so I pretended at first. The photo was of an adolescent girl at some kind of school function, standing with two boys who were half a head shorter—an awkward time in a girl's life that I could relate to. Olivia's hair was glossy blond, expensive-looking for a girl her age, same with the formal dress she wore and elbow-length white gloves. She was so tall, she stood slope-shouldered to disguise her height. Not ugly but certainly not pretty—not at that stage of her life, anyway. With one gloved hand, I noticed, she tried to shield her mouth to hide her braces. With the other arm, she tried to cover her woman's breasts on what the mirror must have told Olivia was a beanpole adolescent body.

What grabbed at my heart, though, was the expression on Olivia's face. *Sullen,* is the way some would have described it, but she was actually showing the camera a whole stew of emotions that come with hormones and a girl's first blooming. Self-doubt, impatience, anger, worry. The difference was, Olivia Seasons struck me as one who wouldn't fast outgrow that clumsy, unattractive stage. If ever. Some women don't. That truth was in her eyes. Old, wounded eyes that appeared sad and already weary with the life that lay ahead.

It had been a while since I'd seen similar eyes and that same expression. But I had many, many times . . . even though I've managed to leave that troubled girl behind—most days, anyway.

Had Olivia?

# Ten

From behind me, Mr. Seasons's voice said, "Olivia doesn't look anything like her old photos now," which caused me to jump, I was concentrating so hard. To reassure me, he patted my shoulder, which was unlike him, then opened the computer, adding, "Here comes Martha—finally."

The woman's jewelry—a wrist bracelet, it turned out—made a rhythmic maraca sound as she came through the shadows, returning from the marina, which my ears tracked while I looked at the computer screen. It showed a page of thumbnail photos, mostly of Olivia, but some of Olivia and a few friends.

"She hated having her photo taken," Mr. Seasons explained as I opened the first photo, then began swiping through rows. "Olivia never considered herself attractive. I don't know why it mattered so much. She was decent-looking enough. Not beautiful, obviously, but not ugly. She could have been popular in the way some young women hope to be if she'd only tried. Even my late brother—Olivia's father—would admit that after a few drinks. Olivia chose to be an outsider. That's the way she's always been."

My face starting to warm, I said, "Her own father said she wasn't pretty?"

The man started to reply, then raised his voice to speak to Mrs. Calder-Shaun. "Sorry to pry you away from your new cabana boy, Martha! But Hannah and I have been waiting. I didn't bring the scotch, you'll have to go upstairs for that. Or ask Carlotta."

Yes, the man was definitely perturbed at her for some reason.

Silhouetted by the pool lights, Mrs. Calder-Shaun called to me, "Pay no attention to the old crab. He's not mad, he's just thirsty—pour him a drink. Can't wait to hear what you've found out, kiddo!" The woman was still laughing as she hurried toward the stairs.

"She's a first-rate lawyer but can be a first-rate pain in the ass, too," Mr. Seasons said, watching her go. "Martha has a few drinks, then starts shopping for new boy toys. Like it's a sport because she's not in the city."

137

I caught myself before asking why a married woman would behave in such a way, but the man must have read my puzzlement because he said, "Don't be naïve, Hannah. In the business world, people spend more time in hotels than at home. I'm not saying it's right—but Martha's more . . . open-minded than most. Everything she does, she does to extremes."

The man's strong words were unexpected, and I wondered for the first time if there was something more between the two than just business. He simmered for a moment, then returned his attention to me. "Where were we?"

"I'd asked about Olivia's father—"

"No," he interrupted, "the important question is, is Olivia in danger? Is she doing this because she's bitter about her father's death and trying to get attention? Or because some construction worker is forcing her? Unusual behavior is typical for that girl—that's why it's hard to be sure. Take a look at the pictures, they'll tell you."

Rather than letting me look, the man pivoted the computer away and opened a new page of thumbnails. "Olivia has always been angry. Angry because she's not pretty. Angry at her father because she lived a privileged life. Angry at his wealthy friends. That attitude of hers caused her to rebel early on, which some of these photos show. She went through a Goth stage—piercings but no tattoos, thank God. Then drugs and an abusive boyfriend, but that lasted only a few months. Organic foods and anorexia came next. For the last year it's been religion, almost nun-like, and raising orchids. Painting oils and watercolors, too—her Georgia O'Keeffe period, that's the way I think of it. She'd damn near become a recluse by the time—"

"I don't need to see more pictures to answer your question about safety," I cut in. I'd been itching to say what I was about to tell him and was done waiting. "You should call the police tonight. That's my opinion. And have them find your niece as soon as possible. You don't need to pay me. Do whatever it takes to get Olivia home—that's how sure I am she's in a bad way."

"Police?" the man said, distracted by Mrs. Calder-Shaun, who was descending the stairs, a drink in hand. "Hannah . . . we need more than personal opinion to get the local sheriff's department involved. I've called them, Martha's called them, we've had friends of friends try. But Olivia's not a missing person by their definition. If you have some personal juice that I don't have, by all means light a fire under them, I'm all for it."

Now I was watching Mrs. Calder-Shaun, too, her auburn hair worn long for the first time. It was surprising how striking the woman looked in a white satin blouse and beach skirt compared to her starched appearance on my fishing boat. I

139

hadn't realized she was so fit and busty under all the clothing she'd worn to protect her skin from the sun. The satin top revealed her bouncing breasts when she walked, which the woman knew and was enjoying as she crossed the deck in the Caribbean glow of the pool.

"Isn't that a gorgeous blouse, Hannah dear!"

For a short, dumb moment, I thought the woman had figured out why I was staring at her. Wrong. She was speaking of the blouse Mrs. Whitney had given me.

"This?" I touched my fingers to the top button, worried I should have undone only one, not two. "This was a gift from . . . someone. First time I've worn it and I haven't even had a chance to—" I was about to say *look in a mirror,* which was true but would require some explaining.

No matter. Mrs. Calder-Shaun was already saying to Mr. Seasons, "You're right about her. She has an unusual sort of beauty—so obvious when she isn't wearing fishing clothes. And so natural. Who's the designer, Hannah? I could swear I saw something similar at a boutique in the Village."

I remembered the name on the label of the blouse because I'd looked at it closely, searching for directions on how to wash it. "Dolce and Gabbana," I said. "Maybe I didn't pronounce it right, I'm not sure."

I'd never heard of the designer, but Mrs. Calder-

Shaun undoubtedly had. It caused her to stop in her tracks, give Seasons a sharp look, and then take a moment to recover. "It's pronounced *Gah-bannn-yah.*"

After another glance at the man, she added, "What a wonderful present, and it certainly shows off that body of yours. Who's the friend? He must be special to be so generous."

I didn't like the woman's tone, but that was okay. I'd already thought about how I'd handle the situation if she tried to trick me into revealing Mrs. Whitney's name. "Just a friend," I replied, which should have been the end of it.

Not for a tough one like Mrs. Calder-Shaun, though. I realized I'd have to be just as tough, or spend tomorrow rebooking charters I'd canceled —and, worse, worrying about Olivia, whose photo had just hooked me into her life in ways I could not yet guess. The woman was smiling, not catty, more like a challenge. "A hunky young man, I hope," she continued. "Larry told me you don't date much—but he's so oblivious to women, I'm not surprised he got it wrong."

Mr. Seasons started to speak, but I told him, "It's okay. It's natural to be curious—" Then turned to Mrs. Calder-Shaun. "The friend's name is personal—and that's the way it's got to stay. There's no point in me saying much more if you're not okay with that."

The woman raised her eyebrows, pretending

surprise but her flinty expression was telling me *You don't know who you're dealing with.*

That was okay, too. Growing up around rough fishermen, their wives and girlfriends, a hard look from a woman doesn't faze me any more than a hard look from a man. However, I also know that once I've stood my ground, it's smarter to offer a friendly hand than to make an enemy. So I added, "I don't mean to be disrespectful. And I do appreciate the compliment about the blouse. Olivia's what I came to talk about—her and convincing you that police need to start looking. Once I explain, I think you and Lawrence will agree." The man's name slipped out as if I'd said it a thousand times but only because I was trying so hard to hide my irritation.

*"Really,"* the woman said in a flat tone, but giving me a look that now seemed to show admiration for the way I'd stayed strong.

"Really," I replied, then nodded to an empty chair, meaning she should sit. The beautiful Martha Calder-Shaun could fault me later if she wanted. But first she was by God going to listen to what I had to say.

# Eleven

At Fishermans Wharf, where the shrimp fleet docks, I said to a man who was barefoot in the shade of a ficus tree, working on a diesel generator, "I'm looking for a boat called *Sybarite*. I was told she's moored somewhere around here."

A commercial yacht—no matter the size—wouldn't be easy to find in the two hours I had before Nathan arrived in his truck and drove me to Olivia Seasons's home in Naples. Mr. Seasons had arranged for me to have a look at Olivia's bedroom and personal stuff, and I expected it to take a while. Fishermans Wharf isn't a huge place, but it's busy. There's a clustering of maritime businesses, storage barns, and piers set among a forest of sailboat masts, net seiners, barges, and charter boats. Three marinas, plus a restaurant called Doc's Rum Bar, all offered dockage, so I was trying to narrow my search.

I had no choice. Unfortunately, Mr. Seasons had been right about the sheriff's department. He'd even suggested I speak to a missing persons officer myself. So I did—spent twenty minutes on the phone that morning before leaving in my boat. Now I was more determined than ever to find the girl.

When I spoke, the old man glanced up from the generator, eyes gathering information from my gray chambray shirt, paint-stained, my fishing shorts, the worn Top-Siders, and the canvas bag I carried over my shoulder. Then his eyes moved to a nearby slip where I'd just tied my boat. "That your skiff? I've seen it before."

"Yes, sir, it is," I told him, being polite to this seventy-some-year-old stranger because that's the way I was raised.

"Scientist what lives on Sanibel used to own it. Quiet sort of guy with glasses. He comes here sometimes, goes out with the shrimpers to see what they cull from their nets. Nice man—but I wouldn't cross him."

The old man obviously didn't want to discuss *Sybarite* until he'd figured out who he was talking to. I replied, "That's Dr. Ford. I took over my uncle's charter business two years ago. Can't imagine a better boat for the sort of fishing I do."

"You're a good friend'a his, I suppose." The man was testing me, which was just fine. Truth was, I'd been trying to invent a reason to talk to the biologist again, who was a solid-looking man with a strong face, but I had yet to summon the courage. Maybe this was my chance.

"My Uncle Jake knew him better. I haven't seen Dr. Ford since we made the deal, but I've got his number on my cell if you want to call and ask about his skiff."

The man took that as proof enough, which was a disappointment. He glanced at the bag I'd placed on the ground, SAGE FLY RODS emblem showing, and asked, "You got sponsors, huh?"

"A company in Washington State that makes really fine reels and fly rods," I answered, not expecting the old man to be impressed.

He wasn't. "Kills me these days how some supposed guides dress like race car drivers. They pay you?"

I told him no, but I got to try all the new gear, plus I made a little doing casting clinics, then added, "I'm one of the few women field testers in the country." It was something I was proud of and didn't mind letting it show.

The man thought about that for a moment before getting back to a subject he knew about. "Strictly bay fishing, I suppose."

I replied, "This time of year, I go offshore for tarpon sometimes," aware this was another test. "Tripletail and mackerel if it's glassy. Tarpon'll eat a fly in deep water even better than on the flats. Some of my clients won't believe it till it happens."

The man's face showed distaste. "Wouldn't waste a minute on tarpon, what good's a fish you can't eat?" which was typical of old-timers who'd made their living on the water and refused to accept fishing as sport. I was talking to one of those people now. He had the thick, heavy hands of someone who'd pulled their share of nets and crab traps, and brown eyes fogged blue from too much sun off the water. Those eyes focused on me for several seconds before he said in a friendlier voice, "Took over your uncle's charter business, you say?"

I nodded.

The man's face brightened. "By gad, you're Jake Smith's daughter!"

I smiled at the mistake but let the man talk.

"Jake spoke about you sometimes. I heard he'd passed away, but I've stopped goin' to funerals. Figure a dead friend wouldn't want me to waste what time I've got left in a graveyard. I sure as hell don't want 'em to waste time coming to mine."

"Jake's niece," I corrected as we shook hands, listening to the man introduce himself as Cordial Pallet, which made sense once I noticed the Star of David around his neck, the big jaw and deepset eyes that resembled dozens of other Pallets in the area. The family was well known among commer-cial fishermen because they'd owned packing-houses and a string of shrimp boats before federal fishing laws chased most of the shrimp fleet to Mexico. What was left of the fleet was docked right here, bayside of Estero Island, in the shadow of the Sky Bridge that hurdled Estero Pass onto Fort Myers Beach. Mr. Pallet smiled as we talked and exchanged a few more

146

names, but then the smile faded abruptly. "You say your name's *Hannah* Smith?"

Before he could pursue it I told him, "You might be thinking of my late Aunt Hannah. She died 'bout nine years ago."

"Boat explosion," the man nodded, thinking back while he inspected me. "I'm not one to speak bad of the dead, but some say that girl had a wild streak. That she got mixed up with bad men. Excuse me for talking straight, but I'm starting to wonder the same about you."

I didn't know how to respond. It was 9:30 Saturday morning and was aware I didn't look my best. And I certainly didn't feel my best because I hadn't slept well in Mr. Seasons's guest cottage, particularly after overhearing an argument between him and Martha Calder-Shaun— she was convinced he'd given me the expensive blouse. Then, around three a.m., the woman had come tap-tapping at my door, wobbly drunk, wearing only a T-shirt and panties.

After that, I hadn't slept at all.

Before sunup, my boat was pointed south toward Fishermans Wharf, the next barrier island down, running free in the chill of a glassy blue morning, eager for wind to clean away the tension and upset I felt after a night at Lawrence Seasons's place.

"My aunt was a strong-minded woman," I said finally, wanting my words to sound sharp. "I wish

I had half her spirit—not that it gives anyone else the right to judge how she lived her life."

"Now, don't go gettin' mad," Mr. Pallet said, apologizing with his tone. "Reason I said it is, why in the world you down here asking about *Sybarite*? I know they're advertising what they call a 'server's' position, and a mate's job, too. But those ain't jobs for you, young lady. Unless"—the man took a slow step back to get a better look at me—"unless you're on hard times. Unless you took to smoking them damn drugs like half the island kids I see stumbling around. I'll have no hand in getting you work on a boat like that. Now, tell me the truth, and I promise I won't call no cops. You in trouble, I'll do what I can. My people know people who specialize in helping young folks outta this sort of bad business. By gad, I'll give you a job myself before pointing you toward a berth aboard *Sybarite*. It's the least I can do for your uncle."

The old man said the vessel's name as if it were a profanity, so I finally understood why he'd thought the worst of me and had said what he'd said about Hannah Three. It caused me to chuckle, and say, "You're a nice man, Mr. Pallet. But you've got nothing to worry about when it comes to me and what you might be thinking." I motioned toward the generator he'd been working on. I could see he'd changed the water filter and had the sort of tools laid out on a towel

148

that told me the engine still wouldn't start. I asked, "You find water in the fuel?"

Instead of answering, the man pressed, "It just doesn't make sense you asking about *Sybarite*. There's no need to lie to me, girl. I haven't talked to your mamma in years, but I'd know her if I saw her. Met your daddy once or twice before he—" The man was about to say *before he ran off* but stopped himself in time to finish, "—and your granddaddy was a fine man, too."

There was a moment of awkwardness, which I shrugged off without much effort. I had no memory of my father. He'd left Loretta when I was three—an insult I'd fumed about until I was old enough to understand my mother's irritating ways better. The fact that Loretta continues to blame me with her snide comments about my gift for losing men only makes it less of a mystery why a handsome, smiling Army paratrooper would slip out the back door, desperate for freedom.

I knelt by the generator, looking at clamps the old man had removed from the fuel pump's tubing, and the nut to the high-pressure fuel line. I said, "If you want, I'll explain my business while I help you bleed the air out of these injector lines. It's easier with two people. Or have you already tried the lines?"

Mr. Pallet had a lot of kindness and wisdom behind those rheumy eyes of his, and he still appreciated women, judging from the quick peek

149

he stole down my blouse as he squatted beside me. "Dang kraut engines," he said. "I had to drive all the way back home and get metric wrenches. Guess I should'a tried burping her first."

"No, sir," I replied. "Water would have been my first guess, too." Actually, I would have checked to make sure there was fuel in the tank first, but I didn't want to insult the man.

He said, "You sure you're not after quick money working aboard that dang boat? 'Cause if you are—"

I interrupted to ease his mind, saying, "I'm looking for a missing woman. She's the niece of a friend of mine. I've got reason to think the man she's with might have tricked her into booking a night aboard *Sybarite*. Might even try to get her to do it again. If one of the crew remembers the woman, maybe they'll have an address written down or something. That's the only reason I'm here, Mr. Pallet. I promise."

"What's the girl's name? I've still got a good memory for faces and names."

"The family wants the name kept private," I told him. "Plus, if word gets around I'm looking for her, she might just run harder." Sensing the man's approval, I added, "But I'll trust you because of who you are."

When I'd told him Olivia's name, he said, "Beach people," which is how old-timers refer to wealthy families who've wintered on the islands for generations.

"Her uncle has a place on Captiva, but Olivia lives in Naples. Port Royal. I brought a picture of the man she might be with if you wouldn't mind having a look."

"Beach people," he repeated, meaning it didn't matter where they lived. As I reached for my equipment bag, though, he said, "Show me later. Meantime, you can explain some important left-out details while we burp these lines. Like why'd a rich family put someone like you on the girl's trail, not a hired detective or the police?"

As I explained, I was thinking that Lawrence Seasons had been righter than I'd suspected about the value of local contacts and local knowledge, which is why I added, "Main reason they hired me is because of people like you, Mr. Pallet. And that's the truth."

In reply to the puzzlement on his face, I added, "You want me to crank the engine while you pull lines? Or I'll pull lines while you crank. I don't mind diesel on my hands if that's a worry."

The old man liked that. "Good for you. I can't abide people who waste time yapping away while they could be doin' something useful."

So that's what we did. Talked while we got the generator running.

At a boarding ramp that angled up onto *Sybarite*'s deck, Mr. Pallet said to a man who looked more like a Colorado ski instructor than a boat captain,

"I told this girl I'd skin her alive if she took the mate's position you're advertising, but she's a stubborn one. I've made the introductions like promised. Now I'm washing my hands of the whole danged matter."

The old shrimper and I had become friendly during the thirty minutes it had taken us to get the diesel running. Now he was trying to help me, but his bold approach was unexpected.

Mr. Pallet's comments, however, struck the good-looking captain as humorous. In the patient way some use when speaking to the elderly, he chuckled, "If you spent more time working, less time listening to gossip, Cordie, you might be able to afford shoes. Maybe a clean shirt to go with it. Cordie . . . ? Cord!" Cordial Pallet had already pivoted and was striding away but finally stopped to listen when the man yelled, "Hey . . . I'm talking to you, old man!"

Mr. Pallet did a slow turn, his expression blank, but his eyes had the glittery focus of a pit bull watching a trespasser climb a gate. "You talking to me?" he asked, voice soft. Then raised it just enough to interrupt the man's response, saying, "The name's Cordial—*Captain* Pallet to you. Unless you wanna go home and explain to your mamma how some old man stripped the skin off your ass with a strap."

Mr. Pallet didn't have shoes, but he was wearing a leather belt and he began unbuckling it, which surprised me because I could see it wasn't an act. The boat captain realized it, too, which is why he said uneasily, "I was joking, for Christ's sake! I wanted to ask a simple damn question, that's all"—the man paused to swallow before adding —"*Captain* Pallet."

The old man nodded, his expression showing nothing, but began rebuckling his belt. "What you wanna know?"

The boat captain made a few joking remarks to convince me this sort of exchange happened all the time between him and Mr. Pallet, who he called "this salty old coot," but Mr. Pallet, stone-faced, finally interrupted, "You got a question or don't you?"

*Sybarite*'s captain swallowed again, a nervous man for having a body so tall and lean, muscular-looking in his nautical slacks, canvas belt, and a white short-sleeved shirt, *Capt. Robert Simpson* embroidered above the pocket. "Is she qualified?" he asked, forcing a tough tone. "Does she have papers and is she qualified? Or does that piss you off for some reason, too?"

Pallet took a slow look at *Sybarite*, an exotic-looking passenger yacht, three decks high, with sleek black windows that gave the steering room and cabins a secretive look. There was also a tower of electronics spaced between radar cones high above the flybridge where there was what looked like a service bar and a Jacuzzi.

"She's a hell of a lot more qualified than you, I imagine," Mr. Pallet said finally. "What you're really asking is, will I vouch for her? Answer is yes, she'd be first-rate—if I wanted her working for the likes of you and your owners. Which I don't. But she's a stubborn one, I wasn't lying. Whether she takes the job or not, that's up to her."

For an instant, just an instant, the old fisherman flashed me a private glance that told me he was manipulating Robert Simpson, giving him a stronger reason to consider me for a job I had no intention of taking. Cause him to hire me just because Mr. Pallet didn't want it to happen. Which was smart. In reply, I touched an index finger to the side of my nose as a private *Thank you,* then waved as he walked away, calling, " 'Preciate it, Captain! If you have any more trouble with that engine, you've got my cell. I'll be in touch."

Which was true. In the time we'd spent working on the diesel, I'd grown fond of the man. He was smart, he actually listened to what I had to say and didn't mince words, yet there was a gentlemanly quality about him that I appreciated —maybe because it's so rare in men my own age. Whatever the reason, I trusted Mr. Pallet enough to tell him details regarding Olivia Seasons— minus Mrs. Whitney's name, of course. He'd probably figured out right away why I wanted to get aboard *Sybarite*, but didn't let on until I'd showed him the photo of Ricky Meeks. After wiping his hands clean on a rag, the old fisherman had held the photo close, squinting to get a sharper look, then said, "You did good to come to me first, young lady. Wouldn't be smart to show a thing like this around the boatyards."

I asked, "Do you remember what he calls himself? The man's using a couple of names."

Pallet had replied with a quick shake of the head, then used the towel again, wiping his hands until I'd slipped the photo into an envelope and zipped my canvas bag closed. "You sure he's the one this rich girl ran off with?"

"No, sir. But my suspicions are getting stronger. You must've seen him around."

The man nodded as I added, "He lives on a boat, maybe he's got some friends. I wouldn't ask about him right out, of course—"

Mr. Pallet interrupted, "It's enemies you've got to worry about—man like him doesn't have friends. People he owes money. Some mad husband who wants to chunk him on the head. Folks think you know a man like that, they'll assume you're trash, too. Or you're an easy way to get some questions answered."

"You met him," I said.

Another shake of the head. "Didn't bother. He owns a beat-up Skipjack cruiser, thirty-footer with a low flybridge, anchored here three or four times in the last year. Paddled ashore in a bluish sort of cheap dinghy. I know the kind'a man he is

155

by the way he handles himself and handles that boat."

A cabin cruiser with a dinghy stowed on the bow—it matched Lawrence Seasons's description, I noted, listening to Cordial Pallet continue. "That sorta man, he's all show and big mouth with women around. Otherwise, he stayed to himself, avoided men. That's always a bad sign—*remember* that, young lady. A man without men friends, there's usually something bad wrong about them. That one"—he had nodded toward my bag, which contained the photo of Meeks—"he reminds me of a thing with teeth that hides in a hole and waits for bait to swim by."

After that, it was comfortable for me to tell Mr. Pallet what I had in mind. I wanted to board *Sybarite* in hopes of finding out if Olivia had gone on the Key West cruise, as I suspected, or had booked a future trip. It would confirm that I was right about why she had used her special credit card and that Mr. Seasons was wrong in thinking it meant she'd gotten rid of Ricky Meeks.

I didn't expect anyone I met to name names, of course. And I couldn't come right out and ask whether Olivia had been on the boat, but the guest list would be somewhere aboard if the boat's captain kept proper records. And when Mr. Pallet manipulated the good-looking captain, Robert Simpson, into wanting to hire me, my hopes brightened. Like it or not, men tend to be sloppier about paperwork than women—a boat is no different than an office when it comes to that—so maybe a few months of names were hanging on a clipboard somewhere right out in the open.

That's what was on my mind as Captain Simpson watched Pallet stride away, the scowl still on his face when he turned to me and said, "You helped *him* fix an engine? According to locals, there's nothing that obnoxious old bastard can't do when it comes to boats. What kind?"

Ignoring the insult, I told him the brand of diesel, saying it in a way that suggested I was being modest.

"You have your Coast Guard papers with you?" Simpson asked the question, trying not to sound impressed, but he was.

I had a copy of my Merchant Mariners 100 Ton Ocean Operator's license aboard my skiff, which I explained as the good-looking captain waved me up the boarding ramp onto the boat's deck.

"What're your operating restrictions? We sail from here to Key West a couple of times a month, but sometimes we do a week trip to the Bahamas. And, about twice a year, the owners fly over to Campeche and meet the boat in Mexico. I make the decisions, but I expect my mate to spend a lot of time at the wheel. If your ticket doesn't cover the area, we could maybe apply for an extension, but I'd rather have someone already qualified."

I hoped to impress the man again by telling him

my license was designated *unlimited,* meaning I had no operating restrictions—thanks to my Uncle Jake, who'd always pushed me—before risking a question of my own. "Who's the owner?"

Simpson had been warming to me, I could sense it, but that changed instantly. He had opened the door to the main salon but now used his body to block my way before replying, "This is a private commercial yacht. Everything about it is private. That includes the name of the owners, the names of our clients. It includes what goes on before charters, during charters, and after charters. Especially *during* charters. Understand that? What's your name again?"

I told him, trying not to be obvious about looking past him into the salon, where I was surprised to see a girl about my age whose face seemed familiar. A blond girl, thin as a fashion model, Havana-cream complexion, and what I suspected were grapefruit-sized breast implants straining against a white *Sybarite* blouse. She was standing at a bar that glistened with varnish, folding cloth napkins, the reflection in the mirror behind her showing the most ornate cabin I'd ever seen on a vessel, exotic inlaid wood, brass fixtures, spotless maritime glass.

"Hannah Smith," Simpson repeated before saying, "The first rule aboard *Sybarite* is, my crew keeps their mouths shut. They don't ask questions—not about the owner, our clients, *nothing*—unless the question has something to do with their job. If you don't think you can do that, we might as well stop the tour right here."

I looked into the man's green eyes long enough to say, "A client's privacy and safety, those are the two most important things, I agree," then let my gaze drift past the girl to my shoes, which is something I did a couple of more times while Simpson continued to lecture me.

"*Sybarite* isn't some head boat that hauls tourists a mile offshore to catch trash fish. We cater to an exclusive clientele who demand the best, Hannah, so I only hire the best. It's way too early to start talking money, but I guarantee you won't believe what my first mate makes in tips alone. In return, I demand total dedication to your job. That means *total* dedication to our clients as well. Understood?"

Maybe. The man said it in a way to suggest a double meaning that, knowing what I knew about *Sybarite*, had a whorish ring. I was more interested in the girl who had paused, an unfolded napkin in her hand. She recognized me, too, I realized. She was staring in my direction, her memory probably trying to do the same as mine, attach a name to a face I hadn't seen since . . . college? No . . . high school, more likely. My time at community college was more like a day job than an educational experience. I hadn't socialized at all.

Simpson had finally allowed me into the salon and was leading me toward the steering room, now saying *Sybarite*'s crew was more like a "close-knit little fraternity," which caused the blond girl to roll her eyes as we passed by, her smile not bitter, exactly, but not cheerful either. That's when the name came to me: Gabrielle Corrales, a popular, flat-chested girl (at the time) who had inherited a slight Cuban accent but not much of the language and who'd run for an office of some type, posting cardboard signs in the halls. When I stopped, though, wondering if I should say hello, Gabrielle used a panicked look and a quick shake of her head to urge me to keep moving. So I did. We hadn't been friends in school, so I was neither worried nor hurt. Even so, I was curious about the girl's behavior and determined to find a way to speak with her in private. A girl who folded napkins as part of her job had less to lose by talking about clients than a starched yacht captain who probably made a good living and who clearly was protective of the boat's privacy.

It happened. Half an hour later, when I'd finished my interview and was crossing the parking lot toward the docks, Gabrielle pulled beside me in a red Corvette convertible, top up, engine running to stay cool in the June heat.

"Get in, *chula*," she said, the window cracked only a few inches.

*"What?"*

"You heard me!"

Caught by surprise, I hesitated and checked my watch. Nathan would be arriving in twenty minutes to drive me to Olivia's house, but the girl didn't give me a chance to explain. She pushed the passenger door open and hissed, "Hurry up! Trust me, you don't want him to see us together."

*Sybarite*'s captain, Robert Simpson, I assumed.

I got in the car, which felt cramped with legs as long as mine until I found the power-seat adjustment. After that, riding in Gabrielle's Corvette was more like riding in a spaceship.

"Where we going?" I asked, then was slammed back in my seat when she accelerated.

Upset enough that it fired her Cuban vocabulary, Gabrielle replied, "Someplace safe! We need to talk, *chinga*, or you're screwed!"

# Twelve

Gabrielle was rummaging around in her purse for something as she asked me, "Anyone following us? Take a look over your shoulder." It came out *Teek eeh luke*, the only hint she was part Cuban.

I replied, "They'd have to own a jet airplane to keep up," but twisted around in my seat anyway. "Nope. Just that man with the limp, but he's headed the other way—not that I blame him." I was referring to the guy she'd almost clipped with her fender.

Not bothering to glance back at the old fisherman, who was wobbling toward the shrimp yards, a paper sack clutched to his chest, Gabrielle said, "Old drunks should own Seeing Eye dogs," then, without looking up, informed me, "I go by Gabby now. Clients think it's cute, and it stops people from confusing me with the horn guy in the Bible. If they read *Gabrielle* on paper, it happens every time."

Darren had mentioned Gabby when speaking of *Sybarite*, but I hadn't made the connection. *Gabrielle*, though, sounded better, the way the girl rolled her Spanish *r*'s.

We were in a parking lot between a boat storage barn and a large wooden complex that was perched on stilts overlooking the bay, DOC'S RUM BAR on a green sign atop the building, the area still empty because it was early. No one around but cawing seagulls and a wandering cat. Gabby had parked near a cabbage palm that threw about as much shade as a fence post, so she left the engine running, the volume of "Mr. Saxobeats'" thumping disco too soft to hear above the blast of air-conditioning but with enough bass to feel through my seat.

"Where the hell did I put it?" the girl muttered, still pawing at her purse, then told me, "Robert's a paranoid little dictator, never trust him. He has spies everywhere. Take another quick look, I'm *serious*."

The only other person I knew who would fret about spies on a clear June morning was Loretta. The remark caused me to lose some confidence in Gabby and wonder about my own judgment, having allowed a woman I hadn't seen in years drive me a mile from the docks, tires screeching at every start and stop. In fifteen minutes, I was supposed to meet Nathan. Because he is not a punctual man, however, it was not a troubling concern. Plus, I had my cell with me. Nathan would text if he found my skiff empty.

*"Finally,"* Gabby said, bringing out a pink pillbox that contained three tightly wrapped joints, each thin as a dart. She lit one with a Bic, holding the joint between her lips until she'd replaced the case, then inhaled deeply before saying, "I can't believe you'd do something that stupid. Jesus Christ!"

Spoken without exhaling, her words sounded squeaky, which only added to my confusion.

"What's wrong with applying for a job?" I asked. "Captain Simpson says the first mate job pays pretty good money." I let her watch me survey the Corvette's gauges and leather upholstery while adding, "Looks to me like you're not doing too bad yourself."

"Captain Simpson," Gabby said, exhaling her

163

contempt. "That's a laugh. He's a backstabbing asshole who hates women—never forget that." She extended her hand, offering the joint, and waited until I shook my head before repeating, "What you did was so goddamn stupid! The straightest girl I've ever met, so quiet and polite in school. Hannah Smith—*unbelievable*."

I figured she was referring to me being aboard *Sybarite*, a boat with a bad reputation, until she added, "Knock off the act, damn it! I saw you! Robert would've called the cops if I'd told him." The girl considered me for a moment, then looked at the joint between her fingers as if reconsidering. "Or . . . maybe you are a cop. Is that what this is about?"

"Last two years," I said, "I'm a fishing guide, mostly fly-fishing, that's my specialty. I heard about the mate's job from Cordial Pallet. You can ask him."

Gabby was still staring, thinking about it. A grown woman who worried about spies and smoked weed in public parking lots would need more reassuring if I expected her to open up and explain what she was talking about. I hate cigarettes but remembered liking the taste of marijuana, which Delbert Fowler had finally gotten me to try the afternoon he'd asked me to be his wife. It was one of those rare days when the word *no* didn't seem to be in my vocabulary, which has been the ruin of more than a few good women, I suspect. But all it had cost me was a one-night marriage and a few unpleasant hours feeling like someone had poured syrup on my brain.

"People change," I told Gabby, using my fingers to pinch the joint from her hand. "If you're accusing me of something, there's not much I can say until I know what it is." I put the joint to my lips, took a shallow puff, then another, before handing it back.

The woman murmured a phrase I hadn't learned in college Spanish, then said, "You didn't inhale. Think I'm stupid?"

"I like the taste but not the feeling," I explained.

"You kidding. The guy I buy from calls this stuff 'Sunshine Skyway.' " She took a dreamy drag to illustrate. "Says it's like floating over water on a sunny day."

I shook my head. "I've got my own boat, thanks. The taste, though, it's nice. Sort of an herbal flavor, and it smells good. Like smoking tea, you think?"

"Tequila—" Gabby said, making no sense. Then she took a deep hit and held the smoke in for several seconds before exhaling, "—Tequila's the same for me. I'll order a shooter just to smell and sip it, but I only drink Grey Goose 'n' cranberry. You really don't like getting high?"

"I would if it didn't make me feel so slow and stupid," I answered. "A couple of mojitos with fresh mint, that's a different story."

Gabby took another hit, offered the joint to me again, and this time smiled when I took only the shallowest of puffs before handing it back.

"Sort of sweet and tomboyish," she said. "That's what I remember about you. Can't believe how much you've changed. I stay in touch with a few girls from our class"—Gabby named several names—"and most of them already look like hell. They have kids, got fat, got skinny after their first divorce, and already getting fat again. But you're looking good, Hannah. Not so plain, like in school, so I almost didn't"—the girl stopped, aware she'd said something mean, then finished with a wider smile—"almost missed the chance to make a new girlfriend. We're gonna have some fun, you and me."

My old schoolmate was beginning to relax, I decided, but the smile left her face when I replied, "If that's a compliment, I appreciated it. Now, tell me what I did that was so damn stupid."

The woman sat up straight and got serious again. "*Sybarite* has a video monitoring system, you idiot! A whole closetful of electronics off the main salon. Your interview with Robert, I was *watching*. You still gonna sit there and play innocent?"

"*Oh,*" I whispered, too surprised not to sound guilty. My brain was already sifting through a series of lies that might explain my behavior. I was irked at myself for not having an excuse ready and also because I'd looked for cameras and had failed to spot a single one.

"What were you after, Hannah? You were looking for something. Might as well tell me the truth. I've got the recording"—she reached for her purse again—"the whole thing right here. It's on a memory stick. Downloaded on my iPhone, too. You want to watch yourself opening drawers, going through private papers, when Robert wasn't looking?"

It was all true. Every chance I'd gotten, I'd searched for a passenger list. My best opportunity had come when Simpson had stepped outside the helm area to take what he said was an important call. For the next four, maybe five minutes, I had moved like a thief, going through drawers, files, leafing through clipboards, and had almost gotten caught when Simpson surprised me by returning through a different door. In truth, the man *would* have caught me if he hadn't dropped his cell phone as he entered. All I'd come away with was a shaky set of nerves and proof I'd been right about the man keeping sloppy records. Even the boat's logbook was a mess, hadn't been updated in more than three weeks.

"You want evidence?" Gabby was laughing as she scrolled through her iPhone. "Wait . . . I'm trying to find my favorite part . . . *shit* . . . I had it cued up. Here . . . here it is. I found it!"

Simpson squatting to pick up his phone,

oblivious to me, mule-eyed, fumbling to jam a folder into a drawer before closing it, that was the woman's favorite footage.

"The expression on your face!" she croaked after taking a final hit, fighting to hold the smoke in. "Like you're about to pee your pants!"

I wasn't laughing. "Why are you showing me this, not Simpson?"

"He's a prick, I already told you. I erased it from the computer, so no need to worry—as long as I have the only copy."

My classmate was threatening me.

I turned the radio down until my seat stopped vibrating, then finally found the window button, needing fresh air. After a couple of deep breaths, I said, "What's the real reason?"

There was a thing Gabby did with her face I remembered from high school, fluttering her eyelashes, cheeks sucked in, something she thought looked innocent and cute. She made the face now before replying, "Thing is, sweetie, I don't *care* what you were looking for. The name of your screw-around husband or boyfriend, that's my guess. It wouldn't be the first time. Or cash . . . or you've got some sort of mental compulsion—my last roommate couldn't pass a mirror without touching it no matter how hard she tried. You're not a cop, so who the hell cares? Robert's gonna offer you the job. That's why we're sitting here. It'll be a week or two, but he'll do it. I just want to make sure we've got some kind of arrangement in place when you start working as first mate." Gabby had fiddled with the radio as she talked so my seat was vibrating again, a punk group doing "Missing You."

Her threat was beginning to take shape.

"What do you want?" I asked.

What Gabby wanted in return for not showing Robert Simpson the video was fifty percent of my tips for the first six months, after that twenty percent, which was five percent more than the standard cut between *Sybarite*'s first mate and what she called "the hostesses."

"I don't even know how much money we're talking," I responded. "What makes you so sure I'll get the job? Did he say something?"

Cupping her hands beneath her breasts, Gabby said, "Because of these, sweetie. You're the first qualified woman to apply and you've got a nice set of tits—something I don't remember you having in high school, by the way. On *Sybarite*, a good body means a hell of a lot more than experience." She paused, her eyes moving from my breasts to my face. "So what about it?"

I thought she meant the deal she'd just offered until she continued, "I got my implants six years ago, and they've totally changed my life. Who did yours?"

I told her, "An inheritance from a dead aunt, I guess, but it was a long time before they

169

showed up. Back to the subject of money—"

Gabby interrupted, "That's what I'm trying to tell you! With your body and those legs, my God, Hannah, you'll look so goddamn hot in nautical whites. Or our navy blues, which we wear in winter, except for formal dinners . . ."

The girl went on about uniforms for a while, everything custom-tailored—shorts, blouses, slacks, and blazers—before telling me, "Our clients will eat you up—literally . . . *if* you're willing. That's where the real money is, sweetie. Keep in mind that, you and me, we only share tips you make on cruises. Any sideline stuff you arrange with clients, it's yours to keep. Cut the right deal with Robert, he'll even give you permission to wear a *Sybarite* uniform if it's one of our regulars. More than a few have a fetish for the whole uniform thing."

The new expression on my face caused Gabby to laugh again. "It's not like I'm talking about being a hooker, for Christ sake! It's not like that at all." She paused. "What did Robert tell you about *Sybarite*? About the type of charters we do, I mean." She was having fun being the expert, me the novice.

"Enough," I replied, which was true. The man had hinted around, stressing the importance of confidentiality over and over, before finally telling me that clients paid for a "unique sensual experience" and the crew was expected to make sure it happened, then keep their damn mouths shut.

"Maybe so," Gabby said, "but get the whole prostitution thing out of your head. No one's gonna *force* you. Or even expect it. See . . . the way it goes is, we're out at sea, everyone's relaxed, and things just sort of happen. You meet a nice gentleman aboard, sometimes a man with his good-looking wife or girlfriend, it's only natural they want to party. You'd have as much fun as them, probably more, if you just loosen up. Next day, if they want to thank you for the good time, it's only natural they give you something extra special."

"The tips," I said. "It's always cash?"

The woman flashed a catty smile, and replied, "Take a guess at the biggest tip I ever got for our cruise to Key West. Go ahead, guess. One night, two days, and I personally had a damn blast!" Without waiting, she tapped the convertible's dashboard. "You're sitting in it, sweetie. Last year—from a very, very special couple."

I couldn't stop myself from saying, "A *Corvette*—holy shit!" For the first time, I gave fleeting thought to accepting the mate's job if offered.

"Look . . ." Gabby thought for a moment, then tried a different approach, lowering her voice. "Our clients, they aren't just regular people. We're not talking rednecks and salesmen at a

171

convention. These are some of the most successful people in the country. I'm not naming names. Even when you're part of the crew, no one names names. Not last names, anyway. But I can tell you this"—the joint had gone out and she now took a few seconds to relight it—"some of the names you see in *People* magazine, on TV, the movies. Mostly not, though, because they've got enough money to keep their lives private. If they wanted hookers, trust me, they could hire a bunch for what they pay for two days aboard *Sybarite*." Gabby tapped the car's dashboard again to prove her point. "But when guests are with us, just them and the crew, it's not work. It's more of a *We're enjoying this experience together* sort of thing. A private party at sea, that's the way I look at it. With the best of everything."

Sensing a chance to maneuver the conversation toward Olivia Seasons, I offered, "I've got fishing clients with money, but you wouldn't know their names if I told you. And they live right here in the area. The same's probably true of the clients you're talking about."

Gabby startled me by replying, "Do you know the difference between people with money and people who're actually *wealthy?* Think about it because that's the difference I'm talking about."

I'd gone thirty years without hearing that question, now I'd been asked it twice in less than twenty-four hours. It might have been coincidence, but more likely she'd run into Mrs. Whitney and Ricky Meeks on their trips to Key West. "Classiness?" I offered, thinking it was the answer she wanted and would move us in the right direction.

"Nope," Gabby replied, her expression mellow. "It's right here," then clasped a hand to her breast. "They're classier, sure. But the real difference is, they have huge hearts. You would not believe how polite and generous they are. Once you get to know them—most wealthy people, I'm saying. They're fun and totally *real*."

My schoolmate was stoned, if the hand squeezing her left implant meant anything. Too stoned now to keep on track—I'd been through it enough with Delbert Fowler to recognize the signs. I looked at my watch and said, "Whoops, I'm late. You mind taking me back to my boat? I want your number so I can call later. Tonight okay?"

Agreeing as she fumbled to start the car, Gabby repeated herself about wealthy people being real and having big hearts, which I expected to hear a few dozen more times if she was anything like Delbert. Instead, she varied it by saying, "A couple of clients, they've become two of my closest friends. That's the truth, sweetie. You'd love 'em. The wife, she's more like an older sister now. Doesn't make any difference I work as a hostess and she's worth a few hundred million."

Because I was watching traffic as Gabby accelerated toward the exit, instead of asking *She bought you the Corvette?* I reminded her that a truck was coming so don't forget to stop.

"I see it, I see it," Gabby grumbled, then snapped her fingers as if she'd just remembered something. "In fact, they're having a party tomorrow night. Tomorrow's Sunday, right? Not big, just a few people. Want to be my date?"

When traffic was clear, I told her, "You can turn now," then waited for her to do it before saying, "Your client friends, you mean?"

"They own a mansion in Naples—but they've got houses all over the world. It's a pool party–barbecue sort of deal. Bring a suit if you want—or *not*. It'll be very laid-back." Gabby grinned, eyes a tad droopy, both hands on the wheel while she turned right again toward the shrimp yards, now driving way too slow. "Where you living these days? We can meet somewhere around seven and take my car."

I already had an excuse waiting and was shaking my head until she pleaded, "Please, Hannah! It's only forty minutes, a gated community with some of the most beautiful homes you've ever seen. Port Royal—you've heard of it?"

Suddenly, I was interested. Rather than answering, I reminded her it was best to pull over before we got to the docks or Robert Simpson might see us and get suspicious. Gabby liked that.

"You know, sweetie, I had a feeling we were gonna hit it off. *¡Mejores amigas! ¡Amigas para siempre!* Know what that means?"

In formal college Spanish, I replied, "It is nice to have friends who have trust and share secrets," which came out stilted but not too bad.

Gabby liked that even better, clapping her hands a couple of times in applause. "*¡Mejores amigas siempre, sí!* My last girlfriend, we had a big blowup six months ago, and I've been bored as hell ever since. A regular bitch, too—so forget what I said about splitting tips for six months. Make it three months, then the regular split . . . and all the dinners and drinks are on me. How 'bout it?"

Gabby was a tough one when it came to money, something I admire in a woman, but she was also lonely like most single people our age. She struck me as tricky, a tad neurotic and sad but not a bad person. The same, I suspected, could be said of me at times. Mostly, though, I was thinking about tomorrow's party. It wouldn't interfere with my plans to stop at marinas between Vanderbilt Beach and Naples as Mr. Seasons had suggested. The party might be a waste of time, but there was also a chance I would meet someone who knew Olivia. Port Royal couldn't be that big . . . maybe one of her neighbors had spoken with her recently. On the other hand, Lawrence Seasons had told me that Olivia had no close

175

friends. Undecided, I decided to take a chance.

*"Bored?"* I said, being sympathetic. "Try being a fishing guide. I don't meet any girls our age. The few I know, all they talk about is their kids, their husbands, and how nice their house is. Makes me feel like a loser. Or like I'm from outer space."

Excited by my confession, Gabby replied, *"Tell me about it.* Honey, we've got so *much* in common!" then asked if I was married, if I was dating someone special, all the regular questions I have learned to dodge with as few words and lies as possible. She had pulled into a vacant lot a hundred yards from the boat docks, where I could see a muscled giant in a tank top pacing and checking his watch. Nathan Pace.

"I've gotta run," I said, unzipping my equipment bag and taking out the envelope that contained Ricky Meeks's picture. "You sure you really want me along tomorrow night? I'd love to go, but I've never hung out with the sort of people you're talking about. I might be nervous."

Sounding happy and very stoned, Gabby told me to relax, wear a nice blouse and shorts—not *fishing* shorts, for God's sake—or a summer skirt that showed my legs, and I would do just fine. Then she asked, "What's that?" meaning the envelope.

"If we're going to be friends," I said, "I don't want to start out with a lie. When you asked if I was looking for someone's name? You were sort of right." I then proceeded to tell several lies after showing her the photo, saying that Ricky Meeks owed a friend of mine money, that someone had mentioned seeing him aboard *Sybarite*, which is why I'd been asked to check the crew roster while I was interviewing for the mate's job.

"If Simpson hadn't left me alone, I wouldn't have bothered," I added. "I like doing favors for people when I can, but I wouldn't have risked a good job."

Sneaky and guilty, that's how I felt when Gabby, in her eagerness to be friends, pretended to believe me, even though I sensed she had her doubts. After listening to what she had to say about Meeks, I felt better in some ways, worse in others. But it didn't compare to the electric spark I experienced when she concluded, "For all I know, the guy might even be at the party tomorrow. He shows up sometimes, but only if he's the guest of a guest."

"Your friends would invite a man like that?" I replied, the electric sensation still moving through my spine.

"Not them, sweetie. I doubt if they know he exists. But there's always a few losers around. Some women—wealthy, older women usually—can't get enough of what a guy like him's got to offer. Go figure. But you've got to promise you won't make a scene if he shows. You can't say a damn word about money, it just wouldn't be classy."

"Promise," I told my new girlfriend, a little dizzy because of my good luck . . . or possibly the marijuana smoke I'd inhaled just from being in Gabby's car.

# Thirteen

That afternoon, I was standing with Nathan inside Olivia's "room" and had just seen for myself that Gabby Corrales was right about Port Royal. Every mansion was a gated island, crowns of brick or stone poking through the trees, with winding driveways shaded by oaks or, in Olivia's case, a quarter mile of royal palms, solid as cement, the trees spaced like shaggy utility poles.

Voice low, Nathan said to me, "Even *he* can tell. Did you see the way he stared? We need to get you home and put you to bed before he says something. Or calls the DEA."

My friend was referring to the uniformed guard who had signed us in at the security pavilion after stubbing out his cigar. Then he'd let us into the Seasonses' mansion, using keys he had taken from a lockbox, and was now stationed at the door.

"I am *not* stoned," I whispered for the

umpteenth time, which was untrue, possibly because I now at least *imagined* feeling spooked and sort of fuzzy. When I saw that Nathan was grinning, though, I slapped his shoulder and told him, "Stop doing that . . . *please.* You're making me paranoid. Look around the rest of the house . . . or wait outside. I need time to concentrate."

Nathan was doing a slow three-sixty, still marveling at the spaciousness of Olivia's suite and also the monkish way she had stripped the walls of decorations and painted everything white.

"Chastity and virtue," he said. "That's the message I'm getting. And a ton of guilt—you two ladies have a lot in common."

"Olivia goes through phases," I explained, ignoring the gibe. "Mr. Seasons said a Goth stage back in high school. In her midtwenties, she got into yoga and meditation, then drugs and nightclubs for a while—but only a few months, it didn't take her long to snap out of it. Because she was dating some guy, he says. Lately, it's religion. Religion, growing orchids, and painting. He says Olivia lives like a monk. Or did before Ricky Meeks came along."

"A monastery," Nathan agreed, "that's what this place reminds me of. But where's all her personal stuff? Things she doesn't want anyone else to see?" He motioned toward a rostrum in the corner that held a lone orchid. "A single flower—

179

the only color in the whole damn room, which would drive Darren nuts. And her paintings? Where're her paintings?"

Looking at the orchid, I shrugged, no answer to offer. The orchid's petals were white ivory fringed with pink, not much color left. Wilting from lack of sunlight and attached to a vertical base, the plant leaned like a shepherd's crook . . . or a weary question mark. It felt strange to be in Olivia's room, talking about her, poking into her privacy with only her uncle's permission. I wouldn't have tolerated it. Even reminding myself it was for Olivia's own good didn't make me any less eager to get this over with. But it would take a while. Her part of the house consisted of most of the mansion's east wing, which included an office, a bathroom with a bidet and sauna, a living room that opened out onto a waterfront porch and orchid house, a full kitchen, and a vaulted-ceiling bedroom with a walk-in closet that was larger than any two bedrooms I'd ever had.

"Why would anyone run away from this?" Nathan asked, then opened venetian blinds to look out a window. "Christ, she's even got her own lap pool and Jacuzzi. How do you think you'd handle it? Being this rich."

Rather than answering, or explaining the difference between *rich* and *wealthy,* I put my hands on his back and steered the man toward the door. "Out! Get serious and try to find something useful. This girl's in real trouble. Hasn't that sunk in yet?"

On the drive to Naples, I had shared what Gabby had told me about Ricky Meeks. She had not only seen Meeks on several cruises, she'd asked Robert Simpson to ban him from the boat after clients had complained about his behavior.

"Robert wouldn't do it, of course," Gabby had said, then explained the reason.

"Ricky is what we call a 'teaser pony.' He finds a woman who's super-wealthy, talks her into a cruise, and Robert pays him a percentage or maybe a flat fee. The woman never knows, of course. Even I wouldn't know for sure if I didn't tally the bar receipts after a cruise. All the guy's drinks are comped—what's that tell you?

"I'm guessing we have maybe a dozen teaser ponies," she'd continued, "mostly women and gays who do five or six cruises a year. Regulars who're good at what they do, never cause any trouble. Ricky is more of a freelancer. He did some bottom work on *Sybarite* a few years back. You know, went down with tanks and scraped barnacles or something and has been around ever since. Robert says he's good at that sort of work. Lifting, painting, boatyard stuff, so he's useful. But why he puts up with the guy's bullshit on cruises, I've got no idea."

The problem with Ricky Meeks, Gabby told me, was that he was pure West Texas trash, nothing classy about him, although he could act the part up to a point. The more he drank, though, the meaner and louder he got. That wasn't all bad, depending on the clients, because "rough trade" was Ricky's specialty, a term the girl had to explain to me, which was embarrassing. The look of disgust on my face had obviously amused her.

"Live and let live," Gabby had warned. "If I judged people by their secret fantasies—knowing some of the crazy things I've seen on our trips?— I'd be afraid to leave the house. That's one thing I've learned working aboard *Sybarite*. Even the nicest, best sort of people—men and women both—have a dark little place in their brain just aching to be itched." The girl had looked at me for a long second before asking, "Are you saying you're any different?"

No, I could not—particularly after what I'd experienced when a drunken Martha Calder-Shaun had come tapping at the guesthouse door last night, wearing only a T-shirt and panties. I hadn't admitted that to Gabby, of course. I hadn't even shared it with Nathan and wasn't sure I would, although I had debated it in my head for the hour it took us to get to Port Royal. If anyone would understand, it was him.

"Robert's gay," Gabby had informed me after talking awhile about people's behavior in a way that sometimes sounded mean but more often fair and thoughtful, which had impressed me. "He won't admit he's gay, of course—and Ricky goes both ways, which I know from at least one trip for sure. So maybe that's the answer. Ricky probably has something on Robert. Plus, he brings in money. That's what it always comes down to, sweetie: money. If anyone tries to tell you different, they are totally full of *mierda*. Money, money, *money*. Know what that means?"

Even if I didn't, I'd have understood from the way she said the word.

All of these thoughts and snatches of conversation were colliding inside my head while I attempted an orderly search of Olivia's rooms, occasionally taking photos with my cell phone to help me remember what I was seeing. It was difficult to keep my mind focused, and the little I found was upsetting instead of helpful, although it meshed with what I knew about the girl.

"You come from opposite backgrounds," a buzzed Lawrence Seasons had confided last night, "but Olivia and you strike me as similar in at least a few ways. Subtle similarities, unusual, and hard to put into words. You both have a sort of attractiveness that . . . well, it takes some time to appreciate. Unique, you know? And the look in your eyes when your attention wanders. Olivia was detached from people, even in a crowded room. My guess is, the same's true of you."

*Unusual similarities despite our differences.* That part, at least, was soon confirmed.

Olivia's dressing room closet, which was large enough to stock a women's department store, was so empty my footsteps echoed off the tile floor. Inside were hundreds of empty hangers but only a few simple dresses, mostly in earth colors—which I happen to prefer—and several careful stacks of shorts, jeans, and blouses that were suitable for gardening and hiking—or even fishing—all neatly folded.

I snapped a few photos, which was useful because the flash revealed something my eyes had missed. Against the far corner were three over-stuffed garbage bags covered by a white sheet, which caused them to blend in with the walls.

*Donations to Goodwill* was the first explanation that came to mind. If so, Naples had the luckiest store in Florida, judging from what I found. Inside were some of the most beautiful jackets, dresses, blouses, and women's suits I'd ever seen. Rather than hurry, I began transferring garments to hangers, telling myself that creating an orderly display from the jumble was better than scattering Olivia's personal things on the floor. It showed respect, and also provided a cleaner overview of the girl as a person—the way her mind worked, her private preferences.

This was the first discovery that proved how similar our tastes are. Or were. Olivia was a jeans girl who liked her pants snug fitting, low on the hips, tapered lean at the calves, which is best for wearing boots. Same with me. She preferred understated clothing to the ornate. Many of the designer labels were foreign, but some I recognized from clothes I had admired in stores and catalogs but were too crazy expensive to buy—several Versace blouses among them. A few labels I knew from my own closet: Calvin Klein, Polo, and a cocktail dress that was almost exactly like a black Donna Karan I'd discovered on sale at T.J.Maxx and had guarded on my way to the checkout as if it were stolen treasure.

I snapped more photos, then couldn't help but carry Olivia's version of the dress to a mirror and hold it up to see how it would fit. She was a tall girl, too, but thinner—a diagnosed anorexic, Mr. Seasons had told me. Even so, I liked what I was seeing. The dress was elegant but informal . . . and sexy in a tasteful, flirting sort of way, so I'd yet to find an occasion, or the nerve, to wear it.

As I looked into the mirror, I imagined Olivia modeling this same dress right here where I was standing—she undoubtedly had. I imagined her striking similar poses, her face replacing my own so totally that I had to give my head a shake. To clear my mind, I thought about tomorrow night's party and remembered that Gabby had told me to wear something classy but comfortable—a black cocktail dress would work.

*"Maybe,"* I whispered to the girl staring at me from the mirror. *"We'll see."* Then I returned to the closet to check the other garbage bags—a decision that affected me in a way that was more emotional than expected.

I'm not as crazy about shopping and clothing as some women, but I do have a love for shoes— boots especially—as well as fine purses and wallets. The odor of soft leather and the feather lightness of shoes or boots beautifully crafted can lift my spirits faster than anything I know. More than once when feeling depressed or lonely, I have bought new shoes or a handbag I couldn't afford, indifferent to the guilt I knew I'd experience the next day when I returned it.

Olivia was much the same, which was soon obvious, but wealthy enough to avoid the humiliation of standing in line at the return counter. I found dozens of pairs of shoes—sandals, espadrilles, heels, and boots. My God, the boots! Beautiful handsewn leather from Italy, butter-soft in my hands, several pairs I would have loved to own. Especially a pair of black butch-looking faux biker boots that were ankle-high with silver pirate buckles on the sides. I'd coveted a similar pair at Saks—eight hundred dollars! Thank God, Olivia wore a size 9, which was a size too small for me or I'd have been tempted to try them on. There were also purses by Kate Spade and two fine wallets, one *exactly* like the brown clutch wallet I'd bought for my birthday only a few weeks ago. T.J.Maxx again. On sale, half retail.

As I took more photos, I wondered if Olivia had enjoyed the same feeling I got when finding such treasures in a store. Of course she had. The proof was right here. The connection gave me a strange feeling, but not so strong it erased obvious questions. Why would Olivia dispose of so many beautiful things in garbage bags? Tired of wearing them? That struck me as improbable. Every garment smelled and looked so new. More likely, it had to do with her recent monkish behavior. Even so, no matter how religious, it didn't make sense. A pious woman who had gained or lost a lot of weight might donate fine clothing, stuffing it into garbage bags, but no woman in her right mind would part with a pair of classic boots.

*In her right mind . . .*

Was that the only explanation?

*No.* I wouldn't let myself believe that a girl who was about my age, with similar tastes, had actually lost control of her own brain. Olivia had been lonely—I could relate. She had some neurotic quirks—who doesn't? But insane? Just thinking the word gave me a chill.

It took a while, but I settled on other possibilities. Olivia had been so unhappy, she'd decided to sever herself from the person she had once been, so she had thrown away her finest clothes to prove she no longer cared about material possessions. Or . . . or she'd done it as a form of penitence, a way of punishing herself for what-ever guilty things she had done or imagined. That possibility, at least, might explain why she could allow herself to fall under the power of an abusive man like Ricky Meeks.

I thought about it as I finished with the closet, then went from room to room, snapping pictures, but found nothing else interesting or revealing. Finally, I entered Olivia's office and sat at the desk, where, as I already knew, Mr. Seasons had found the laptop computer and the few photos he'd shown me. The office chair was on rollers, covered in soft stressed leather. I leaned back, put my feet on the desk, and let my mind wander.

*Where are the things she doesn't want anyone else to see?*

Nathan had asked that question and he was right. Everyone has a secret place where they hide their most personal possessions—myself included. Unless Olivia had anticipated her rooms being searched, I had missed something. *What?*

I sat up and took a closer look at the desk. It was an antique office desk made of oiled oak, too masculine for most women but exactly the sort of thing I liked. Had Olivia sat here when she'd made entries in her journal? It still bothered me that her diary had ended so abruptly. Two entries on the same page, dated the week Ricky Meeks had arrived, then only blank pages afterward. Was it possible that she had written about their relationship but had torn the pages out for safekeeping? *Yes.* More likely, though, it was Meeks who had found the diary and destroyed any entries that had incriminated him.

I scooted the chair away from the desk and looked at the floor. For a diary, Olivia had used a common spiral notebook like students use in school. The kind that scatters tiny shards of paper when a page is ripped out. On my hands and knees, I found several such shards scattered like confetti beneath the desk, hidden from the maid's broom.

Did it prove someone had taken pages from the diary? No . . . but it was evidence that it *might* have happened. If so, where were the missing pages?

I took a photo, then stood and checked the trash basket. Empty. Meeks wouldn't have hidden the missing pages inside the desk, but Olivia might have done exactly that if the desk contained a safe hiding place.

I sat in the leather chair and went to work. One by one, I opened drawers, testing each for a false bottom. There were no secret compartments, but the large bottom file-sized drawer was locked. It didn't take me long to find the key, which was hidden on a hook beneath the desk.

Inside the drawer was the private cache I'd hoped to find minus the missing diary pages—at first glance, anyway. There were several packets of letters tied in bundles with red ribbon. One batch might have been from the guy Olivia had dated during what Mr. Seasons referred to as "her rebellious stage," the short period where she'd experimented with drugs—the dated postmarks matched up. They contained greeting cards or birthday cards, from the looks of the envelopes, the sort of stuff people don't send by e-mail. There was a smaller stack from Olivia's father—one letter from France, two from Monaco, one from Madrid—along with a few dozen envelopes that dated back to her middle school years, all from what were probably old girlfriends.

I didn't take photos of the envelopes nor did I open even one. The prospect of reading Olivia's private mail gave me the creeps, so I refused to invent an excuse to do it. After placing the letters on the desk, I then took out an ornate wooden box that might have been a jewelry case. Maybe the missing pages of her diary were inside.

Not even close. When I opened the lid and saw what was inside, my ears began to warm from embarrassment for Olivia . . . plus a mixture of embarrassment and guilt for myself. The day before, I'd experienced a similar reaction. It was when Loretta had intentionally shamed me by talking about the "electric candle" she'd found hidden among my clothing. Olivia, though, had been smarter. Instead of shoving her pleasurable items into a drawer, trusting that all people are decent, she'd protected her privacy with a locked door and a hidden key.

I felt sneaky and rude when I realized what I had stumbled onto. Even so, my eyes couldn't help lingering on the items the girl had collected. There were several what Loretta had referred to as "gadgets." Different shapes, petite sizes, two of them so unusually designed that it took me a moment to decipher their purpose. Only one was cheap enough to rely on a plug-in cord—a brand available at most pharmacies but that also could be found in a shoe box I now kept hidden on my top closet shelf. The other objects, though, appeared either soft and expensive or as complicated as computer games, which possibly explained why they required wall chargers.

*Good for you,* I thought, feeling even closer to Olivia than when I had fixated on her photo as an awkward, unhappy child. *No risk of disappointment, or guilt, or clumsiness.*

How well I knew the freedom that the privacy of my aloneness offered . . . and the comfort only my own imagination could provide. Olivia's life was the same in that way, too. She had experienced the same physical loneliness. Probably the same frustrations and fears as well. It was such a powerful secret to share that my feelings of sneakiness vanished. I would not take photos of what I'd found, of course, but it felt okay to do what I was doing.

No longer embarrassed, I noted what else the box contained, using just my eyes, not my hands. Wedged among the pleasurable items was a vial of lotion, several DVDs in plain paper sleeves, what might have been magazine photos, and sheer lace panties folded on the bottom. True, I felt more sisterly toward Olivia, but I wasn't going to rummage through her intimate things for the sake of lace panties or pictures of movie stars wearing tight jeans. The DVDs, though, were a different story. They were stacked faceup, easy to see if I was willing to use an index finger to flip through them.

I was willing. The nosy, bawdy woman who hides inside my head, though, was soon disappointed. Instead of sensual, erotic titles, the DVDs were unlabeled except for one, upon which, in Olivia's hand, was written *Orchid House*, along with the date *May 17*.

The date caught my eye because it was about two weeks after Meeks had arrived in Naples. Was it possible the girl had been recording the progress of her new orchid house and had accidentally—or intentionally—included video footage of Ricky?

Mr. Seasons had told me I could remove useful material from Olivia's room as long as I cataloged it and returned it. I was holding several DVDs in both hands, my brain arguing with my conscience, when a voice asked from the doorway, "Find anything juicy? I did—*maybe.*"

The DVDs jumped from my hands and clattered to the floor, I was so startled. It was Nathan. Laughing as I knelt to retrieve the things, he said, "You're not the only girl with a guilty conscience who's sat at that desk. I found Olivia's art studio."

Too irritated to wonder what he meant, I replied, "How's a man your size move so quiet? It's not human—and just plain rude. Someone should tie a bell around your neck."

Unfazed, Nathan was walking toward me, saying, "I didn't risk asking the security guard why the studio's padlocked. He was out back for some reason when I got there. So I had to wait until he was gone. Did you see him?"

I glanced at the window as I shook my head. Was there a chance the guard had seen me at Olivia's desk? The possibility troubled me, but it was unlikely. I had checked the window several times.

"Her art studio's the cottage next to the orchid house," Nathan continued. "So I used a screwdriver and took off the hasp. He'll never even know we were there unless you—" He stopped in midsentence, watching me slam the wooden box closed before he could see what was inside. "Hey," he said, "what'd you find? You're hiding something."

Ignoring him, I returned the box to the drawer, stacked the packets of letters as I had found them, and then locked the drawer in too much of a hurry to remember I'd left the DVDs on the desk. "Turn your back," I told Nathan.

*"What?"*

"You heard me. I found something of Olivia's that's private. And that's the way it's going to stay. Private."

Exasperated but in a good-natured way, Nate spun around. While I hid the key under the desk, he couldn't help chiding me, saying, "You'll probably want to buy a new lock for her studio, too, if you're feeling that protective. There's a reason she doesn't want anyone to see her paintings. You two ladies have a lot in common, Hannah. Just like I said."

# Fourteen

Too stubborn to ask Nathan to explain his remark about Olivia Seasons's paintings, I remained silent as I followed my friend out the private entrance, past the orchid house, then into a one-room studio that felt smaller because its windows were shuttered.

"See?" Nathan said, pulling the door closed. "She didn't want anyone peeking in here. That alone should tell you something."

I didn't reply. In appearance and mood, the

studio was the polar opposite of the orderly rooms where Olivia lived. It was a chaos of color and canvases, most of them stretched on frames, several sitting unfinished on easels, many more hanging limp as animal skins, tacked as a patchwork mosaic on every wall. The space had a nice odor of linseed oil and wood, but it did nothing to disperse the atmosphere of shadows and secrecy.

Voice low, Nathan said, "Personally, I think she's pretty freakin' good. The orchid stuff, she was copying Georgia O'Keeffe, that's obvious. But her original stuff—it looks pretty recent— she's a troubled girl, but she's got talent. You mind if I take some shots to show Darren?"

I shook my head no and hissed, "Shush!" which froze Nate where he stood.

For more than a minute, I stood motionless, letting my eyes adjust, allowing details to come into my head without seeking anything in particular. Even in silence, the room echoed with Olivia's presence, a frantic energy that had been trapped inside these four walls even as she, using paint and brushes, had sought to escape from . . . from . . . from what in my soul I felt to be the truth . . . or at least suspected was true.

Even so, I tried to comfort myself with answers that were easier, less personal. Had Olivia painted such sensual, potent images to escape the captivity of her father's home? His wealthy friends? Escape the boredom of a life that provided her with everything yet demanded nothing?

*Yes.* That was an important point—a separate truth that had not yet registered in my heart because such an existence was outside my experience. Growing up wealthy, I realized in that instant, was dangerous for an outsider like Olivia—as it would have been for me. It might be a clear advantage for women who grew comfortably into their own skins, who inherited confidence as naturally as I'd inherited size 10 feet. But for a young girl who was awkward and shy, wealth might rob her of the need to fit in with the outside world, as well as the strength and gradual courage required to strike out on her own, and make a living.

Beside me, Nathan asked softly, "You okay?" He was asking for permission to at least move, if not talk.

I nodded. "I needed some time, that's all. I didn't expect this."

"There's nothing crude about her work," Nathan, the boyfriend of an artist said, defending an artist I already empathized with more than he would ever understand. "They're impressionistic . . . sensual," he added. "Sure, obviously sexual, too. Lots of frustration . . . maybe even rage. You think?"

No—I *knew* but didn't reply. When Olivia was

done painting orchids, banyan trees became her subject. No, her obsession—there were dozens of photographs tacked up on the easels and walls, mostly close-up shots, which reflected the micro-view she painted from. Whole canvases devoted to a cluster of leaves or a single muscled bough. Banyans are unlike other trees in that they claim increasing amounts of ground around their trunks by dropping air roots to support the weight of their limbs. After many decades, a banyan tree resembles a luxurious mound of green that sits on an acre of poles—a visual mix of masculine and feminine that Olivia recognized and had used.

In her paintings, a lone branch resembled legs partially spread, a single leaf created a feminine triangle. A buttressed trunk had the muscularity of a strong man's thigh, a dangling root thick as a hawser was so unmistakably phallic that it caused me to turn away but also sparked inside my abdomen a familiar burn that had been with me off and on for the last several days.

"Before the gym rat came along, you say, she dated only one other guy?" Nathan was following me as I moved around the room, which was irritating because I had to guard how I reacted to a painting or risk one of his all-too-accurate gibes.

"Gym rat?" I said, then realized he meant Ricky Meeks. "There was a guy a few years ago who got her into cocaine, but he didn't last. She was smart enough to dump a loser like that and move on."

"She's about the same age as us?"

I replied, "A year younger, born in late May."

"God help us," Nate said. "One Gemini hunting for another Gemini—there's four times the chance you'll both end up lost. And she's dateless and single just like you."

"Mr. Seasons isn't paying you to crack jokes," I answered with a chill. "He's paying us to find his niece. A fact you might consider is how careful someone like Olivia has to be when it comes to men. I'm referring to these paintings, how it might explain her frustrations. Do men want her for who she is? Or are they only after her money?"

"From what I've heard so far," Nathan replied, "it's neither. No wonder she ran off with the first guy who came along."

"Stop being mean," I shot back. "We don't know for sure she's with Ricky Meeks. Or that it happened like you're saying."

"Bull crap. She's with him, and you know it. Look around the room—that girl had so much sexual tension built up, I'll bet she went shooting out of here like a balloon."

I faced Nate, hands on hips, and squared my shoulders. "So what! Even if she's with him, Olivia didn't leave with a man like him because she wanted to. She's got her own mind and she's too smart. He drugged her or forced her, or something. I'll bet you money on *that*."

Nathan smiled and was remarking on my

protective attitude but then stopped and squinted at me, his bald Buddha head shining. "Why's your face flushed? It's not hot in here. And it's not because you're mad." His smile broadened while his face swiveled from me to the painting of the engorged dangling root I had been ignoring but was still close enough to see from the corner of my eye. "Hannah," he said finally, straight-faced, "I think you've found your soul mate. Good news is, he's hung like a fire hose and won't leave the lid up. Bad news is, he's a freakin' tree."

I started to say something sharp in reply but then began laughing. Couldn't help myself because of the boyish look of innocence on Nate's face that was pure fakery but also reminded me of our school years when he had been puny and I'd backed down more than one bully who was tormenting him.

"You're a mess," I said. "Go wait in the truck and play video games," then gave him a shove to clear my path. I had noticed another garbage bag in the corner and wanted to have a look.

Several minutes later, Nathan was asking, "What'd you find? What are you reading? From the look on your face . . . *Hey,* you want me to call the cops?"

I had found the missing entries to Olivia's journal, ten detailed pages crumpled into a ball so tight that only a strong man could have done it. Much of it was written in her shorthand code, which would take me a while to decipher. "Quiet," I replied, then nodded to the contents of the bag, part of which I'd dumped onto the floor. "Take a look. There's a balled-up canvas in there, too. Why would she throw away her own paintings?"

Even before Nate had gotten the canvas spread out on a desk, I recognized the charcoal curves of a man's broad bare shoulders and a face that was featureless but for two ears like spiked horns, a spit curl, and a wolfish leer.

"He didn't let her finish it," I said, feeling a building anger, "because Olivia was painting the truth about who he is—not just what her eyes saw."

Nathan replied, "You wanted proof they're together. I guess this is it."

The same might be true of the missing pages I'd found, but I needed time alone to decipher the girl's shorthand. "We shouldn't be in here," I said, "she wouldn't like it. Where's the screwdriver? You need to fix that hasp."

Nate did it while I moved the sickly orchid from Olivia's bedroom to the orchid house, where the air was dripping hot on this June afternoon but still felt fresher than the studio where the missing girl had locked away her secrets.

I was so preoccupied with what we'd seen and found, we were halfway home before I took a break from the missing pages and checked my messages. There was one from Gabby Corrales, asking me to call about tomorrow night's party; several from Loretta, who was swearing, she was so mad, the neighbors had hired a backhoe to destroy the rest of the Indian mound; and one from Cordial Pallet that provided some hopeful news.

"An old fishing partner of his knows where Ricky Meeks fuels his boat!" I told Nathan, who was driving.

*"Where?"*

I said, "At a little marina near Marco Island," but was thinking, *Just like Mr. Seasons hinted at to begin with.*

"The Ten Thousand Islands?" Nate said. "Did he name a place? The area's huge."

I was thumbing numbers into my phone. "That's what I'm going to find out right now."

# Fifteen

Sounding businesslike and efficient, nothing at all like the party girl who at three a.m. had invited me to swim naked with her in the pool, Martha Calder-Shaun said, "Do you mind telling me again how you know this? I want to make sure we have all the information straight. In fact, I should record it." There was the bong of a digital button being pushed before she added, "For the investigation time line, it'll help. Do I have your permission?"

"Not if you expect me to use names," I replied. "Later, depending how it goes, it might be okay. But it'll have to wait." I was in my apartment, pacing, phone cradled between shoulder and ear, feeling jittery now that the cloudiness of marijuana had worn off. It was an hour before sunset but felt earlier, despite my busy day.

Because of what had happened the night before, I had been dreading this call to Mrs. Calder-Shaun but had finally summoned the nerve. Up until now, though, things had gone okay. I'd told her about the party I'd been invited to in Port Royal, about what I'd found at Olivia's house (minus a few details kept private for Olivia's sake), but had saved the best for last—new information about where to find Ricky Meeks. So far, there'd been no hint of embarrassment from the New York attorney, no references to what she probably considered my prudish ways or my stern reaction to her behavior in the swimming pool last night.

Martha used a long silence to communicate her displeasure at my refusing to name names but finally stopped the recorder, saying, "Fine, Hannah, have it your way. But don't go so fast this time, I'm taking notes."

I repeated what I'd just said but added more information. On a tip from a friend at Fishermans Wharf (Mr. Pallet), I had phoned a pompano

202

fisherman, who told me that for the last three Monday afternoons a boater who fit Meeks's description had tied up at a marina south of Marco Island. The man always left the marina on foot, then returned about an hour later loaded down with bags from a nearby 7-Eleven. If there was a woman aboard, no one at the marina had seen her, although it was possible a passenger could have stayed below in the boat's cabin. The man bought fuel, filled up his tank with water, and always paid in cash using hundred-dollar bills.

*"Interesting,"* Martha said, not missing the significance.

"The boat's a thirty-foot Skipjack cruiser," I added. "An older model, with twin Mercruiser engines. White hull with blue canvas, no name on the stern—exactly the way Ricky's boat was described to me by my friend at the shrimp docks. His physical description matches, too. A little over six feet, lean, lots of muscles, dark wavy hair, probably two hundred pounds. At least, that's the way I picture the guy from the only photo Lawrence gave me."

Using first names, Lawrence and Martha, had become easier for me after what I'd heard and experienced the night before.

"The name of the marina," the woman said, "say it again. I've heard it before, I'm sure I have—a strange name, but I forget where."

"Caxambas Fisherman's Co-op," I repeated,

then spelled it for her while my phone chimed with an incoming call—*Lawrence Seasons*—which I ignored, explaining to Martha, "It's a little village south of Marco. There used to be a clam-processing plant in the old days. And there's still a tiny little post office but not more than a couple of stores, if you count a tiki bar. If it hasn't gone bust. When I was a girl, my uncle usually stopped at Caxambas on our way back from camping in the Ten Thousand Islands."

"A *post office*," Martha said in a way that meant something. "Now I know why the name's familiar. Put your phone on speaker if you want. It may take me a minute to call up the right file on my computer."

I crossed the room to the desk where my own laptop was open, the DVDs I'd found in Olivia's office already neatly logged into a notebook, and also noted in a folder I'd created to store documents regarding the case. Later, I would decide whether to erase those entries or not. There was a reason. The DVD labeled *Orchid House*, as I already knew, contained nothing personal unless you counted Olivia's preference for the mildest sort of romantic sex scenes—some from the *Red Shoe Diaries* and other short videos she had downloaded from the Internet.

The same with the other DVDs, although I hadn't had time to make a thorough check. Instead, I had fast-forwarded through snippets of couples making love, one man, one woman usually, but sometimes a pair of classy-looking women kissing or fondling, which had caused me to feel uncomfortable even though they contained nothing graphic. As I drifted past the desk, I wondered if I would have reacted the same if Martha Calder-Shaun hadn't tried to seduce me after talking me into swimming with just bra and panties. Something like that had never happened to me before—although there *might* have been two incidents in college I was too naïve or disinterested to recognize.

"Are you there, kiddo? I found it." Martha had returned to the phone.

"This has to do with Caxambas, right?" I asked. I was leafing through the old history book I had taken from the briefcase Lawrence Seasons had been keeping for my Uncle Jake but had forgot to return. Why my uncle would ask a fishing client to "keep" something as innocent as a book made no sense unless it was because the binding was of much finer quality than the reprinted version I'd seen at Darren's. The same was true of the second book, which was leather-bound, embossed in gold, and the size of a family Bible. Maybe they were valuable and Jake hadn't wanted them around during his nasty divorce from Mary.

Martha said, "A week after she disappeared, Olivia mailed a donation she'd promised to a church but had apparently forgotten to send. The minister contacted our office when he couldn't get in touch with Olivia. I've got a photo of the envelope right here. The postmark is Caxambas. It was a check for a thousand dollars sent June sixth, a Monday. That was . . . twelve days ago."

"Then it *is* Ricky Meeks!" I said, so excited I shoved the history book away, which knocked the second book off the desk. The thing landed with a heavy thud, then an unexpected metallic clatter.

"Her check bounced," Martha continued. "That's why the minister called our office. It was written on a personal account we didn't know she'd opened. Larry hasn't been able to confirm exactly how much she'd deposited, but it was a money market account that required a minimum balance of fifty thousand."

Several seconds later, I was still staring at what lay at my feet when the woman asked for what was, I realized, the second time, "Hannah . . . are you still there?"

"Ricky . . . he cleaned out Olivia's account," I replied, struggling to refocus, which required some effort. The book had spilled open when it landed, ejecting a semiautomatic pistol that was like no handgun I'd ever seen. The barrel and slide were stainless steel, which isn't unusual, but the trigger guard was a customized hook, and the handgrips had transparent windows that showed the magazine was loaded with a stack of hollow-point cartridges. Nine-millimeter, it looked like, although I wasn't expert enough to be sure at a glance.

Martha said, "It's all coming together now, kiddo. I think you're right. I think you found that son of a bitch."

Kneeling to retrieve the weapon, I replied, "Fifty thousand dollars missing, that ought to be enough to convince the police, don't you think? Have them waiting when the guy shows up in Caxambas day after tomorrow."

"To question Ricky Meeks, you mean. We don't have enough for an arrest warrant, but shake him a little and see what falls out. Yeah, I agree." The woman sounded excited.

I said, "I'd want to be there, Martha. I feel like I know Olivia already and I won't feel right until I'm sure she's safe." Which was true, but I was also worried. I feared the girl wouldn't want to be rescued unless someone who understood her predicament was there to help—and I was the only person who knew the truth. Some of it, anyway. I hadn't been able to decipher all of Olivia's shorthand entries in the missing pages, but I'd read enough to know that Meeks had seduced her the same way he had taken control of Mrs. Whitney's life. At first, he'd all but forced Olivia, then he'd kept her so dizzy in the bedroom that a strange, unhealthy bond had formed. Maybe the girl was still under the man's spell, which was an upsetting possibility. I probably should have shared the information with Martha right then, but I felt too protective of Olivia to reveal such an embarrassing secret. Plus, I was rattled by what my Uncle Jake had kept hidden inside this old book that lay open on the floor.

Jake and I had been closer than some fathers and daughters, so my ego was bruised. He had given this unusual gun to Lawrence Seasons to protect instead of someone of his own blood.

Why? Why hadn't my uncle trusted *me?*

I hadn't put the phone on speaker but now I did so I could use both hands to unload the pistol. Thumb on the release button, I ejected the magazine while I listened to Martha tell me, "If the sheriff's department tries to ignore this, I've got contacts at the governor's office through friends in D.C. They haven't helped much yet, but now that we know where the asshole is—you know, show them the bad check, the envelope and postmark. The least they can do is loan us a couple of deputies to . . ."

While the woman continued talking, my phone chimed again with another call. *Gabby Corrales.* Her earlier phone message had asked me to call about the party, but party talk could wait. I shucked the pistol's slide and with my left hand caught the cartridge before it hit the table. Yes, a nine-millimeter hollow-point. What I thought was the slide lock was actually a decocking lever.

Still listening to the attorney, I gripped the pistol in both hands and swung its weight toward the door, eyes open, index finger parallel the barrel, my feet automatically moving into combat stance just as my uncle had drilled into me as a teenager —and also later when I took a concealed weapons class he said might be useful if I pursued law enforcement. The pistol was shorter, lighter, better balanced than any I'd ever held. Jake had been a sheriff's detective in Tampa before retiring on disability, but this was not the sort of weapon an underpaid cop carried. No cop I'd ever met, anyway. I placed the gun on the desk, then picked up the book where it had been concealed. On the leather cover, embossed in gold, was a one-word title: *Negotiators*.

My phone chimed a third time: *Elka Whitney*. I couldn't remember getting so many calls in such a short space of time. I'd called Elka earlier and left a message, asking how she was doing. I was worried about the woman and determined to help see her through this. But Elka was a talker who required a lot of time, so I refused the call and put the phone to my ear.

Martha was saying, "I've got to be honest about something. You've impressed the hell out of me, Hannah dear. My instincts told me you might be good, but, my God, in less than forty-eight hours you've accomplished more than what our so-called professional from Miami did in ten days. Let me ask you something. The investigator I'm talking about—according to his reports, anyway—interviewed people in Caxambas last week. At the post office *and* the marina, and they didn't tell him a damn thing. But you found out exactly what we needed to know with just a few phone calls. *How?*"

A private investigator was already working on the case? It was news to me, although I didn't let my surprise show. Tracking Ricky Meeks had taken a lot more than a couple of phone calls, of course, but I didn't want to rebuff Martha's compliment after refusing this powerful woman's advances in the swimming pool.

"Day before yesterday," I replied, "when Lawrence invited me to lunch, he said something really smart, but I wasn't smart enough to understand. Not at the time, anyway. Lawrence said—I won't get the words exactly right—he said, 'Never underestimate the importance of local knowledge.' Which makes sense when it comes to fishing, but I'd never thought of it in a bigger way. My family's lived on these islands forever, so I know a lot of people. They trust me, I guess, so they were willing to talk. And they know I won't—"

Martha interrupted, "Reveal their names to a nosy New York attorney?" She said it with a smile but also a hint of irritation.

I had opened the book titled *Negotiators*,

which, in fact, wasn't a book. It was a leather box with enough real pages to be convincing. The inside was black velvet and contained a formfitting depression that matched the shape of the pistol exactly. There were also a couple of other unusual items the box had been built to hide—a steel dagger among them—but I would take a closer look later. Right now, I had to concentrate on Martha, who could set subtle traps and knew how to use words like they were weapons. She was being nice, sure, but her tone also warned that she was being tricky.

"Something like that," I replied, trying to turn the tables on her. "What I'm wondering is, why didn't you tell me about the other investigator? We could have pooled information and helped each other."

"You didn't need his help, kiddo!" Martha shot back. "Besides, that guy wasn't much of a professional. He was an oddball from the start, then dropped off the radar a few days before we hired you."

That struck me as more than just odd. "The man disappeared, you mean?"

"At some bar on South Beach probably," Martha answered. "But at least he didn't balk at giving names to the people paying his salary."

The woman was a ball breaker, just as Nathan had described. I stayed calm, determined to promote my innocence by playing innocent.

"Since I don't know all the rules about ethics—what clients have a right to expect, that sort of thing—I don't fault myself for protecting the people who helped me. Martha . . . ?" I paused as if not sure how to ask what I wanted to ask. ". . . There *is* something on my mind you might be able to help with."

The woman sensed my uneasiness but confused her own guilty feelings with what was bothering me. "This isn't your last job, kiddo, not if Larry and I have any influence." She said it with forced confidence that is something confident women do only when they're nervous. Then she proved it by adding, "If you're worried about what happened in Larry's pool last night—or *didn't* happen—forget it, for Christ's sake! It's all so fuzzy, I can't remember the details anyway. And I'm sure you can't either." After a tick of silence, she asked the question again: "*Can* you?"

Her lie was so obvious and purposeful, my line of thought was successfully derailed for the moment. Instead of staying strong, I responded, "It happens sometimes when people're drinking," and was instantly irked by my eagerness to please a woman who had manipulated me so easily.

"In the money world," Martha lectured, "the higher you climb, the smaller the net. You reach a certain level, all we want to do is let our hair down and relax when we get the chance. I'm telling you because this *isn't* your last case. You'll be dealing with Lawrence's problems again, or the problems of people who are on the same financial level. And there are some things you need to by God understand about our crowd."

I said, "I'm starting to," careful not to give it an edge.

"*Good.* I had too much to drink last night. Maybe you did, too. Who cares? Business is business, fun is fun. Never confuse the two—or apologize for what you do when you're off the clock. Money doesn't give a damn about morality, success can't afford a conscience, so it's not something I judge people by. What I don't have time for is the passive-aggressive types who think being polite is more important than speaking plainly. You with me so far?"

"I think so," I replied. By exonerating herself, Martha was letting me off the hook with a slap on the wrist, but in a way that was troubling. Unprincipled behavior was preferable to narrow-mindedness, that was her point.

"Far as I'm concerned," she continued, "there's nothing wrong with experimenting with personal . . . *pleasures.* It's nobody else's goddamn business! Or helping someone else enjoy them-selves, it's the same thing. Work hard enough, people earn the freedom to do whatever the hell they want when they're not doing business. Does that help?"

No. But it did help me turn my question into a

statement. "I was worried it wasn't fair of me to accept the deal we worked out, the bonus Lawrence offered. After only a few days' work, I mean, if we find Olivia on Monday like I expect—"

"She hasn't signed the papers yet," Martha reminded me, sounding like herself. "Until it happens, spend more time concentrating on your job and less thinking about how you'll fix up that damn moldy boat Larry promised. Just keep on doing what you're doing."

"I planned to anyway," I replied, again fighting the habit of looking at my shoes when being scolded.

"Tomorrow's Sunday, a whole day to gather more information in case Meeks doesn't show on Monday. You do *work* Sundays, don't you?"

Without mentioning I would have to first take Loretta to church, a weekly ritual, I said, "Of course."

"Then go to that party in Port Royal. I think it's a good idea—just don't say anything obvious that'll tip off the guests . . . *or* embarrass Larry's family more than that idiot girl's already put them through."

I felt my face beginning to warm but said nothing.

"Olivia mailed the check from Caxambas less than two weeks ago, remember? You have time to work the phones or interview your sources in person. You *have* already figured out why that's important, I hope?"

I had, but let Martha cement her authority by explaining, "Somebody had to see Olivia get on or off that asshole's boat. One of your fishing guide buddies, or some distant uncle's cousin who married a niece. One of your good ol' boy pals maybe. *Someone* saw her."

My face was red, I could feel it, but the woman's tone suddenly changed while I fought the temptation to stiff-arm her with a sharp response. "Hannah?"

"Yes, ma'am," I replied, settling on sarcasm.

"Oh, come on, now, grow up. Don't get pissed off at me, dear. This is business. Remember what I just told you? Maybe *you're* the one who should've been making notes."

That did it. I couldn't hold myself back any longer. "Mrs. Calder-Shaun," I replied, "I stopped taking tests when I left school. I didn't grow up in a double-wide—although I know some fine people who did. And I don't happen to find it businesslike to lecture the woman who you said yourself accomplished more in two days than a high-paid attorney and a Miami investigator managed in two weeks. Now, if you have something to say, say it—that's *my* definition of acting grown up. Otherwise, I've got important calls to return."

The woman's laughter was so genuine, my

215

anger was instantly replaced by the embarrass-ment of having stepped into a trap I'd been expecting all along. "I wondered how far you'd let me push," she said between breaths. "See how much time you waste being polite? Had to do it because I knew you'd missed my point."

Teeth clenched, I said, "Martha, games are for playgrounds. Don't ever do that to me again."

"I know, I know"—the woman was still laughing—"but I *like* you, kiddo. You've got a temper and you're tough as nails when you need to be. You'd make a hell of an attorney—the pasty-faced Wall Street types would dribble down their legs when you walked into a room."

That was a compliment, I realized, but I still had to say, "Talking mean about a person's family isn't funny. Keep your mouth off my friends and family 'cause I won't tolerate it."

A smile still in her voice, the woman became serious. "That's all the more reason to be friends, kiddo. I don't have many who'd stand up to me like you just did. Two . . . ? Hell . . . maybe none." She sighed. "It's living in that damn city. Money has no conscience—I wasn't being dramatic. It's true. Not that it's always a bad thing in the real world. Just keep it in mind."

I cleared my throat, not sure what to say, which is when my phone chimed again, this time the caller unexpected: *Dr. Marion Ford*. It was the biologist I'd bought my skiff from—maybe

Cordial Pallet had told him to telephone for some reason.

"I need to take this one," I said. It was a good excuse to end a conversation that was making me uncomfortable.

"Of course, dear. But just one more thing. Truce, right? We've got all our little misunderstandings cleared up?"

"I appreciate what you and Mr. Seasons have done for me," I replied, my tone formal. "I'll call tomorrow, okay?"

The hint wasn't strong enough. Martha kept talking. "You sound restless for some reason. Why don't you stop by tonight for a drink? The guest cottage is still yours, and the pool's still warm as soup. We can discuss the case with Larry. Let him hear your story firsthand."

I listened, feeling rushed, although I expected my phone to chime several more times before it went to voice mail. Wrong. Three rings was all the biologist waited before hanging up. An impatient man, apparently. In my mind, I whispered, *"Shit."*

"I've got calls to return," I reminded the attorney. "But later . . . around sunset, maybe we'll get together." I was eager to ask Lawrence Seasons about the pistol, but I now had a private agenda, too. Captiva Island is connected by bridge to Sanibel, where the biologist lived. I'd only spoken with him a few times, but he was an interesting man. Solid-looking, all muscle and sharp eyes, a man to be trusted or avoided depending on a person's intentions.

Martha was right. After discovering the gun, seeing Olivia's paintings, then fast-forwarding through her DVDs, I was restless. *Very* restless. And my need to move didn't improve any after I'd returned the first of four calls.

"Instead of Port Royal tomorrow, my friends are having their party aboard *Sybarite*," Gabby Corrales told me, not actually squealing but close enough, she was so excited. "Just a sunset cruise—not enough time to have any serious fun—and no crew. But a perfect chance to see why you'll love being first mate!"

In any other mood, job obligation or not, I would have refused to leave the dock on a boat with such a dark reputation.

Instead, I heard myself ask Gabby, "You think a black cocktail dress will be okay?"

# Sixteen

Even though I got only three hours' sleep because I stayed late on Sanibel—the biologist had invited me into his lab—I awoke at sunrise on Sunday feeling as alive and full of energy as I'd ever felt in my life. At my antique vanity, I smiled into the mirror, then set about rehanging the dresses I'd tried on earlier that morning prior to bed. It wasn't until Loretta called, though, that I remembered the shoe box. It was under my nightstand instead of in the closet where it was usually stored.

"You sound so light and cheery, honey," my mother purred through the phone, "like someone lifted an anvil off your shoulders. Or you had yourself a real *special* time last night. Maybe there's no need to hide the axe before you pick me up for church this morning—thanks to that snake Lawrence Seasons, I suppose."

No, Lawrence had nothing to do with my good mood, although it was irksome to be read so easily, but that was nothing new. There were times as a girl I seriously wondered if my mother had X-ray vision. And I still have suspicions that God has gifted her with witch's powers to compensate for the clot that damaged her brain. My strip mall apartment is separated from her home by condos, billboards, six miles of asphalt, and a Kmart, but after hanging up the phone I used a pillowcase to conceal the shoe box, then hid my private property on a closet shelf safe from Loretta's prying imagination. As I did it, I imagined an approving smile from Olivia when we finally met, sure that she would have behaved the same.

My mother's stroke has at least softened her attitude about church, which is odd, but no odder than some of her other behavior. After ending a decade-long affair with a married man, Loretta became a devoted member of Foursquare Pentecostal, where guilt and anger could be purged by "happy rapture," which is Pentecostal talk for speaking in tongues and Christ dancing. That church did the woman a lot of good, in my opinion, brought a peace to her mind that I envied as a girl but unfortunately didn't share, although I did think highly of the minister and most of the congregation. Church rules were strict, which probably kept me out of more trouble than I realize even now. And it forced an orderliness into our lives that living around the schedule of a married man had all but destroyed. Loretta has never admitted her affair, of course, and I've never mentioned it, although it is a secret comfort to me to have such powerful ammunition in reserve.

Attending church is still an important part of Loretta's life. Mine, too—a fact I don't mind sharing when the rare person asks. By college, though, Foursquare Pentecostal's uninhibited rejoicing made it an awkward place for an introvert. And the surgery to remove Loretta's aneurism made it impossible for her to tolerate all that rapturous noise. So, during the last two years, we'd attended a smorgasbord of services but had recently settled on a white clapboard church that overlooks a cemetery on the beach, Chapel By The Sea, Captiva Island. Several

Smiths are buried there, including Ann Savage Smith, who may or may not be a relation, but just seeing my family name chiseled on a tombstone has created a bond and causes me to leave flowers after every service.

On this Sunday morning, Reverend Nyman read from a Unity Church publication, *The Daily Word*, a lesson entitled "Empowered." It was a strong message that promised guidance and protection to those who behaved boldly with faith when challenged by adversity. I liked the quote from the 91st Psalm so much, I found it in Loretta's Bible, then stored it nearly word for word in my memory.

I will not fear the terror of night, nor the arrow that flies by day, nor the pestilence that stalks in darkness . . . A thousand may fall at my side . . . but evil will not touch me . . .

Afterward, in the cemetery, I left gold frangipani blossoms I'd picked from the yard, then returned Loretta home, where Mrs. Terwilliger, her day nurse, and four others were standing at the edge of the property, looking down into a pit the size of a swimming pool. Loretta hadn't exaggerated about what her new neighbors had done. They'd hired a backhoe to dig up what remained of the Indian mound, hauling tons of shell, earth, and whatever artifacts it contained away in dump trucks. The house they were building had seven bathrooms, I'd heard, and required a septic tank.

As I walked my mother up the mound toward the porch, I saw that it was not a cheery-looking group. There were two local archaeologists, one of them a nice woman, Dr. Caren, who I could see had been crying. There was also an Indian-looking man in a Seminole jacket standing next to a skinny long-haired man I recognized. I'd met him the night before on Sanibel and had enjoyed a long talk—me listening mostly, of course.

"Tomlinson?" I called as if surprised, although I wasn't. The man had been so upset when I'd told him about the backhoe's digging, he had vowed to come view the destruction for himself. He had been floaty drunk, true, but I had seldom met a more sweet-natured person, nor a man with bluer eyes, so I was hoping he would remember come morning. Now here he was.

"Miz Smith!" he said to my mother in a comforting way, focusing instantly on Loretta after smiling at me. "No wonder you can't sleep at night—all these voices calling out for help. Did *anyone* understand when you tried to explain?"

For an instant, Loretta shared my puzzlement, but then her expression changed as if realizing she'd finally found an ally. "Not my daughter, that's for damn sure!" she said, giving me a triumphant look. "How'd you know about this god-awful nightmare I've been living?"

The skinny, hippie-looking man was tugging at

222

a strand of hair while he frowned at the concrete monstrosity, and the pit the backhoe had dug. "It's unholy what's happened here. The sacrilege of too much money in the hands of the unenlightened —that's a mausoleum they're building, not a house. Defiled three thousand years of sacred ground, which is why only the purest of souls could help. So they chose you, of course, Miz Smith."

"My Lord . . . it's true!" my mother cried, walking toward Tomlinson with outstretched arms. "No one believed me even when I painted the truth on those cement walls. I *hear* them. I hear them dead Indians crying all night long!"

The man replied, "They used you as a conduit, dear lady," lifting Loretta off her feet with a hug. "Now the cavalry has arrived. The Seminole have a purification ceremony—I'll tell you all about it. The temptation, of course, is to zap these swine with a pestilence curse—but revenge is bad mojo. Soon enough, though, bad karma will infect them and anyone foolish enough to step inside that pre–death chamber, so leave it to the experts. I want you to meet a friend of mine, Billie Egret. He's a Skin, a native shaman—" Tomlinson motioned to the man wearing the brightly colored Seminole jacket. "Hey, Billie, come meet my new sweetheart!"

Loretta was still grinning and acting girlish thirty minutes later when my strange new friend disentangled himself in time to intercept me as I

223

headed for the dock. Nathan was driving me to Caxambas, so I could ask questions in person as Martha had directed.

"I've got a present for you!" the man hollered, waving, something in his hand. As he approached, he was smiling with sharp old eyes that looked inside me, but in a way that was kind, not nosy. What Tomlinson had was a small box, my name written in precise block letters on the label. It was the biologist's handwriting, which I recognized from the night before. He'd left a notebook open in his lab next to a tank full of sea horses.

"Doc told me to give you this," Tomlinson said. "He would've been here, but he had to split for Colombia before sunup. One of those last-minute deals."

"Columbia, South Carolina?" I asked, opening a cardboard flap. The biologist and I had spent two hours together alone in his stilthouse and he hadn't said a word about having to drive in the morning.

"Colombia, South America," Tomlinson replied in a way that told me *Don't ask.* "He wanted to come, though. The guy's never been what you'd call talkative, but I gather you two, uhh . . . had a very good time last night."

"He said that?" I tried not to sound overly hopeful, although I was. Sitting in Marion Ford's laboratory, watching him work, listening to his voice, I'd never felt so comfortable and at ease with a man in my life. We hadn't done anything improper, of course. He hadn't even attempted a kiss when we hugged good-bye despite my best effort to make my lips an easy target. It was the memory of the biologist, the size of his shoulders, the shape of his hands, I had taken to bed with me after trying on my best dresses when I got home.

"Maybe that's not the phrase he used," Tomlinson muttered, trying to remember. "He said you're . . . that you are a very nice lady. That you have a nice laugh. And to give you that." He nodded at the box.

*"Nice?"* I said. I was thinking, *So are cats,* but hid my disappointment.

"Trust me, that's effusive for Doc. Oh!" The skinny man snapped his fingers, a look of discovery on his face. "There was something else. He said you're a *man's* woman. His exact words. A *man's* woman—and there is no higher praise. Not from him, anyway. And that you were a competitive swimmer, so he might have a new swim partner."

I nodded, pleased the biologist had spoken of me but also aware that Tomlinson was suddenly uncomfortable.

"Hannah, there is something I want you to know. *We* want you to know because Doc feels the same. It's . . . not easy to talk about, which is why the coward couldn't bring himself to do it. But the fact is—"

I interrupted to spare him discomfort. "My Aunt Hannah wrote about Dr. Ford in her journal. If that's what you're trying to tell me, I already know. I saw no need last night to mention her private business."

"She *did?*"

I nodded. Actually, Hannah Three had written about both men, which was why, the night before, it had required a ton of willpower on my part not to go through my bawdy aunt's diary and review her scoring system. I couldn't remember the numbers she'd awarded the two men—if any— and truly didn't want to know, although she had obviously preferred one man over the other. She'd put that in words, not numbers.

"And you're . . . you're still comfortable with having us as friends?" Tomlinson's face had the kindly, weathered look of a marble angel, which made it impossible to enjoy his embarrassment.

"Sure . . . as *friends,*" I replied, stressing the word. "Apparently, I'm not as prudish as some folks who live alone on sailboats."

That caused the man to grin, then look at what I'd taken from the box. The grin faded. "He gave you a *garage opener?*"

No, it was a spare remote for the wireless spotlight on the boat I'd bought. Dr. Ford had been meaning to get it to me, but it had taken a phone call from Cordial Pallet to jog his memory and also to provide my cell number. Stupidly,

I'd gone off and left the thing—or so I pretended as I explained events to Tomlinson. In truth, the lapse was sneaky. It was intended to provide me an excuse to return to the biologist's stilthouse, which was in Dinkin's Bay, Sanibel.

"Doc said there's a note in there, too," Tomlinson offered, indicating the box.

I found it, a handwritten note, which I opened and read privately by turning my shoulder as if needing more sunlight.

*You are valuable, Hannah, please remember what I said: If you surprise a dangerous man, expect to be surprised. Tarpon on Friday?*

I folded the paper and gave Tomlinson a quick hug. "We've got a fishing date," I said, grinning, then hurried off toward my boat. I was flattered the biologist was worried for me even though, as I'd explained to him, there was no longer a need. Early last night, the county sheriff's department had finally given in to Martha's pestering. If Ricky Meeks showed up at Caxambas to buy fuel and supplies tomorrow, there would be two deputies waiting—along with me, Martha, and Lawrence Seasons.

Now the only question left to answer was, would Olivia be aboard his boat? We'd find out soon enough, but pride told me I would come closer to earning my paycheck—and a year's use of the Marlow yacht—if I provided my employers with that information, too.

# Seventeen

The tiki bar in Caxambas was named RUM 'N' COKE, which had the dirty sound of smugglers and meth addicts, so fit a tile room with fake palm thatching, two video games, and initials carved into the tables.

"Heart attack in a basket," Nathan said, disappointed by the menu. "Why not stop in Marco and get a smoothie? There's a vegetarian restaurant, too. Lots of decent places to eat."

It was hard to believe that Marco Island, with its million-dollar sky-rise condos, silver beaches, and golf courses, was five miles north of this trailer park village, separated only by mangroves and a shell road. To the east was Goodland, an historic fishing village, another nice place my uncle liked, but not as close by boat.

"The lady's grandson said he'd have her call," I reminded Nathan. "I'd hate to come all this distance and leave without something new to tell Martha." I was referring to the Caxambas post-mistress, who wasn't at work, of course, this being Sunday. We'd asked half a dozen locals before finding the right house, then knocking on the postmistress's door. A snotty-nosed ten-year-old had answered, telling us, "Maw-maw will be back soon, write your number on this match-book." Turned out the kid's Maw-maw was a notary public who did weddings when she wasn't sorting mail.

This was after the disappointment of confirming that no one at Caxambas marina had gotten even a glimpse of a passenger on the white Skipjack cruiser with blue canvas that showed up Mondays for fuel. The same was true of Cordial Pallet's friend, a nice old man who smoked a pipe and had hands the color of sugar-cured ham from being in the sun, fishing pompano and pulling crab traps, all his life.

"Martha, huh?" Nate said, smiling up from the menu. "You sure mention that woman's name a lot for not liking what she did in the swimming pool. Come on, be honest. You didn't tell me *everything*."

"Now I'm sorry I said anything at all, the way you're acting," I replied, tapping my foot on linoleum, looking from my menu to the woman ignoring us behind the bar. "The least she could do is bring napkins and water," I said. Then raised my voice to call, "Excuse me, miss! Could we get a couple of iced teas over here? Sweet tea if you have it."

Nate wasn't going to miss this chance to goad me about secretly preferring women, a topic he enjoyed and often hinted at. "I think Martha's gorgeous," he said, "but in a frosty, ball-breaker sort of way. You said yourself you find her attractive. *And* that you were flattered."

Being honest has its risks, and my friend had caught me at a soft moment during our ninety-minute drive south. First, he'd impressed me with background information on three ex-cons who *might* be using the name Ricky Meeks, as well as a paragraph that seemed to describe the unusual gun I'd found. Twenty years ago, a gun-customizing company named Devel had produced a concealment weapon for a State Department agency that was still classified. Fewer than two hundred of the guns had been made. The weapon was a shortened Smith & Wesson with a hooked trigger guard and "window" grips, plus some other tweaks for fast shooting.

"I'm not sure if the name's pronounced *Dee-vel* or *Devil,*" Nate had added, telling me with his tone that he preferred the second. There was no photo, but it sure sounded like the mysterious weapon I'd brought along for him to see.

Then my muscular friend had softened me more by giving me a photo of Barbara Stanwyck framed in polished aluminum. The frame was too modern for my taste, but I was touched by his thoughtfulness and loved the picture. It was different from the one in Darren's magazine, but I'd seen it on the Internet when researching the actress. I'd never been compared to a beautiful Hollywood star before so, naturally, was hopeful of finding other similarities that would support Darren's compliment. To my surprise, I'd discovered a couple that even the skeptical girl inside me couldn't deny.

As I'd told Nathan, "Barbara Stanwyck's father ran off when she was a little girl, too. Went to Panama or someplace when she was barely three, never saw him again. And she was a real outdoorsman. Owned a ranch, rode horses, and loved to trout-fish. Plus, she lived most her life as a single woman after divorcing. Didn't feel the need to hook her star to a husband to be happy." As a secret compliment to myself, I'd almost added, "She was an independent lady. A *man's* woman," but unfortunately did not.

That was the slip that had led to prying questions from Nathan, then me revealing how Martha had tried to seduce me. Worse, I'd admitted I had found it flattering—as unwelcome as Martha's behavior was—to be picked out by such a successful, attractive woman when there were plenty to choose from on a night when live music was being played at Jensen's Marina just down the road.

I'd sworn Nate to secrecy! Instead, he was jabbing me with more questions, and in a public place, where the woman ignoring us behind the bar could hear if she'd bothered to put down her cell phone and pay attention.

Now he was asking, "After she tried to kiss

you, what happened? Jesus, Hannah, the details! You *slapped* your boss. What'd she say?"

Yesterday, I would not have revealed to Nate, or anyone else, the exchange that took place between Martha Calder-Shaun and myself two nights ago. What the woman said had troubled me so much, I'd left the Seasonses' estate sleepless and was still wondering about my feelings the next day. But that was no longer true.

Even so, teeth clenched, I leaned forward and spoke in a low voice, saying, "I *pushed* Martha's hand away—more of a whack than a slap. Then the two of us agreed to forget it. If you're so darn nosy, I'll tell you the details—but later, when we're in the truck. I've got nothing to be ashamed of. It's kind of funny, really."

"Oh, come on! Tell me now." Nate's huge head swiveled toward the bar. "Our waitress is too busy texting to hear."

I sighed, confirmed that it was true, then wiggled my index finger to summon him closer. "You're a mess, you know that?" I said.

*"Please?"*

"Okay!" I hissed, then whispered what the New York attorney had said after I'd knocked her hand off my breast.

"Hannah, you beautiful, unusual girl. Ninety percent of all women are bisexual, they just don't know it. It's the most natural thing in the world. You're afraid to let go . . . risk finding out how

232

sexy and tender it can be. Why? Because you *know* you'd love it."

To Nathan, I added, "Those aren't her exact words. But close. It isn't true, of course."

Nate said, "That's awesome! The woman's crazy about you. My God, she was still trying to get in your knickers even after you slapped her."

"Martha isn't one to quit easily," I agreed. "You don't get to her level unless you've got some grit."

"Listen to yourself! You're defending her!"

"A woman who comes right out and says what she thinks? I admire that. I wish I was more like her. Why not?"

Nate was loving it. "You were *tempted* to let her kiss you, I can tell. Just a little? Admit it, Four."

I shrugged and shook my head, comfortable with what I was about to say. "Like I told you, I was flattered. Sure, I've thought about what it would be like. Do something that's fun and feels good—especially with someone I admire—I don't see anything wrong with that. But my body makes the rules—so far, at least—and I don't see that changing. My body tells me I'd have a lot more fun and feel a lot better with a man who has something between his ears and between his legs."

I shrugged again, adding, "There's no doubt in my mind about what I like." Which wasn't a lie —especially after last night, sitting in a small, warm room with the biologist, listening to his voice and watching the way his hands and shoulders moved. If Dr. Ford had a woman in his life, there was no evidence of her in his manner, or in his bathroom shower soap caddy. I'd checked.

Nate parroted Martha's words, wanting to remember them: *"Ninety percent of all woman are bisexual, they just don't know it."* Then asked the same question I'd made the mistake of asking: "What about the other ten percent?"

I quoted Martha Calder-Shaun, getting it almost perfect. "They're lesbians, kiddo. Don't fret— most of them are a hell of a lot happier than we are."

The dumb grin on Nathan's face told me he was trying to commit the conversation to memory, but then his expression changed. I realized he was looking beyond me at a man who had just come through the door. Short man, with muscled fore-arms, wearing a turquoise Miami Dolphins cap and white rubber fishing boots.

"I think that guy's following us," Nate whispered. "He was hanging around the marina. Then drove past when we were at the door where the postmistress lives. Remember the old pickup with the loud muffler? Red one. I saw his face." My friend made a subtle hushing motion with hands. *"Quiet.* Here he comes."

To balance Nathan's timid body language, I sat taller on my seat and didn't disguise my interest as I watched the man stop for a moment, silhouetted by the bright day outside. His eyes moved around the room until he found me, then he smiled, teeth whiter and straighter than expected.

"You're the folks been asking questions," the man in the Dolphins cap said when he got to our table. "We're looking for the same guy, I think. Ricky Meeks. That crook owes me money. How much he owe you?" Spreading like a cloud over our table floated the smell of beer and lighter fluid or what might have been sweat.

Nathan was a foot taller when he stood to shake hands, which caused the man to puff up and try to appear larger, his eyes still fixed on me. "Name's Eugene. And you're Hannah Smith. Don't look surprised. I sell fish to the marina, and the boys told me what a famous family you come from." He still hadn't craned his neck to look up at Nate but said to him as an aside, "Place as small as Caxambas, people talk. Everybody knows everybody else's business. That ain't always a bad thing . . . unless you *do* bad things—like that boy you've been asking about. Mind if I sit down?"

I couldn't place the accent. It was Southern, but not Central Florida, and definitely not Deep South. One of the Western states, maybe. Something else I couldn't put my finger on was why I felt an instant distrust for this drunken man who, so far, had been open about why he was looking for us. Unless . . . he was lying.

The waitress, at least, liked him. She called him

by name, still ignoring Nathan and me, but soon Eugene had a beer in front of him while I sipped sugarless tea that tasted of plastic. Nate had made a safer choice ordering bottled water.

"What's your last name again?" I interrupted when the man went right back to the subject of Meeks owing him money. The way he hesitated before responding, "Schneider . . . Eugene Schneider," caused more suspicion, which must have registered on my face.

Like a curtain falling, the man's genial manner disappeared with his smile. "You got a problem about something, darling?"

Nathan winced, but I felt right at ease. "I'm not your 'darling.' And you're the one who came to find me. If you've got something to say, say it."

Schneider pushed the cap back on his head, his expression broadcasting disbelief. "Just 'cause you're sitting with muscle boy here doesn't give you call to be snooty . . . darling. Especially to a man who's only trying to help." For the first time, Schneider looked up at Nate, whose face I noticed was mottling just like in school when older boys picked on him. "What about it, biggun? Your girlfriend always this ornery?"

"Always," Nate said, "except for when she's worse."

"There you go!" Schneider's smile reappeared as he toasted the ceiling with his beer. He took a sip, spread his arms to claim more table space, then returned his attention to me. "You want to find this Ricky Meeks character or not? Cops won't listen to me because I loaned the guy five thousand cash and didn't get a receipt. If you've got something in writing, though, *I* know where the guy is." The man leaned closer. "Trust me, he's not staying where some folks might have told you. I know that for a fact."

I didn't believe for a moment that Eugene Schneider had ever owned five thousand in cash, but his claim was worth exploring, so my brain told my mouth not to say anything else to offend the liar. Instead, I tried a lie of my own, saying, "If someone told us where to find Ricky Meeks, it's because they trusted me and I trust them. So I don't see how we can help each other." I gave Nate a look to make sure he understood what I was doing. He understood.

Standing, my friend said, "Thanks for the offer, but we've already found out what we need to know."

Eugene ignored the outstretched hand, preferring to keep his drunken eyes on me. "You sure you don't want to at least listen? Might save us both some time."

I exchanged another look with Nate, who handled it exactly right. "Wouldn't hurt to hear what the man has to say, Hannah. Besides, if he leaves, the waitress probably won't be back to take our order." My friend, playing the good cop, grinned and took his seat as a way of answering for me.

Schneider rewarded Nathan with a fraternity boy cackle, then lowered his voice to stress the importance of what he was saying. "A few weeks back, some local Crackers *might* have seen Ricky's boats anchored back side of East Drake Key. Sure. His Skipjack cruiser, and he's got an over-powered little jon boat. But that was two weeks ago, and these know-it-all Crackers don't work after sunup like me."

A jon boat is a flat-bottomed aluminum skiff built for running fast in shallow water. This was the first I'd heard of Meeks owning anything more maneuverable than his thirty-foot cruiser and a blue dinghy, but I didn't want Schneider to know the information was useful. "You remember Drake Keys," I said to Nathan. "They're south of here, part of Cape Romano."

To Schneider my friend said, "So far, you haven't told us anything new."

"Biggun," Schneider said, getting impatient, "I'm not finished yet. What I'm trying to tell you is, I fish around Cape Romano a lot. I know Drake Keys like the back of my hand, and Ricky's not there anymore. I know where he went, though— but you've never heard of the place. Dismal Key. It's southeast a few miles but hidden so far back in the islands you couldn't find it if you tried. I'd have to take you—if we come to some agreement."

238

If Uncle Jake hadn't taken me to explore Indian mounds on Dismal Key—an island dense with cactus, mosquitoes, and heat—I would have thought Eugene had stolen the name from a movie or was making it up. Dismal Key was a real place, though, and there was never a more accurate name. Now my brain was telling my mouth *Don't say anything stupid, keep him talking.*

"Interesting," I responded as if I wanted to believe this drunk with angry pale eyes. "What you're saying is, you expect us to pay you for your help."

"The guy owes me five thousand cash. How else you expect me to recover what I lost? Either that or tell me the truth about why you're looking for Ricky. If you've got enough dirt on him—or receipts for the money he owes you—maybe the cops will listen if we join up together."

Schneider was still lying. If the locals had told him my name, they'd also told him we'd been asking if there was a passenger on Meeks's boat, not looking to recover a bad loan. But why? The man wanted something—money, of course. Or maybe he was just nosy and liked being the center of attention. Ricky Meeks wasn't the type to win loyal friends, so Schneider had no reason to put us on a false trail. But after taking our money, he could always claim that Meeks had moved to another spot when we failed to find him.

"I'm kind of fussy about who I do business with," I said, no longer worried about making the man mad. "Nathan, instant tea is all the lunch I'll get if we stay here. You ready to find a place that's more particular about its customers?"

Eugene Schneider's temper had been sparking all along. Now it flared. "You little bitch!" he snapped, pushing his chair back. "I ought to slap you across this room for that."

Nate was instantly on his feet. "Shut . . . shut your mouth, mister!" he stammered, looming over the little man. "Lay a hand on Hannah and . . . and you'll regret it!"

I'd never experienced such behavior from my friend before. It was so unexpected, I couldn't speak for a moment, then had to hide a smile because of the way Schneider was cowering, looking at his dirty fingers, the table, anything but Nate's red face.

"Now, now, boys," I said in the tone of a grade school teacher, then waited until Nathan had taken his seat. "Eugene? You need to be careful who you taunt. Nate doesn't get mad quick, but he's a dangerous man when it happens." Not making eye contact with Nathan was the only thing that kept the smile off my face.

"Smart-ass woman," Schneider mumbled, his expression sullen. He was still inspecting his fingers.

I told him, "There's no reason I should tolerate

240

that sort of talk, but here's what we'll do. Tell me who Ricky's got on his boat and there might be a business arrangement. But no promises."

"Lady, you just got all the free information out of me you're gonna get. I have things to do this afternoon, but I'll run you down to Dismal Key after sunset. You can see for yourself—but it'll cost you . . . a thousand dollars. Five hundred if his boat's not there."

Nathan answered for me. "We can't. Hannah's going to a yacht party, but maybe tomorrow—"

"Party?" Schneider interrupted. "I'd know about it if there was a party on a boat anywhere near here."

"Fishermans Wharf, not Caxambas," Nathan explained, laughing because he was nervous. After showing such strength, my friend seemed to be seeking peace through camaraderie. I didn't appreciate him mentioning my personal business to a drunk, but I was busy thinking about Schneider's offer to take us to Dismal Key. Not that I intended to go with him, of course, but we could rent a boat at the marina ourselves. I'd just have to get approval from Mr. Seasons for something that expensive.

The problem was, Schneider had told us so many lies it was impossible to pick out the small bits of truth—if any. If Ricky Meeks had been anchored off the Drake Keys, why would this local drunk reveal the exact name of Ricky's new hiding place? Schneider either didn't suspect I could boat to the place on my own, or he was intentionally trying to nudge us off the trail until he'd had time to warn Ricky to move—not out of friendship, but because of what remained of Olivia's fifty-thousand-dollar checking account.

As I sat there thinking, the party aboard *Sybarite* no longer seemed important . . . but that suddenly changed. It changed when I noticed how curious Schneider was about the name of the yacht hosting the party.

"Nate!" I interrupted. "Eugene was about to tell us who else is on that Skipjack cruiser. You mind letting him answer?"

Schneider was disappointed. I could see it. The man finished his beer, his mind working hard at something, no telling what, then finally said to me, "I know the person you're talking about."

"On Ricky's boat?" I countered.

"She's a woman about your age. A rich young woman, or so that asshole claimed. I only got a quick look at her—she was coming out of the post office. Her and Ricky together. She reminded me of a stork, all bones and legs. Can't imagine what the dude saw in a piece like her."

My face warming, I replied, "We can't all be short and soft, now can we?"

The man missed the sarcasm. "This was . . . two weeks ago or so. But she took off."

I said, *"What?"*

"You offered to pay if I told you about Ricky's passenger. So I told you. He had a woman with him—I just described her—but that was a while ago." The man's eyes moved from Nathan to me to see how we accepted the news. "I'll be damned!" he said after a moment. "*She's* the reason you're here! Well, you're wasting your time, darling. The woman got pissed off at Ricky, or he got bored and kicked her out. Who knows? But she's been gone at least two weeks."

"Gone *where?*" I demanded.

The man was shaking his head. "If you want more details, it'll cost you . . . two hundred dollars cash. Now."

Confident after seeing my reaction, Eugene Schneider was smiling again, back in control. Within a few hours, I'd get my first look at Ricky Meeks whether I paid or not, but there was no way of knowing that. No way of predicting or even guessing at events that would soon follow.

So I did what I thought was prudent. As I reached for my wallet, the little man was signaling for another beer.

# Eighteen

More than an hour before sunset, I tied my boat at Fishermans Wharf, dressed for the party aboard *Sybarite*, but I was not in a party mood. As I crossed the bay from Sanibel, my cell phone had buzzed, so I had shut the engine off and drifted so I could hear Lawrence Seasons.

"Hannah! I've got something important." In contrast to the man's urgent tone, a few yards from my skiff a pod of dolphins rolled in slow unison, their blowholes spraying a genie mist into a silver June sky.

"You found Olivia?" I asked. Part of me hoped it was true, part of me felt guilty because of my disappointment.

"Listen closely," Lawrence replied. "The P.I. from Miami we hired, the first guy on this case? He's just been listed as a missing person. Officially. His agency called, state police are looking. I had a feeling something was wrong—that's why I was so tough on you today."

I replied, "Martha told me the guy was an alcoholic. Said he was probably barhopping on South Beach." As I spoke, gulls hovered above the dolphins, bickering about who owned the rights to any bait that was flushed. Watching the birds, I recalled how odd the news about the investigator had struck me earlier, yet Martha hadn't seemed bothered.

"That's what the agency manager told her. The guy has a history of binge drinking, so they were giving him a last chance—and probably time to surface. But it's been a week. They found his dog half starved. Even his family hasn't heard a word. According to the logs, he planned to rent a boat in Everglades City but hasn't been heard from since. How far's that from where Ricky Meeks buys fuel?"

Everglades City was only a short drive from Marco Island, which I told Mr. Seasons, but didn't mention it was ten very complicated miles by water to Dismal Key, plus a few miles more if the investigator had actually gotten a boat and tried to find Cape Romano.

"Understand now why I couldn't let you do it?" Lawrence was explaining again why he'd refused to authorize the expense of renting a boat in Caxambas. I'd been so disappointed, I would have paid the money myself if Nate and I could have pooled the five-hundred-dollar cash deposit required. It was because of what Eugene Schneider had told us—or hadn't told us. After listening to the surly man, my hopes and fears for Olivia were more mixed than ever, and I wanted to find out the truth with my own eyes. Was Ricky Meeks still anchored near Cape Romano, hidden in a bay formed by the Drake Keys? Or had he really moved his Skipjack cruiser to Dismal Key, where there was a dock, as I remembered, and the remains of a shack? More important, was Olivia still with him?

Maybe Schneider actually believed the girl had left the area two weeks before, maybe he didn't. Either way, it didn't matter. Ricky Meeks could have lied to him about Olivia being gone, hoping the rumor would spread among the Caxambas fishing community. If Ricky had done something bad to Olivia—a crime even worse than the way he had treated Mrs. Whitney—it was a way of buying time. I didn't want to wait another twenty-four hours before joining sheriff's deputies on the docks, hoping Ricky Meeks would bring his cruiser and the truth to Caxambas.

Lawrence Seasons, though, was a stubborn man when he'd made up his mind. In the conference call I'd made from Nathan's truck, I had shared Schneider's claims with him and Martha as well, but neither would budge. "I don't want you anywhere near Meeks," Lawrence had told me for the second or third time. "We're paying you to find Olivia, not some con artist who might be dangerous. Until tomorrow, at least, we're assuming the drunk you talked to was telling the truth. Olivia is free, finally. She's safe."

When I tried to argue, the man had cut me off, saying, "*Think* about it, Hannah—his story fits with Olivia's credit card records. Two weeks ago, she started using the Centurion card again. Why? Because she's traveling alone. Without Meeks looking over her shoulder, she doesn't need to be so careful about covering her tracks. Your theory had merit, but you were wrong. Is that what this is about? If that's the problem, get over it. It's time to shift your focus and move ahead."

To Lawrence Seasons, that meant calling the list of Olivia's friends he had sent by e-mail. To Martha, it meant sticking with my plan to attend the party, where I might run into someone from Port Royal who had seen or spoken to Olivia recently.

I wasn't convinced. First, Olivia disappears, then a trained private investigator? The possibilities my imagination conjured up gave me a shaky feeling in my legs, made it impossible to focus on anything but what the girl might be suffering now . . . this *instant*. I'm not the sort of person who can force a fake smile and pretend to have fun when someone I care about needs help —help I might be able to provide.

Which is why I wasn't in a party mood as I strode along the seawall toward the dock where *Sybarite* was moored, its sleek hull and black windows glowing like molten metal, caught in the spotlight of a west-setting sun. On the vessel's top deck, a few elegant-looking couples were already lounging against the rail, sipping drinks, while another half dozen guests made their way up the boarding ramp. Greeting them was a lean, busty woman in a white summer uniform consisting of slacks and a collared blouse.

It was Gabrielle Corrales, who had phoned me four times that afternoon, she was so excited about the party.

*"HANNAH?"* Gabby called when she spotted me. "Hannah!" Soon the girl was galloping down the ramp, saying, "*¡Mi mejor amiga!* So glad to see you, honey!"

I didn't expect my old classmate to fall into my arms so I could swing her around, but that's what happened, which wouldn't have bothered me if I wasn't in such a sour mood. Worse, couples on the top deck were pointing at us and whispering, probably guessing that Gabby was either stoned or drunk.

I pulled away and blocked a second bear hug by stepping back to inspect the girl, saying, "You told me you weren't wearing a uniform—not that you don't look sharp. 'Cause you do."

"It's just temporary," Gabby confided, but without much confidence. "Only until all the guests are aboard—I *hope*. Then I'll change. It's because most of the crew's been invited, and Robert's pissed off he's so shorthanded." The powdery smell of marijuana on the girl's breath, I noticed, was as mild as her perfume.

Gabby was embarrassed about being dressed like hired help, not a guest, so I tried to reassure her, saying, "If I looked as nice, I wouldn't bother changing. White's such a good color on you." The compliment had a purpose, but it was also true.

Gabby had been right about *Sybarite*'s tailored clothing. Creased slacks, crisp cotton blouse, sleeves the perfect length, and a firm starched collar that framed the girl's pretty face. Buttons on the blouse, I noticed, had been spaced in such a way that it was impossible not to show cleavage—particularly on someone like Gabby, who was proud of the way success had improved her body.

"Aren't they awesome?" she said, just a touch of Cuban accent. I wasn't sure if she was talking about her uniform or her breasts until she explained, "I've got my formal blues in the crew quarters. Later, after we've had a few drinks, I want to watch you try them on just to prove how hot you'll look. My slacks'll be too short, but—" The girl hesitated, seeming to look at me for the first time. "Hey . . . why aren't you wearing your cocktail dress?"

In my apartment, I'd spent twenty minutes admiring how the sheer black dress transformed me into a shapely woman who had taste but wasn't afraid to show off a little or hint she might look even better naked, taking a bubble bath, or in some strong man's bed. But I had decided against it. The fact I was traveling to

Fishermans Wharf by boat wasn't a problem—I almost always wear a dress to church. Problem was, the cocktail dress had a carefree look to it, which was the opposite of how I felt.

Instead, the photo of Barbara Stanwyck, in its brushed-aluminum frame, had told me what to wear. I'd chosen low-cut jeans tapered at the calves enough so as not to hide my Laredo boots of maple brown. The closest I could come to the actress's wrangler blouse was a cross-dye shirt with Navaho patterns, copper and desert primrose, I'd bought with Uncle Jake at the Clewiston Rodeo, which is a big affair in Central Florida. I seldom wore the shirt because of its Western pockets and buttons, so I had forgotten how soft the material felt against my skin and how the Arizona earth tones and ancient symbols added a gloss to my black hair.

I couldn't wear boots on my skiff, of course. Dark soles scuff white fiberglass. So I had carried them, changing out of my Top-Siders only after I'd reached the dock. Gabby was eyeing my boots now, but I was wrong about her reasons.

"I've got boat shoes," I offered, "if you're worried about those varnished decks."

The woman laughed, hooked her arm around my waist, and walked us toward the dock. "We're going to have so much fun together, honey. I was admiring your outfit, that's all. Envious, really. I wish I had the balls to dress so butch. And I

would if I thought I could pull it off. But I can't
—not like you. Think we could go shopping
maybe Wednesday or Thursday? Weekends are
bad for me, but I could sure use your help doing
the jeans-and-boots thing because . . ."

As Gabby talked on about clothing, then
switched to the wealthy guests we were about to
meet, I felt her hand squeeze my waist, then
slide to my ribs, which caused a moment of
tenseness that my mind instantly blamed on
Martha Calder-Shaun. My uneasiness didn't last,
though. What did Gabby's intentions matter if I
had my own thoughts under control? Besides, I
liked her. She was a tad wild, true, but the woman
was making her own way in a hard world, and
she had proved herself fair-minded when it came
to judging people.

Even when Gabby gave me a soft pat on the
butt, it was okay. It felt comfortable to be with a
girl I knew, especially with so many well-dressed
strangers filing out of the parking lot toward
*Sybarite*. I had never seen so many attractive
couples in one small space—nor so many
expensive cars. There were Bentleys, a bunch of
BMWs, a Rolls or two, plus a few makes I
couldn't identify. Sleek luxury rockets as shiny as
trophies, designed to impress, or as bedroom
lures, not meant for practical transportation.

"They make my 'Vette seem sorta plain," Gabby
said when she noticed where I was looking.

251

"My legs wouldn't fit into that little maroon job," I observed. "Never mind fishing rods or grocery bags after shopping. How much you think it cost?"

"A Ferrari Testarossa?" The girl raised her eyebrows in a way that told me it was better not to know.

"I've got a Ford Explorer with a hundred thousand miles, so I've been thinking about a truck," I said. "You seen the new GMC short beds?"

Laughing, Gabby squeezed me closer, which felt natural. Her family had been just as hard-up for money as mine back in school, so it was a sisterly bond we shared. "Robert gets his rocks off strutting through that lot before a cruise," she smiled. "Just watch him! He does it every time. That's why he makes the crew park way the hell down there." She motioned toward a chain-link fence separating the marina from the road. A moment later, though, because I hadn't responded, Gabby pulled away and asked, "What's wrong? Hannah . . . ? *Hannah!*"

A rusty old pickup truck that I recognized was turning in to the marina, that's what was wrong. A red truck I'd seen earlier that day in Caxambas, a lone man behind the steering wheel. Even from a distance, I could tell it wasn't Eugene Schneider.

I took Gabby by the elbow. "Did anyone call this afternoon and ask if I was on the guest list?"

Flustered, the girl stammered, "I don't know . . . and what's it matter? You're my date, no one's going to care."

"It matters, Gabrielle. Or I wouldn't ask."

On the shell road, the truck was kicking dust, the driver indifferent to speed signs, one hand on the wheel, the other holding what might have been a cigar.

Gabby said, "This is a private party, so I'm not even sure there is a guest list." A moment later, she grunted. "Hannah, you're hurting me!" then yanked her arm free. "Honey, who's in that truck? What in the hell is going on?"

Ricky Meeks was driving the truck, which Gabby confirmed after watching him park among the expensive cars. "Oh, because of *that* creep. Now I get it. And . . . my God"—Gabby was staring at me—"you're *afraid* of him, honey. Why?"

She said it because I had pulled her closer to an aluminum storage shed so we could watch Ricky without being noticed. "I've never seen him before," I replied. "Just that picture I showed you." For some reason, my chest had tightened. It felt harder to breathe.

Hands on hips, Gabrielle studied me for a moment. "*Chica*, tell me the truth. He scares the hell out of you—it's on your face."

"Not really—not for myself, anyway," I replied, which wasn't true, and Gabby knew it.

253

"That son of a bitch! He hurt you somehow, didn't he? You weren't snooping because he owes a friend of yours money. Ricky did something to you. *What?* Don't lie to me anymore, Hannah. We can't be friends if you lie."

My eyes were fixed on Meeks, thirty yards away, as he banged the truck door closed, flicked his cigar aside after a last puff, then used the side mirror to comb his hair. The smoke reached us seconds later and caused me to flinch—not just the stink, but because it had come from Ricky's mouth.

"Some of what I said was true," I replied, "but you're right. Mostly, I lied."

*"Why?"*

"I wasn't sure I could trust you. Even if I was sure, I probably would've lied anyway. Just to be on the safe side."

"Safe side, hah! You intentionally fed me a line of bullshit."

"Sorry. I don't blame you for being mad."

"Don't *blame* me, why . . . you two-faced little *chinga!*" Gabby sputtered but kept her voice down. "I saved your ass, erasing that security tape before Robert saw it. You've had a dozen chances to tell me the truth, all the times we've talked on the phone. *Hey*"—she began backing away—"you *are* a cop, aren't you? Hannah, if you're trying to trap me into some kind of shitty sting operation, I'll . . . I'll . . ."

The girl shrugged my arm away when I tried to wrap it around her shoulder, but calmed a bit when I took her hand and pressed it between my hands. "This is serious, Gabrielle. I need your help. Please? At least let me explain."

Gabby glanced over her shoulder toward *Sybarite*, heaved a sigh of frustration, then steered me behind the storage shed. "This better be good, sister! If I lose my job because of you—"

Ricky Meeks was walking toward the dock, straightening the collar of his gray dress shirt, checking the buttons of a navy blazer, as I interrupted, saying, "I'm not a cop. That man kidnapped the niece of a friend of mine. Probably raped her, then kept her drugged somehow. So drugged up, she might be waiting for him on your boat right now."

Gabby shot back, "Aboard *Sybarite*? A private party . . . a party that friends of mine are hosting?" Her tone accused *You've got to be kidding*.

"You said yourself the guy's trash. That's the only way he can get aboard—if some rich woman invites him. Do you remember a passenger named Olivia Seasons?"

Gabby was muttering, *"This is insanity,"* not wanting to believe it but still listening.

"Olivia's a tall, thin girl about our age. She's worth millions, and her uncle is"—I hesitated, reluctant to tell this smart woman another lie— "he's my employer. And he's a friend, too. Olivia

255

is either aboard your boat, or Ricky Meeks has come here looking for me. That's why I asked if someone called about the guest list."

Gabby's expression changed. "He knows you're looking for . . . what's her name? Olivia?"

I nodded. "I think so."

The girl stood taller to get a better look at Meeks, who was sliding through people to get to the boarding ramp. "No wonder you're afraid. That guy's a sicko, you ask me. Olivia's tall and thin, you said? What color's her hair?"

As I did my best to describe the missing heiress, Gabby was shaking her head. "I haven't seen her. But I got here a little late, so maybe she's somewhere on the boat and I missed her. I doubt it, though."

"I have to find out for sure," I said. "If she's here, I need time alone so we can talk. I think the guy's screwed up her mind so much, it's like she's under a spell. She's in bad trouble, Gabrielle. Will you help?"

Gabby thought for a moment. "There's another possibility, honey. Because of the party, Robert's so short on crew, maybe he's paying the guy to handle lines and stuff at the dock. As a sort of first mate. That would explain his ugly damn blazer. Or . . . could be one of Ricky's other teaser pony ladies wants him around. My friends sure as hell didn't invite that bastard—you're right about that."

I was watching Meeks move toward the boat's sleek, wide stern, astonished at how smoothly guests snubbed him without making a show, turning their backs at just the right moment or staring past him as if he were invisible. Their behavior validated my loathing for a man I'd never met but also made me apprehensive. I, too, was an outsider. Would they treat me as coldly?

Gabby threaded her arm through mine, a serious look on her face as she gave a pull, then walked me toward *Sybarite*. "Don't worry, honey, I'll look after you. But don't lie to me ever again. That's what my last girl did—plus she was screwing my boyfriend behind my back. Now we don't even talk anymore. See what happens when best friends don't trust each other?"

I replied, "If Olivia's not on the boat, I need your help even more. I'm so nervous, maybe we should talk about it now so we don't get confused later." My mind was flipping through options, gauging the minutes until sunset, while my eyes moved from Eugene Schneider's old truck . . . to *Sybarite* . . . then to my fast boat only a hundred yards away. If Olivia wasn't here, waiting for Meeks, he might have left her alone on his Skipjack cruiser somewhere in the Ten Thousand Islands.

"That's what worries me," Gabby said. "Let's go straight to the crew lounge and smoke a joint. You're way, way too uptight, honey. Once we're

257

away from the dock, how will you handle it if Ricky tries to make small talk? I don't want you freaking out on me. Or he starts hitting on you?"

That's when I shared with Gabby a decision I'd just made. If we didn't find Olivia, I was getting off the boat before *Sybarite* left the dock and headed for open water.

"Without him noticing," I added, meaning Ricky Meeks. "Can you help me do that?"

"You'll miss the party!" she said.

"If it were you, Gabrielle, in real trouble, would you want me to stay here having fun? Or expect a friend to do something?"

"And if Olivia *is* aboard?"

"Keep Ricky busy while I take her somewhere private to talk. I'll keep it all real quiet even if she agrees to go home with me. We'll sneak her off somehow—you know, figure it out later. I won't embarrass you, though. Promise."

I liked the look on my friend's face and her fierce reaction. "*¡Es tan sencillo, cariño!*" she nodded, then offered a loose translation. "Honey, you just leave that white trash loser to me."

# Nineteen

A little while later, I was following the plan—but I was a mess.

In my imagination, I could feel Ricky Meeks's black eyes drilling a hole in my back as I idled my skiff away from Fishermans Wharf and *Sybarite*, which was just leaving the dock. The yacht's upper deck was loud with reggae music and the crowded laughter of a party amping up for sunset, eager for the freedom of open water.

Ricky was up there somewhere. Maybe he actually was watching, startled to see I'd left the yacht. Hopefully, though, Gabby was keeping him occupied or he was busy helping Robert get under way as he was being paid to do. I couldn't risk turning to look, of course. So I sat hunched at the wheel, trying to will my body to stop shaking. I'd been shaking ever since finally meeting Meeks, face-to-face. The man had caused me to behave like a helpless fool and I was still suffering the effects.

Ricky had surprised me when I was alone in Gabby's tiny cabin, waiting for her to return from *Sybarite*'s steering room. Olivia wasn't mingling with the other guests, so it was up to my friend to check the crew area and finally confirm that the missing heiress wasn't aboard.

Sitting on Gabby's bunk, feeling nervous and antsy, I had heard a man's heavy footsteps pause outside her door. There was a long silence punctuated by a soft snorting sound. The rhythm of the sound reminded me of a dog sniffing for the blood trail of wounded game. Into my head came Elka Whitney's words . . . *he can smell weakness. It's like an animal thing* . . . as I watched the doorknob slowly twist right, then left—someone testing for a lock. I wanted to do something, anything, to stop what was happening, but my brain and body felt mired in glue. Then, *BANG!* the door slammed open, hitting the bulkhead hard, and Ricky Meeks suddenly filled the cabin, greasy spit curl on his forehead, his black eyes shining as if he'd known all along where I had been hiding.

"Hannah Smith, you nosy bitch! Guys in Caxambas say you've got a skinny ass, but they've seen worse. I want to look for myself—on your feet!"

Never in my life had a stranger leered at me with such confidence nor spoken such rude words. I sat there frozen, too shocked to speak, and yet, *stupidly,* I had managed to stand exactly as the man ordered me to do. Worse, I had remained frozen, numb as a mannequin, when Meeks cupped my face in his rough hands, saying, "Let's just hope you taste better than you look," and forced the stink of cigars against my lips.

Then he was wagging his big index finger at me, saying, "You and me are gonna have ourselves a little talk when we get back. Then you're going to show me around your boat. I've got some questions need answered."

An instant later, the man gave me a push, then was gone, leaving only the odor of his cheap cologne and his locker room laughter to linger in the hall.

I felt furious with myself and embarrassed. Too stunned to tell even Gabby or confess my fear that Meeks had put his hands on my breasts before pushing me. *Had he?* Everything had happened so fast, the details were so blurred, I couldn't be certain—or was my memory blocking the shame of tolerating such an offense?

Now my brain was still raging about what had happened, punishing me with clever words I could have said, the brave things I *should* have done with my knee, my fingernails, my teeth. In the past, I'd been mystified—secretly contemptuous, too—of women in the headlines who had been assaulted without fighting back or even reporting what had happened. Now, for the first time, I understood. The realization added guilt to the fury that was causing my body to shake. How could I have been so unfair, so cruel in my thoughts, to women who'd been humiliated by what I was too callow to imagine?

Behind me now, *Sybarite*'s horn gave three

blasts to announce she was backing. Then I heard the yacht's diesels accelerate and I knew that, finally, I was safe from Ricky Meeks's mean hands. Even so, I didn't turn to look. I kept my skiff pointed southeast, toward Estero Bay, frustrated by the *No Wake Zone* markers but pleased that *Sybarite* was moving in the opposite direction, headed for the mouth of Matanzas Pass.

*If you surprise a dangerous man, expect to be surprised.*

The words of Marion Ford returned to my head, and I clung to his voice for several seconds, which calmed me. *Surprise.* That's exactly what had happened. That's why I'd been unable to fight back. Never in my life had a man caused me to feel so weak, so helpless, but it wasn't because I lacked courage—or so I wanted to believe. It was because Ricky Meeks had skipped the normal bullying steps that usually precede a confrontation. Instead, he had shocked me into submission by doing the unthinkable—but something I should have expected! I had listened to Elka Whitney. I had read Olivia's journal and seen the hatred in her painting of a faceless, leering man with horns instead of ears. All the facts I needed were stored in my brain, yet I hadn't anticipated —*or even believed*—that I, too, could become the victim of such vicious behavior.

Ricky Meeks had caught me unprepared once, but it would never happen again. That was the

262

promise I made to myself as I sat at the wheel of my skiff, considering the weather, picturing how the sea would feel far offshore. On this June afternoon, the bay was so gelatin slick that bait pocked the surface like rain. Shock waves of a pelican diving echoed for miles, expanding rings on the Gulf's silver veneer. It was the perfect afternoon for a long trip in a small boat—if I could summon the courage. As I thought about it, something else Elka had said helped finalize my decision: *Forgiveness is for women who don't have the balls for revenge.*

Meeks had surprised me. Now was my chance to turn the tables. Do it right, I could blindside the bully who had hurt me, Olivia, poor Elka Whitney, and God only knew how many other women.

I glanced at the sun, then checked my watch: *6:45 p.m.* Sunset was at twenty to nine, which meant I could fly the forty-some miles to Marco Island and still have enough daylight to look around Cape Romano and possibly even get to Dismal Key if I hurried. Returning by night was no problem—Dr. Ford had equipped the skiff with the best lights and electronics, even a single-sideband radio, which I'd removed in favor of a handheld VHF. It was getting to the Ten Thousand Islands fast that was important.

I couldn't fly yet, though. The Coast Guard station was too close to risk ignoring the *No Wake Zone* buoys. They extended for another hundred yards before I reached the channel. So I paid attention to Marion Ford's warning and spent the idle time going over my equipment. I had lights, extra clothes, and food if I decided to anchor for the night, plus an item I'd stored beneath the console to show Nathan, then forgotten—the Devel pistol, book case included, all safe in a waterproof bag.

I opened the console, then opened the bag. The weight of the gun in my hand, rather than giving me confidence, brought a couple of worst-case scenarios into my mind that I took time to consider. What if I found Olivia and, instead of welcoming my help, the troubled girl turned against me and called the police? Much worse, what if Meeks had seen me leave *Sybarite* and was in his truck right now racing me to Marco Island?

In my head, I calculated how long it would take him to make the drive, then cover a few back-country miles in a small boat. If Ricky had left right away, I decided, he would beat me to Cape Romano by ten or fifteen minutes. More if he was hiding his Skipjack cruiser at Dismal Key.

Not good.

Police and an angry rich girl didn't bother me at all. But the thought of being intercepted by Meeks in his fast jon boat was spooky. Just the two of us alone in the Ten Thousand Islands, one of the largest uninhabited wilderness regions in

America. Nothing but black water, mosquitoes, and mangrove tunnels snaking deep into the sawgrass of the Everglades. At night, probably no cell phone reception—only seven cartridges in the pistol I was holding if I got into real trouble, plus a handheld VHF that was an expensive Lowrance but still only a six-watt radio with limited range.

But that *wasn't* going to happen. Meeks was being paid to work as first mate, which Robert, *Sybarite*'s captain, had confirmed. Unless . . . unless Meeks had accepted the job not just to try to scare me off, but also track me as I continued to search for Olivia.

For the first time, I risked turning my face toward Fishermans Wharf. *Sybarite* was already several hundred yards away, the party guests a blur of pixelated shapes. It was impossible to see if Ricky was among them. Closer was the marina parking lot, but much of it was screened by a stand of casuarina pines. If the red truck was still there, I didn't see it.

For several shaky seconds, my courage wavered. Then my anger at what Meeks had done fired a burning drive in me, that grew stronger and stronger as I imagined what Olivia Seasons had suffered and might still be suffering. As Nathan and Lawrence Seasons had both observed, the missing girl and I had some unusual ties in common. Now there was one more—a mean, wolfish man by the name of Ricky Meeks.

As mad as I was, though, I wasn't about to do anything foolhardy or stupid. That's what I kept telling myself, anyway. To prove it, I took my cell from its waterproof pouch and called Gabby, hoping to be reassured that Meeks hadn't left the yacht. I wasn't surprised she didn't answer, and so left a message asking her to call me first chance she got.

I couldn't call Martha or Lawrence Seasons and tell them where I was going—they would have stopped me—but I wanted someone to know. Nathan would try to talk me out of it, too, of course, so I called his apartment instead of his cell and left another message. In detail, I told him where I planned to search, and what he should do if I didn't make contact before noon, which is when Martha, Lawrence, and I were scheduled to meet sheriff's deputies in Caxambas.

"Cell phones probably won't work down there," I explained, "but I'll monitor channel sixty-eight on the VHF if there's some kind of emergency." Nate is experienced with boats and water so wouldn't have found my mention of the radio as comforting as most. Handheld radios transmit at low wattage with a line-of-sight range that's rarely more than five miles, depending on how many islands block the signal. Even on Sanibel, I sometimes receive Key West weather a hundred miles away. But transmitting a solid signal to even nearby Captiva is considered a lucky day.

Even so, I had taken all the precautions available to me. As a reward, I allowed myself to do something personal. I dialed Marion Ford's lab, even though I knew he was in South America, just to enjoy the comforting sound of his recording. His was a low voice, so calm and solid that I found myself replying with the same details I'd left on Nathan's machine, which pretty much guaranteed the biologist would call the moment he got back.

"I'll tell you the whole story when we fish for tarpon on Friday!" I added with some spunk, then returned my cell phone to its waterproof case.

Reassured by my solid behavior, I stood at the wheel as I neared the channel, feeling some confience for a change and the first spark of excitement about the trip I was about to take. Within easy reaching distance, I had secured a thermos of cold sweet tea and a Tupperware container that held two blueberry yogurts, a banana, and an orange I'd packed for the ride home after the party. I hooked the ignition safety lanyard to my belt in case I fell overboard, checked around for Coast Guard boats, then shoved the throttle forward—too fast in my eagerness. The rocket sled acceleration caused my cell phone to jump off the console, then skitter overboard despite my desperate lunge to catch it.

Too late. The case was waterproof, not sink-proof, and it was gone.

*No reception down there anyway,* I told myself, then buried the mistake by opening the throttle wide. Minutes later, after shooting beneath Big Carlos Pass Bridge, I entered the Gulf of Mexico doing fifty-plus according to my gauges, my eyes blurring from speed.

To my left, windows of distant hotels and condos mirrored a brassy westwarding sun. Afternoon storm clouds were building, I noticed, but I ignored them, preferring to concentrate on my destination. A mile offshore, safe from sandbars, I checked my GPS, then the compass switch, just to make sure my electronics were a hundred percent. The compass glowed a mild red for nighttime navigation. The GPS told me that at current speed, estimated arrival time at the sea buoy off Marco was 19:47 hours, which would put me off Cape Romano around eight p.m.

Good! My guess had been right. I would have more than an hour of daylight to search for the Skipjack cruiser and Olivia.

Feeling more confident than ever, I turned south. Checked fuel, oil pressure, and water temp —all fine despite the engine's blistering fifty-five miles an hour—then sat behind the windshield to dry my eyes and take a swig of tea. Overhead, a jetliner banked to land at Southwest International, and it pleased me to imagine how my fast boat looked to passengers peering down. Like an arrowhead, I hoped, that cut a feathered wake as it cleaved a straight line toward its target. The Seminole shaman, Billie Egret, and Tomlinson would have both liked that.

I finished my tea, tweaked the trim tabs to nudge more speed from the engine, and felt my skiff settle beneath me, a Kevlar hydroplane, only its chines and propeller connected to the water.

Ahead, there was no horizon, no buildings to use as range markers. There was only the emptiness of water and my teenage memory of the wild islands that lay beyond.

# Twenty

If the makeshift markers I remembered at the entrance to Drake Keys hadn't been moved, I never would have spotted the Skipjack cruiser. Instead, a fast loop around the bay would have convinced me the boat wasn't there before I hurried deeper into the islands toward channels that zigzagged toward Dismal Key.

A thirty-foot boat with Mercruisers required depth for safe anchorage, especially on a falling tide. As I approached the entrance, though, a glance told me there wasn't enough water inside those islands to float a canoe. Plateaus of turtle grass, blades combed smooth by the tide, leaned toward gutters of deeper bottom, but there wasn't a boat in sight. There were two navigable cuts, however, that sliced Cape Romano, and the shortest route to the nearest was through the shallow bay. That's when I began to look seriously for the markers I remembered from my trips to the islands with Uncle Jake.

Normally, I don't need poles or floating milk bottles to direct me through thin water. Even in unfamiliar regions, I have confidence in my abilities. But visibility had changed during the hour it had taken me to raise the shoals of Cape Romano. Now a flotilla of squall clouds muted the sky above while sunset painted the surface from a low angle, cloaking sandbars and nervous water with a blinding film of gold. I backed the throttle . . . squinted through my polarized glasses . . . thumbed the jack plate higher while searching for the best line to run. No matter how hard a boat passenger tries to pay attention, only the driver's brain is actually branded with the self-taught ranges and contours of bottom required to navigate backcountry. I had run this little cut several times while Jake steered, but the placement of those old markers now refused to take shape in my head.

Twenty yards from the island, I knew I was in trouble. The hull lifted beneath my feet, as it always does in thin water, then my engine's skeg banged bottom. Rather than kill the motor instantly, I got aggressive because I'd come too far to be stranded here in the middle of nowhere. Not if Ricky Meeks might soon return!

Instead, while my thumb worked the trim button, I steered hard to the right, jamming the throttle forward until the engine kicked and bucked us toward deeper water. By the time we'd broken free, my skiff was heeled precariously on its starboard chine, so I spun the wheel to the left, which caused a turn so sharp, I was nearly thrown from the boat.

Gradually, I got my skiff under control but continued steering hard rights and hard lefts until it was safe to run flat, the foot of my engine tilted deep in water that its cooling system required. For almost a minute, I thought I'd dodged a serious mistake. Then I heard *BZZZZZZZZZZ!* as my motor sputtered, then died, a cloud of exhaust steam floating past me while my skiff drifted to a stop.

I seldom say any profanity worse than *shit,* but I made an exception now.

This wasn't the first time I'd been stopped by a warning buzzer and a computer chip that caused overheated outboards to shut down. Summer is the worst time in Florida for fast boats. Lots of dead sea grass adrift on the surface. Chances were good the problem wasn't serious if I took the right steps to clean the water intake and exhaust vents. Trouble was, the time the task required would ruin my chances of finding

Olivia. The sun was setting. Soon the blazing western sky would surrender to slow purple shadows and the pearly glow of twilight. Unless I was willing to poke around after dark, island to island, searching with a spotlight, it was time to turn around and head for home.

That's exactly what I decided to do. In fact, I whispered it aloud. "Hannah Four, you reckless fool. Get your butt home."

Part of me was relieved, part of me was disappointed. But there was something more powerful I was feeling—*fear*. Calm as I pretended to be, the anxiety inside me was a building pressure that required methodical action or I risked panic. My fear wasn't groundless, the reality of my situation was plain enough that it didn't need warnings from my imagination. It had been half an hour since I'd seen another boat or even heard a radio transmission on my little VHF. I was alone, no friendly stranger within hailing distance to help. The crunch and scream of a powerboat running aground is distinctive. Over water, an alarm buzzer can be heard for miles. To a man like Ricky Meeks, those sounds might bring him running like a wolf who hears the squeal of injured prey.

In the new silence of slapping water I did a slow turn, searching the area for a small boat hidden someplace in the shadows. If Meeks had witnessed what had just happened, he'd probably be grinning, his confidence sky-high at the prospect of dealing with a woman who was so incompetent around boats and water.

*Nothing.*

That's what I saw. Pelicans roosting heavy in mangroves . . . snowy egrets aflame against a sunset sky, gliding to roost . . . a cormorant, it's snaky emerald eyes watching from a few yards away while my skiff drifted toward the shallows.

*Ricky's aboard* Sybarite, I reassured myself. The yacht was scheduled to return to Fishermans Wharf at eleven—more than two hours from now. I had plenty of time, if I got my engine running. That was first on the agenda, so I went to work trying all the normal remedies. I waited a few nervous minutes for the outboard to cool, then turned the ignition key. The engine started but was barely audible above the screaming heat alarm. I shifted into reverse and watched the propeller kick a ball of sea grass to the surface. A good sign! I shifted to neutral, engaged the idle button, then throttled forward to increase water flow through the cooling conduits.

*BZZZZZZZZZZZZ!* Instead of stopping, the alarm shrieked louder.

I braved the noise long enough to see that the exhaust vents weren't spewing water—*pissers,* fishermen call the little tubes that jettison hot water. In a rush, I killed the engine, the abrupt silence as piercing as that maddening alarm.

273

Now I had to admit that the water intake hadn't been choked with grass as I'd hoped. Either the engine's cooling ducts were clogged, or I'd burned out my water pump. Fixing the first problem might take fifteen minutes. Replacing the pump required a marina forklift and meant I would be stuck here all night unless I could arrange for a tow.

Slowly, slowly, my eyes scanned the perimeter of mangroves and water that encircled my boat. Other than switching my good boots for boating shoes, I was still dressed for a party in my jeans and Navaho shirt. Even so, I felt naked and vulnerable as if nothing but a shower curtain separated me from some lurking, invisible evil. My chest had tightened, breathing required an effort.

*Nothing.*

Same as before. More seabirds racing darkness toward shore . . . mullet slap-thumping in the shallows . . . the mushroom girth of a manatee breaching the surface, then the farewell wave of its fluked tail.

I put my hands on the gunnel and peered into the water. It was black with tannin but clear, and only a few feet deep. Next step was to push my skiff to a shell ridge that was twenty yards away, mangroves thick on both sides. The ridge had probably been built by the same people who'd constructed the pyramids where I'd lived as a girl. The elevation would give me room to work, plus that ancient connection offered a homey feel. Nathan is right when he accuses me of being superstitious. In my superstitious heart, I believed I would be safer there.

From my toolbox, I took a Phillips screwdriver and a length of monofilament almost as thick as the line used in a weed trimmer. If I snaked the monofilament far enough up the pisser holes, maybe I could auger the cooling ducts clean. It was my last best hope of getting my engine running again. Fail, and I was stuck for the night, which was frightening to contemplate. Even if Ricky Meeks's Skipjack cruiser was anchored near Dismal Key, I was close enough that I would hear his engine when he passed by. Close enough that he might even *see me* if he used a spotlight.

Suddenly, my body was shaking again, which made me so disgusted that I stomped my foot, banged the console with my fist, and reprimanded myself with a lecture:

*Stop worrying and get to work! If the man shows up, do what Hannah Three would have done: charm him silly, then slap the hell out of him. Steal his wallet, too, if the fool gives you a chance!*

My aunt wasn't a thief—not that she had admitted in her journals, anyway—but just thinking of how that tough, bawdy woman would handle the situation caused me to smile. It helped me feel better and cleared my head.

*Be prepared to be surprised,* Marion Ford had warned. So that's what I concentrated on instead. I took the pistol from beneath the console, opened the book titled *Negotiators,* and checked to make sure there was a round in the gun's chamber. I engaged the safety, then placed the book on the starboard seat, closing the cover to disguise what was inside, yet kept the weapon within easy reach if needed. Then I laid out a spotlight and slipped a powerful little LED flashlight into my pocket because it would be full dark in thirty minutes or so. Finally, I looped the leather scabbard of my fisherman's pliers onto my belt. The pliers had a wire cutter and a knife blade, which might come in handy.

I wasn't sure I'd need a tow, but the possibility was a good excuse to take another precaution. I wanted someone to know where I was, and the tough situation I was in. It had been half an hour since I'd heard a transmission on my handheld VHF, but I tried the radio anyway, using emergency channel sixteen after reducing squelch.

"Break, break, sixteen, requesting assistance from any vessel in the Marco Island area. Any vessel . . . copy?"

In reply, I heard rhythmic static, which meant someone was answering, but too far away to make contact.

When conversing with fishing guides, I don't use the name of my boat or radio call letters, but

I couldn't think of a better time to sound official. So I repeated the call, adding, "This is commercial vessel *Hannah-Belltiva* . . . Whiskey-Romeo-X-ray six-seven-niner-six. Do you read?"

*Belltiva* is a name I'd made up by combining Sani*bel* with Cap*tiva*, and it seemed to bring me good luck. This time the static was decipherable, and I heard: "*Hannah-Belltiva* . . . this is Key West Coast Guard, we have you broken but readable. Please switch and answer twenty-two Alpha."

Instead of raising a local vessel, my weak signal had skipped across eighty miles of water to a tower somewhere near Duval Street and Mallory Square, where another relative of mine, Great-great-uncle Jake Summerlin, had sold cattle to meat buyers from Cuba!

Hands shaking, I switched channels, then spent a frustrating several minutes shouting my location and describing my situation, at least some of which the Coast Guard radioman understood before our frail signal vanished. I tried a couple more times without success, then gave up.

Even so, I felt a hundred times better when I slipped into the water and pushed my skiff to the shell ridge, the mucky bottom trying to suction off my boat shoes with every step. The U.S. Coast Guard knew my name, where I was, and that I might need help! I dropped an anchor off the stern, then went to work, stopping every minute or so to sweep the area with my eyes, then listen for the distant whine of an approaching jon boat.

My engine's tiny exhaust tubes were clogged with gray marl. I could see that right away, which gave me some hope. Clean the pisser holes, and my water pump would probably work just fine. In ten or fifteen minutes, I could be in clean Gulf air headed home!

It wasn't that easy, though. I tried to drill through the marl (which is rough gray clay), using the monofilament. I made a quarter inch of headway before my plastic auger finally bent, so I used the other end. After another quarter inch, it snapped, too. Maybe I'd gone deep enough to get my engine running. Maybe water pressure inside the engine would kick the rest of the muck free, but it was better to do the job right than waste precious minutes on a failed test.

I stood and stretched, still confident but worried. A screwdriver was too thick, the shank of a fishhook wasn't long enough. I needed a drilling tool as thin as the monofilament but stronger.

I turned and considered hunting through the storm detritus that settles at the rim of every mangrove swamp. Drake Key was different though. The shell ridge behind me rose ten or twelve feet above flotsam left by storms. Atop the ridge grew a gumbo-limbo tree, buttonwoods, and a thicket of Spanish bayonet plants, their leaves spiked with three-inch needles.

I didn't have to think about it for long. Bayonet

plant needles are as sharp and tough as darts, and I had hundreds to choose from. Exactly what I needed!

Moving fast but not rushing, I scampered up a cascade of shells, not stopping until I grabbed a buttonwood limb to steady myself at the top of the ridge. That's when I noticed it—the air conditioner kick of a small generator, then a patch of blue canvas visible through vegetation that rimmed the bay below. Odd noises, too, were coming from the area. It was a garbled squawking, like parrots fighting . . . the grunt of what might have been a wild hog . . . and the feathered *whap-whap-whap* of a wounded bird trying to fly.

I felt my breath catch, then fought the temptation to turn and run. Instead, I took quiet steps down the back of the ridge, mangroves so thick that light faded, like slipping into a cave . . . then kept changing angles until I confirmed what I was seeing. The blue canvas was a sun shade on the flybridge of a boat—a low flybridge built atop the boat's cabin. *A Skipjack cruiser.* Ricky Meeks had found a pocket of deep water way back in the mangroves and that's where he had hidden.

As I looked on, the boat floated still as a painting, no one visible above deck. The dinghy that Cordial Pallet had described was missing from its brackets, I noted, but there was no sign of a fast jon boat that Meeks no doubt would have tied to the stern—a huge relief.

My chance to find out if Olivia was aboard! To finally meet the girl face-to-face and urge her to return home with me. The temptation was to call the girl's name. Better yet, climb aboard the Skipjack in case Meeks had left her tied up or locked in a cabin.

But I didn't. There was something else I saw now that I was closer . . . the source of the strange noises. Deep in shadows separating me from the boat, a gaggle of vultures were battling two feral hogs to get at something that lay in the bushes. The area being so dense with mangroves, the vultures were getting the worst of it because their wings kept tangling in vines. And one of the hogs was bigger than me, probably two hundred pounds of muscle and tusks. When it grunted, the sound was so coarse that the shell ridge vibrated beneath my feet.

*Why didn't you bring the damn pistol?* That's what I was thinking as I watched the animals squabble. My Great-great-aunt Hannah One had hunted hogs for meat and money, but I was more interested in self-defense. Boars didn't often attack people on the islands, but it happened, and the prospect of being mauled by an animal that size was sickening. How would the hog react if I tried to detour around it to get to the boat? Or even heard my voice?

I don't know why but into my head came the message from church that morning—the promise that guidance and protection belonged to those who had faith and behaved boldly. I'd been disgusted by my inability to control my shaking nerves and was sick to death of being scared. The bullying behavior of that boar hog, the mean way it strutted, was irksome, too. Maybe that's why my attitude changed so abruptly. Whatever the reason, a mix of anger and cold calm settled into me, a change as solid as it was swift, and for the first time since leaving Fishermans Wharf I felt strong, not flighty and timid. Neither Ricky Meeks nor some damn feral pig was going to bully me!

Hands cupped to my mouth, I stood on my toes and yelled, "Olivia! Are you in there? I'm a friend!"

Startled, vultures squawked and thrashed their wings, trying to scatter, while the boar hog whirled to face me. The animal didn't bother to drop what was in its mouth while sniffing the gloom for my scent—something long and thin, but rounded at one end. A piece of dead raccoon, possibly, or a bloated fish. I couldn't be sure, and didn't much care as long as the animal didn't charge me.

"Olivia, don't be scared! My name's Hannah Smith and I want to talk! *Olivia . . . ?*" I took a few steps closer, straining to see. Was it my

281

imagination or had the curtains inside the cabin moved? Hopeful it was true, I tried again. "Olivia! Please come out!"

This time the boar hog reacted by snorting and lunging stiff-leggedly in my direction, warning me to stay away. But the threat only sharpened my mood. In reply, I made myself bigger by waving my arms and yelling, "Shoo! I'll fry you for breakfast! Scoot!" The pig backed away a step but was still glaring at me as its tusks cracked a bone inside the thing it was eating.

Now I was wondering whether I should get the pistol and shoot the boar or finish with my engine and approach the cruiser by water. But was it worth risking that shallow bay if Olivia wasn't aboard? Had I really seen those curtains move? I needed a solid reason to keep me from heading straight home once my boat was started.

Squall clouds moving toward the island were still purple-pink with sunlight, but it was darkening in this swamp of tangled trees and sulfur. Dark enough that details of the cruiser and everything around me were becoming grainy. I remembered the powerful little LED flashlight in my pocket and used it, pointing the laser-sharp beam at the cabin.

"OLIVIAAAAA!" I yelled, loud as I could. Which was more than the hog could tolerate and caused the thing to trot toward me, crushing tree limbs with its weight. In a rush, I swung the light at the animal. Held the LED in both hands like a pistol, aiming at the boar's eyes as it crashed through brush, closing the distance between us, coming faster, and growling . . . until its eyes strobed like flashbulbs when the light pierced them. Squealing, the hog flung what it was eating toward me, then spun away, taking the other hog with it into the bushes.

"That'll teach you!" I hollered after it. Then, only mildly interested, I checked to see what had been in the animal's mouth before I called for Olivia again. Several seconds later, though, I was only able to whisper, *"Dear God above . . ."*

What I saw was a human hand, fingers missing, attached to what remained of a forearm. Even from the distance of several yards, I couldn't deny what the hog had been eating. I felt eerily calm while, slowly, the flashlight revealed bloody details I didn't want to see, or remember. No . . . I was in shock, but didn't realize it. The same chilly calm stayed with me while I stood my ground and used the light to search the mangroves below until I had found the body.

Yes . . . a human body. Vultures had returned and were now competing with crabs for what had, until recently, been a person, judging from the freshness of what I saw. Man or woman, though, I couldn't be sure because a frenzy of wings and crawling shadows obstructed my view. If I descended the ridge, the vultures would scatter, but my feet wouldn't allow me to move. So I used the flashlight to probe. The victim was an adult, from the size . . . an adult who had sought safety by balling into a fetal position, then was left to die.

My eyes moved from the corpse to the Skipjack cruiser, to the corpse, then swept the area nearby. Hanging from a bush was a raspberry-colored garment that looked feminine enough to have been a woman's blouse. A length of denim cloth covered a portion of the dead person's thigh: *blue jeans*. Now my eyes moved from my own legs to the corpse to the cruiser as I put the details together.

Somewhere deep in my brain, a detached observer was amazed by my analytical behavior and also approved of the rage gathering inside me.

*"Olivia? Oh . . . Olivia!"* I whispered the girl's name, giving it different meanings, while the detached observer advised me, *You can't let that son of a bitch get away with this.*

"I won't," I promised the shadows. "I swear to God, he'll pay."

Slowly, slowly, then, I began backing away, which is when two things happened at once— something confusing, the other startling:

In the lifeless cruiser, a light blinked on, then the cabin door opened. Out stepped a tall, frail girl, mousy hair tangled, her expression, when she turned my direction, that of a child who feared punishment if caught looking at the sky.

Maybe Olivia saw me, maybe not. I couldn't be sure because at the same instant, from the other side of the ridge, I heard a man's voice calling. A voice with a sarcastic edge, ordering, "Hey, you! Hannah Smith! Get your ass down here . . . darling!"

Olivia heard the man, too, and fled instantly to the cabin. A girl so scared would be no help, and I couldn't rescue her by hiding in the mangroves. I took a last look at the corpse, thinking, *It's the private investigator,* then had to decide whether to escape to the cruiser, or return to my skiff and get the gun.

My body didn't want to do it, but I finally turned in the direction I knew I had to go, my conscience urging, *Protection is promised to those who behave boldly.*

# Twenty-one

I had heard Ricky Meeks's voice only once, but it had a taunting slickness I would never forget. It was him waiting for me, which I'd known before I topped the shell ridge. Ricky still wore the gray dress shirt, the tight slacks, and he was grinning because he'd surprised me, arriving in the cruiser's dinghy, which he paddled quietly as a canoe.

Rather than hike through swamp after hearing me bang aground, he'd apparently decided to observe from a distance . . . or was showing off, feeding his ego by humiliating me once again.

*Trying to,* I reminded myself.

"My God, it's a cowgirl!" Meeks hollered with a Texas twang, close enough to my skiff now to fold the oars and drift. "From the look of it, you're better suited to rank horses than fine boats. Need some help?"

The ridiculous spit curl dangled between his eyes, which he brushed back in a showy fashion that suggested practice in front of a mirror. Same with the way he yawned and stretched, flexing his big hands as if tired by rowing, and then said in a scolding way, "I warned you, you wouldn't listen. I'm surprised you made it this far without Injuns scalping you."

Meeks expected me to respond. I didn't. So his tone took a sharper edge, taunting, "Didn't your mamma teach you a boat's no place for a woman? Particularly a cowgirl that dresses like Belle Starr—and who don't know the difference between bottom and deep water." The man gave it a beat before adding the punch line: "Unless the girl's on her back, of course."

Ricky was in a game-playing mood now that he had me alone. Having too much fun with my grounded skiff and Barbara Stanwyck clothes to comment on the bayonet needles I was clipping off with my pliers and storing point down in the scabbard. He had been watching me for a while, I realized, which gave me a dirty sort of chill. Meeks had seen me leave *Sybarite*, no doubt about it now. Or someone had told him. The man had beaten me to Drake Keys with just enough spare time to ditch his blazer and probably warn Olivia to keep her mouth shut. Now here he was. But why the interest in me? And why return to a cruiser that was anchored within throwing distance of a dead body?

One guess was that Meeks planned to blame someone else for the murder and wanted me to witness how surprised he was when he saw the body. It was not the behavior of a sane man, which made it even more likely. Eugene Schneider came to mind as the one to accuse.

But no . . . Ricky was the killer—a killer who realized he wasn't done yet. It was in his voice when, fussing with his hair again, he asked, "What you find up there, partner? Anything real *interesting?* Might as well tell the truth 'cause I'll find out one way or the other." To convince me, he picked up a chunk of axe handle and whapped the palm of his hand a couple of times.

As I slipped the fisherman's tool into its scabbard, I was gauging the distance to my skiff, still deciding the best way to get my hands on that shiny customized silver pistol. Ricky had only a few yards to cover if he tried to intercept me, but he was still in the dinghy, and I had the advantage of running downhill.

"Don't you go try anything stupid," Meeks warned, some animal sense in him smelling trouble . . . or aware I was picking up speed while descending the ridge. Then when I began to sprint, he yelled, "Stupid slut!" and it was a race to see if he could bail from the dinghy and slog through water before I made it to my skiff.

This time I won. But just barely, skidding to a stop on the starboard side of the boat while Ricky charged from the port side, moving catlike for a man his size. For some reason, though, arriving too late didn't seem to worry him.

When I saw what he had done, I understood. My lockers were open, gear was scattered, and there were muddy footprints everywhere. Calling my name from the dinghy, pretending he'd just arrived, was Ricky's idea of being clever. Or he'd wanted time to search for something before I returned.

"My Lord, who could have made such a mess? Poor little cowgirl. Are we having ourselves a bad day?" The man tapped the axe handle against my boat to remind me who was in charge. Then the threat took added meaning when he patted the sleeping bag he'd found in a locker, pointed toward the island, and said, "There's a shady little spot of sand over there. Why don't you and me corral ourselves a little nap first? I brought us some bug juice."

I was thinking about my bawdy aunt, Hannah Three, how she'd handle herself in such a spot. Her on one side of a skiff, knee-deep in water, a man threatening to rape her on the other. Aunt Hannah would want to slow things down, get the upper hand, while her eyes searched the plundered deck for the pistol that was no longer on the passenger seat where I'd left it. What had Meeks done with the thing?

"That's something to think about," I replied without much emotion. "Right now, the only pisser hole I'm interested in is on my engine. I fried my water pump, and need to drop the lower unit—but I didn't expect this." I was leaning into the boat, moving items he had scattered as if looking for tools. My VHF radio was missing, too—along with the keys to my boat, but I had a spare ignition key.

"*Pisser* hole," Meeks said, making it sound like a dirty word. He used one hand to hitch up his pants, the axe handle in the other. "That's the least of your worries, girl, with a bad impeller. You don't know jack shit about motors either! What you need is a marina if you're sure it's fried." His tone told me he hoped it was true.

I didn't stop what I was doing. "If you're such an expert, maybe you could start by finding my ratchet set in all this mess you made."

Ricky smiled. He *liked* saucy women. "You got more fire than the last time I saw you—about shit your panties when I came through that door. But you don't seem to understand you're in a predicament, sugar. *My* pisser hole was first in line, so unbutton your shirt while you march your ass to that beach. Hear?"

The man's stupid jokes and strutting manner reminded me of the boar hog. He'd trashed my boat, I didn't see the book containing the gun, which all made me too furious to speak. When I didn't instantly respond, Meeks shouted, "Get your damn clothes off now!" and clubbed the gunnel of my skiff so hard it chipped the Gel Coat.

"Stop that!" I hollered.

After flicking his hair back, Meeks did it again. *WHAP!*

The book . . . where was the fake book I'd left on the seat? While my eyes darted back and forth, Meeks began circling the boat, which floated the transom toward me. That's when I saw it, the title *Negotiators* gleaming from beneath a life jacket. The book was within reach, but had Meeks tricked me again? Had he opened the cover, saw what was inside, and taken the gun?

"Ricky," I said, leaning to move the life jacket, "I worked hard to pay for this skiff. If you want to have some private fun, something rough and naughty, we can discuss it. But put one more scratch on my skiff, all you're going to get from me is lies and disappointment."

Meeks leaned his hand on the bow. *"What* did

you say? Rough and naughty, huh?" The man grinned.

In any other situation, I would have called the change that came over Ricky amusing. Not looking up, I said, "You heard me. I'm not in the habit of repeating myself."

He laughed, hesitated, then said, "You're lying," and started toward me again. "How dumb you think I am?"

Now I had the book in my hands, knowing from the weight that the pistol was inside. "Not dumb enough to force a girl who's willing," I said into the man's black eyes. Then, with a smile that Hannah Three might have offered, I placed the book on the gunnel and began unbuttoning my Navaho shirt, hoping Ricky would stop to watch.

He did. Stood facing me, half a boat length away, and said, "Bullshit!" before his ego reminded him that he was irresistible. "On the other hand . . ." He paused to give it some thought. "Hey—I get it! You read all the sweet things Olive Oyl wrote about me in her diary—good sex scenes, I'll bet. Real . . . *naughty,* like you say. That's what made you decide you need a dose of Big Rick, huh?"

No . . . it wasn't the grinning man's ego talking, it was his sly brain setting a trap. Someone had told him I'd found Olivia's missing pages— entries that could prove she had been raped and robbed. *That's* why he'd searched my boat. Probably why he'd driven all the way to Fishermans Wharf. Only two suspects flashed into my mind—Martha Calder-Shaun one of them—but I wasn't going to admit anything by asking for names. Instead, I undid another button, touching my free hand to the book for balance, and played the role of a silly girl. "You keep talking about other women, I might tend to my water pump first. Who's Olive Oyl?"

Ricky Meeks had two grins. The one he'd practiced in the mirror and another that revealed who he really was. It was a vicious, pit bull leer that turned him into the painting I'd seen, a faceless head with horns. He spooked me with that grin now, taking another easy step, as he said, "You lying slut, you know exactly the girl I mean. Olivia's so goddamn bony, she's bruised me *almost* as bad as the bruises I put on her."

It was a brag, not a slip of the tongue, and Ricky was disappointed that, instead of cringing, I picked up the book as if bored.

"What the hell you going to do with that?" he demanded, pointing the axe handle. "Plan to read me a bedtime story after I take some skin off your back?" Then, staring at my blouse, smiled, "Not bad, sugar . . . not bad at all."

I had undone a third button, enough for him to see me spilling out of Mrs. Whitney's 34D Chantelle bra, which held his bug-eyed attention while I opened the book and swung the pistol clear.

"No, Ricky," I said, pointing the gun at him, "what I plan to do is shoot you in the chest—if you don't drop that club and start walking backward. *Now.*" My uncle's customized Devel was a double-action pistol, so I didn't have to thumb the hammer back. But I did, making a *click-click* sound that replaced Ricky's leer with a dazed, dumb look.

My favorite part in Hannah Three's journals is where she describes getting her abusive husband so drunk that he wakes up naked, a baited fishing line knotted around his male privates, while hundred-pound tarpon school beneath her boat.

I had memorized what Aunt Hannah said to her soon-to-be-ex: *I don't have a damn bit of use for that thing anymore, so it's up to you. Do you want to discuss a divorce? Or you want to fish?*

The look on Ricky's face had to be similar, but he only gave me a moment to enjoy it before recovering from his shock. "Go ahead, Annie Oakley," he said, squaring himself. "The bull dykes in prison are gonna love you." His knuckles were white on the axe handle, I noticed. He was breaking a shoe free of the muck, ready to move.

"Drop that club, start walking backward," I replied, buttoning my shirt. "I won't tell you again." The calm in my voice gave me strength, but inside my head doubts were forming. I'd never fired this pistol, did it still work? How many years had the cartridges been stacked in the aging magazine? Misfire once, a man like Meeks would crush my head open and leave me for the feral pigs.

"Why, sugar, 'pears to me your hands are shaking. A woman acts tough, what she's really doing is begging a man to take charge. Doesn't mean I'll have to slap you around too much—not if you hand ol' Ricky that gun right now and be sweet."

The oily tone, his vulgar grin, were infuriating. They suggested a growing confidence that threatened to drain mine. *He can smell weakness,* Mrs. Whitney had warned. *It's like an animal thing.* Soon, within seconds, Meeks would charge or hurl the axe handle to distract me. His swaggering contempt, the memory of his hands on my breasts when he'd shoved me, only made me madder. The temptation was to step back and create space. Instead, I broke a foot free of the bottom, took a long step forward, and made it obvious I had selected a new target.

"I won't miss at this range," I said, settling into combat stance. "You've got five seconds! *One . . .*"

Involuntarily, Ricky's free hand rushed to cover his genitals. Then his bully's ego made him pull it away, while also changing his grip on the club. "You're flat crazy, you know that? Let's talk about this. Wait . . . stop counting!"

*"Two,"* I said.

Which caused Ricky to shout, *"You don't have the balls, you ugly cow!"* but he also took a step backward, the club still in his hand.

Or had he?

It didn't matter. Ricky had chosen the wrong thing to say to a person who had comforted a sobbing Mrs. Whitney, and who remembered her words about victims and forgiveness.

*"Five,"* I said, changing my target because I'd skipped a few numbers. Then I squeezed the trigger, both eyes focused and wide, just as my Uncle Jake had taught me to shoot.

# Twenty-two

When I fired, the gunshot was so thunderous, I wondered if the special pistol was loaded with custom ammunition as well. There was a nice, smooth recoil while the bullet chopped the legs from beneath Ricky Meeks and caused panic in the mangroves. Vultures, done feeding, battered the tree canopy with wings and caustic shrieks, finally exiting in a smoky spiral that reminded me of the flying monkeys in *The Wizard of Oz*, or giant Asian bats I'd watched with Loretta on the Discovery Channel.

Even louder than the vultures, Ricky screamed, "You crazy bitch, you shot me!"

*Yes I did.* One round, but was still willing to pull the trigger if necessary. The man knew it and wouldn't bother me again—or so I believed.

"Jesus Christ Aw'mighty—I'm bleeding! Look what you done to me!" Ricky held up a bloody palm to prove it, his hand black, not red, in the swampy twilight.

*Yes, bleeding, too.* Not as badly as he might have been, though. Meeks had been correct when he'd said my hands were shaking. Not much, but enough to let the barrel jump when I squeezed the trigger. I'd been aiming at the meaty part of Ricky's thigh, not his groin, while my eyes had allowed my target to blur by concentrating on the sights, just as I had learned. But I'd shot high, and the slug had either taken the tip off his pelvis or a chunk of love handle Ricky had allowed to settle on his waist. No way to be certain, even though he'd ripped off his shirt in a panic after crabbing his way to the shell beach, then used his fingers to explore the damage. The whole while, calling me profanities and threatening acts so vile they could have hatched only in a brain that was diseased or naturally just as foul.

"Instead of cussing me, you stupid fool, tell me where you hid my radio so I can call the emergency medics." I said it to interrupt his tirade, but somehow it came out sounding flustered, too eager to please. Later, of course, I would come up with a dozen replies more biting and clever. Wave the pistol at him and say, *You don't understand the predicament you're in, sugar* . . . No—tell him, *I don't know when I've seen an uglier man, but even a cow wouldn't leave you to bleed to death* . . .

Not that Meeks was gushing blood, but he was bleeding steadily. From a safe distance, I had already tossed him the first-aid kit, which he was using—sterile pads and tape—so there was nothing else to do but offer to summon help. I was eager to explain my side of the story to authorities—*The man threatened my life, he'd left me no choice, so I shot him*—something I didn't want to ever happen again.

*No, I didn't.* That sensation of actually pulling the trigger, then my ears ringing from the thunderbolt, had shocked me numb at first, but now I was feeling better about what I had done. Good enough to want to rush to find Olivia, pack her things, and get going. One look at Ricky's reaction, though, when I mentioned my radio, and I knew he'd rather patch his own bullet wound than risk attracting police. He was more worried about the body they would find than surviving a night in the mangroves, and maybe becoming a corpse himself.

There was no doubt in my mind as I watched Meeks struggle to his feet and limp toward his dinghy. I couldn't allow that, of course, so I confiscated his oars, placing them on my skiff.

While I did it, there was a glow of hatred in the man's eyes that threatened me every step of the way. And the insults he yelled about my looks, my face and body, were so mean that even my anger couldn't shield some words from their mark. Finally, I used the pistol to motion him back to the beach, hoping it would stop his poison.

Meeks's leer returned for the first time since I'd pulled the trigger. "It'll be dark soon," he told me, meaning it as a threat. "Come morning, you'll be slap-ass crazy with bugs and snakes, scared shitless. Couple big gators on this island, too. *That's* when I'll put you out of your misery." He turned his back to me then, and headed for the slab of beach, not the shell ridge, walking hunched to one side, the gauze he'd taped over his wound a dark square beneath what remained of the gray shirt.

Meeks didn't stop at the beach, which worried me at first, but then didn't. He might be pretending to be hurt worse than he was, but there was nothing pretend about the blood soaking his slacks. Even so, he kept walking, slogging along the edge of the island toward the cut where I'd nearly run aground. I knew he was either headed for his missing jon boat, or taking the long but easier route back to the cruiser where Olivia, I suspected, was worried sick about the gunshot she'd heard.

Something else I couldn't allow was the man

298

to get to the girl or his fast boat. In the western sky, the last citrus streaks of twilight were fading; stars had appeared in the east. Meeks was twenty-five yards away, moving slow but steady, when I raised the pistol and squared the notch sight between his shoulders.

"Ricky, stop right there! You called my bluff once! Want to try it again?"

In reply, I heard more foul names, then a challenge to shoot him in the back, his words fuming with contempt.

"This is the last time I'm saying it—stop!"

From over the man's shoulder: "Ugly stork! Go join a freak show!"

I yelled, *"Ricky Meeks!"* dropping my index finger from aside the barrel to the custom hair trigger.

His answer: "Why don't you move to Key West with the other carpet munchers!"

Once so balanced and light in my hands, the precision Devel pistol—pronounced *Devil* by my friend Nathan—was becoming barrel-heavy and refused to track straight. I couldn't shoot the man in the back. Just *couldn't*. But I had to do something. My Uncle Jake had told me warning shots were only for Hollywood actors or cops willing to risk their own funeral, but that's what I was considering now. Skip a round in front of the man. Then say something clever for a change.

*You won't hear the next one!* Or: *Your*

*pecker wasn't much of a target, but . . . but . . .*

My clever tongue had been blunted by events, so nothing good would form in my mind. I lowered the pistol to reset my feet, then sighted a few paces ahead of Meeks. Thirty yards, though, was a long shot with a pistol. If I attempted a near miss, there was a fair chance I would hit him accidentally. How would I explain that to a jury? Or when I did miss, Ricky would think I'd done it on purpose, which was further proof I'd lost my courage.

*Wrong*—I hadn't lost my courage. Some shaky moments, sure, but I no longer doubted myself. All I doubted was how long my good luck would hold. That, and my engine's cooling system.

*Licensed investigators obey the law,* I reminded myself. *Panic, and he wins.*

I lowered the pistol, engaged the safety, then returned to my skiff in a hurry. My eyes and ears never leaving Meeks for long, I used bayonet needles to clear the exhaust tubes but didn't risk a quick test of my engine. I didn't want him to hear what I'd done. Meeks still hadn't reached the bay's entrance, barely visible in the fresh darkness, but soon would. Leaving a potential witness alone—me—meant he was convinced I'd ruined my water pump, and that he didn't know about the spare ignition key hidden in my tackle box. Something else his behavior suggested: Meeks still intended to kill me—after killing

Olivia most likely. I wasn't the only one who knew about the body that lay in the mangroves.

I grabbed a second flashlight from my skiff, then jogged up the shell ridge to find Olivia. Ricky Meeks and I were racing again.

# Twenty-three

What I needed for Jake's customized pistol was a holster, I decided. A book case was a waste on such a fine weapon, and I wouldn't have to wedge the thing into my jeans to free my hands like I was doing now.

It was because of the rough country I was in: a tangle of mangroves, the cruiser visible through a cavern of mosquitoes and black leaves. The boat was only yards away, but getting to it required gymnastics. The use of tree limbs, grabbing one, then another, to monkey myself over roots to the water was the only way unless I had brought a machete.

So that's what I did, after securing the pistol between the small of my back and my belt. Got both hands around a limb, swung my feet over a hooped blockade of mangrove roots, then repeated the process several times. By the time I got to the water's edge, my shirt was soaked from the sulfuric heat that settles into a swamp at night. My jeans were torn, my shoes were ruined, and mosquitoes tickled my face, my hands, the canals of my ears, despite the spray I'd used.

No wonder Meeks had chosen the easier route. But there was no chance he had beaten me here. Even if he had *sprinted* around the island's edge —impossible for any man, healthy or wounded— I still had a big chunk of time to use safely. Twenty minutes . . . half an hour. Plenty. Question was, would Olivia come with me?

A light was on in the cabin, but weak as a candle behind drawn curtains. The air conditioner was running, too, the generator a mild hum compared to the screaming hush of mangroves. Cicadas, frogs, growling cormorants . . . the baritone *Oomph-Oomph* of an alligator, too—or a crocodile. Could be. There were saltwater crocs in the Ten Thousand Islands, although the only croc I'd ever seen was on Sanibel.

Just thinking the name *Sanibel* made me want to be gone from this dark place where, only a light beam away if I'd chosen to look, was a fetal mound of bones and human flesh—if any flesh remained.

No . . . I hadn't looked and wouldn't. So far, I had used the flashlight sparingly. Didn't want to risk being seen.

*Private investigators behave professionally. Panic, and Ricky wins.*

I kept reminding myself of that. Stay strong, be bold—the combination had worked so far, and I wasn't stopping now that I was almost close enough to touch the cruiser's hull.

I grabbed another limb, swung my legs, then lowered myself until I was standing in water that flooded my jeans to the waist. The bottom was shell here, at least, not muck. After three strides, I was out of the water again and leaning my weight against the bow of the boat. I'd made it! Now all I had to do was convince Olivia to trust me.

Meeks had nosed the cruiser into the mangroves, then used heavy lines to secure it. Before I could scale the railing, though, I needed to create room by pushing the hull back from the awning of tree limbs. As I did it, someone inside noticed the movement. I could feel the thump of footsteps through the fiberglass. Soon, I heard the cabin door open and a voice call, "Is that you? I was worried . . . *sugar*."

I felt a sick feeling in my stomach. Not because I associated the word with Ricky, but because it was Olivia Seasons speaking. Her voice had the parroting eagerness of a girl who was desperate to please after being beaten into submission.

"Down here, Olivia!" I responded, not loud but in a way I hoped sounded harmless, friendly. "Don't be afraid. I'm coming aboard, okay?"

After a shocked silence, I heard: "Who are you—don't come near me!"

"Please listen! Just give me a chance. I've got a boat on the other side of the island. It's safe now,

I can take you home." Fearing she would slam the cabin door and lock it, I spoke fast while positioning myself under the bowsprit. "Olivia, I'm coming aboard. Don't be scared."

With fingers wrapped around the railing, I used my legs to spring high enough to get a foot hooked over the bowsprit. I hung there for several seconds, wrestling with the anchor windlass and a rotted tree limb that finally splashed into the water below. Then I scooted across mooring chocks so fast that my bottom plopped into a doughnut of anchor line as if it were a bucket. As I sat there resting, I heard the hush of bare feet moving along the safety rail, so I looked up. It was Olivia: long skinny legs in a white robe, facial features indistinguishable in the darkness, her hands squeezing the robe tight around her neck, a girl too scared to come any closer.

Mentioning Lawrence Seasons, I had already decided, might cause trouble, so I got to my feet, telling her, "My name's Hannah Smith. If you want out of here, I'll help—and he won't bother you again."

Olivia was shaking her head. "I can't talk to you! To *anyone*—not unless he says it's okay. So you have to leave. Leave right now!" She was speaking for Ricky's benefit, I realized, in case he was with me or hiding somewhere nearby. No other reason for her to talk so loud.

So I shocked her by replying, "I shot him. I

shot Ricky Meeks, and that's how I know he won't stop us."

*"What?"*

I said it again, adding, "That was the gunshot you heard."

"You *can't* be telling the truth."

My hands were checking my pockets to confirm I hadn't lost the flashlights while climbing over the railing . . . then patted the small of my back where the pistol should have been. *Damn!* The pistol was gone.

"Is it true?" Olivia whispered. "Someone our age—a *woman* couldn't do that. Is he really dead?"

My heart was pounding. I felt a first tremor that signaled my body was starting to shake. My hands were checking and rechecking my jeans, refusing to accept the fact I had lost the pistol. Then, trying not to be obvious, I checked the deck near my feet, then stepped over the anchor line to check the bowsprit. The pistol wasn't there. I took a deep breath to control myself before turning. If the girl sensed what I was feeling, she would never trust me enough to leave.

"I hit him below the ribs," I told her. "He's wounded, bleeding bad, but we have to hurry. Get your things! You need to wear pants. Boots and a heavy shirt if you have them." My mind was working on the safest way to proceed now that I'd lost the gun.

"We've got five, maybe ten minutes," I added,

which was half the time I believed we had, but I wanted to get the girl moving.

"You're not a policeman—you're lying."

"You heard the shot. He's hurt too bad to cut through the island, but he's still hobbling. That's why we've got to leave now." I reached for Olivia's shoulder, but she backed a step.

"You've got to be sure! He'll kill you . . . maybe kill me, too! This morning, he"—the girl looked at the wall of mangroves behind me where the corpse lay—"Today, he did something . . . really awful. Is that why you're here?"

Some distant part of my brain was aware that Olivia had yet to say Ricky's name—as if no other man in the world existed. In a way, that was more troubling than her reluctance.

"If I wasn't sure I shot the man," I told her, "I'd be headed home alone, not helping you. Can I come in the cabin? Mosquitoes are eating me alive."

The best hope I could come up with was use the cruiser's VHF to call an emergency Mayday, then run for my skiff. A vessel this size would have a powerful radio—why Olivia hadn't used it already to call for help, I didn't *want* to understand. Not now, I didn't. Then I would spend a little time, not much, searching beneath the bowsprit for the pistol. I'd heard a couple of limbs hit the water, but maybe I'd actually heard the pistol fall.

A minute later, we were in the cabin, which was a sewer of odors and pornographic photos tacked everywhere. Even in the galley, which consisted of a propane stove and a small fridge, there were pictures so graphic, they belonged in a textbook, not a space designed for eating. It didn't matter. I was finally alone with a woman whose face, whose thoughts and fears, I had been living with for what seemed like weeks, not days.

Olivia's appearance, though, bore little resemblance to recent photos I had seen. Ricky had done more than just bruise the girl's busted lips, her jaundiced left eye. The skin on her parchment arms was poxed with bruises from the man's fingers. The intelligent brown eyes I remembered from her childhood photos had the glaze of an elderly woman who, exhausted from suffering, had already abandoned her body. No wonder she had hung a towel over the only mirror in the cabin. My guess was, she had done the same in the sleeping quarters, which appeared as a black opening forward of the bulkhead.

I expected these symptoms and signs of abuse but not the sudden emotion that rolled through me. What I was feeling only got worse when, after I'd rushed to the boat's VHF, Olivia told me, "Don't bother. He disables it somehow when he leaves. I checked the wiring, the fuses. Once he was gone three days, I still couldn't get it working. Same with the engine, after he thought I'd found a key. The air-conditioning, too—usually."

I nodded, struggling to control myself, thinking, *The antenna.* Meeks had probably disconnected the VHF coupling at the flybridge—not many would think of that.

"You don't want to be here," I said without turning. "If he's hurt you, you should leave."

There was a shrug in the girl's voice. "It's too late for me. And why should you care, anyway?"

"Not yet, it isn't," I started to say, but Olivia interrupted by telling me something else I didn't expect.

"I married him. Last week . . . ten days ago. Everything's a blur. I know he only did it for money—money I don't even have yet. If he caught us and doesn't kill me, that's the only reason. But I said yes, so I've got no one to blame but myself."

I shook my head to refute Olivia's words while thinking, *No wonder she won't sign the papers,* then of the postmistress in Caxambas. "Ricky would've had to apply for the license more than a month ago," I argued, remembering Florida law and all the paperwork I'd done because Delbert Fowler was not a man for details. "I don't believe it was legal, Olivia. Besides, no court would hold you to such a marriage."

"But I said yes—and you don't know him! He'll never stop looking until he gets his husband's share. I'm talking about more money than you'd

308

believe—*that's* what you don't understand. Or what he'll do if I run. He's never wrong when it comes to promises like that. If anything, he'll hurt me worse."

I glanced at the girl's face, then looked away. Her misshapen lips, the swollen eye, gave me a choking sensation, and I had to clear my throat while she said, "I do such stupid things sometimes. I bring it on myself. So he has no choice—from his point of view, I mean. Only a . . . an insane woman would beg to go with a man and then whine. That's something I've heard every day since—"

I couldn't listen to any more. "Stop that right now! I know more about you than you think, Olivia Seasons. You're not crazy. And that's not a fair way to speak of yourself . . . or let yourself be treated . . ." My voice faltered, then I lost the words, even after clearing my throat again.

Olivia was sitting at the galley settee, where a notebook lay open next to a pocket Bible, the sketch of what might have been an osprey recently started. I heard the girl stand, then felt a hand on my shoulder. "Are you crying?"

"I am not!" I snapped. Then as an excuse to clear my eyes, I scratched my forehead and pulled my hair back. "You made me mad, being so stubborn. That's all."

Olivia was trying to put it together but too scared to think clearly. "Did he hurt you, too?

*That's* why you shot him. I still can't believe you did it. How did you find the nerve?"

"For one thing, he knocked a chunk of Gel Coat off my new skiff," I replied. "That's reason enough. I just wish I was a better shot."

I felt a tug at my shoulder, trying to get me to turn. "Did he hurt you? You can tell me the truth. He hurts women—brags about it. Someone like him has had a lot of girlfriends. I won't be jealous if you tell me the truth."

*Jealous?* Her suspicion was so misguided it proved Meeks had branded yet another scar on Olivia's brain. I had been near tears, feeling so sorry for the girl and fearful for both of us, that it was exactly the jolt I needed to get my mind back on what had to be done.

I spun around and took the girl gently by the arms, just as my Uncle Jake had done to me sometimes when I was confused. "Get your clothes changed. If you've got any mosquito spray, soak yourself. I'm going to fix the radio, but we're not waiting on the Coast Guard. Then I want you to help me do something."

I meant hold a flashlight while I searched for the pistol. Instead of questioning me, though, Olivia said in an odd way, "You're . . . you're the one my family sent. I just realized—*Hannah,* right? He was talking about you."

Meaning Ricky, of course. I had already told Olivia my name, but a change in her expression hinted that she might be awakening from this nightmare. Still in a daze, though, which I knew when she started to ramble.

"Yesterday, he went crazy. Drinking before sunrise, then the security guard left a message about you searching my studio. That you found something in the trash, so he had to drive all the way to Naples to check. Now you're actually here—it's hard to believe."

It was a relief to know the guard was responsible for blabbing about the diary pages, not Martha Calder-Shaun, but I realized that talking was Olivia's way of not making a decision. Even so, I ignored the urge to shake some sense into her. That gentleness paid off when she finally returned to the subject of Meeks, saying, "He and the security guard, they like cigars—that's how they met. Plus . . . he probably paid the guy to watch the house. With *my* money."

In my most reasonable voice I said, "Olivia, *listen*. Don't you see he's feeding on you? Pretty soon, there won't be enough left of yourself to fight back—that's why we have to go now."

The girl wanted to leave, no doubt about that. I watched her eyes move around the cabin, the prison that had become her world, then spoke to the ceiling as if arguing with herself. "This morning when he got back from my studio, he swore he'd kill you. Shoot you in the head. Something cruel like that. But it didn't happen.

311

He's never made a threat that didn't happen. That's what's so hard to believe."

I said, "He has a gun?" There wasn't one in Meeks's dinghy, I'd checked.

Olivia ignored me by continuing, "Instead, you shot *him*. For the first time since I met that . . . that pig, he was wrong. I guess it should prove not everything he says comes true. And I did hear the gunshot." The girl faced me. "Sorry I'm having trouble, it's just that he takes up so much *space* in my head, thinking isn't easy. Or to convince myself that someone like you could shoot a man who's so . . . vicious"—a tentative smile appeared, eyes on my Navaho shirt—"even though you're dressed for the part. Does any of this make sense?"

Maybe—but not in the Barbara Stanwyck way she meant, although I hoped I was wrong.

"Olivia," I said, taking her by the arms again. "Does Ricky keep a gun in his jon boat—a little aluminum boat with a motor. Usually green."

"A shotgun, of course," she said as if everyone did. "That's what he used on the man this morning. The one who came asking questions. But *he* said you already knew that he'd killed—"

In a rush, I asked, "Where's the jon boat? The man he shot had to come by boat, too. Where did he hide them?"

I was frightening the girl, but it couldn't be helped. Then it was me who was scared when Olivia explained there was a fisherman who had

312

a camp just across the cut on the next island, about half a mile away. In exchange for borrowing the fisherman's truck, when needed, Ricky left his boat there sometimes because it was faster than a net boat.

"Eugene Schneider," I said.

Olivia nodded, then looked at her feet in a shamed way that told me the jon boat wasn't the only thing Eugene used sometimes. "I don't know his last name. He stays here and watches me when my . . . when the owner's away. This morning, before I heard the gunshots, the man you mentioned, he didn't have his own boat. He paid Eugene to bring him out to find . . ."

"Ricky," I prompted. "No reason to be afraid to say his name."

"Yes. He brought Ricky back from the mainland a little while ago. Then left, saying he'd come back later because we're leaving for Key Largo tonight. And both of them wanted to have some fun with . . . with . . ."

"With me," I said. The two planned to rape me before dumping another body in the mangroves, that was plain.

Now it was Olivia who couldn't make eye contact. "That's where the shotgun would be. In the boat with Eugene." She paused, still embarrassed. "Hannah, I am . . . I'm so sorry this is happening to you. It's my fault. All because of . . ."

The girl's body shuddered, so I held her for a

313

moment before saying, "We can stand here and cry, or we can prove we're not fools. Personally, I'm tired of apologizing for things I can't change." The pocket Bible had caught my eye, so I pointed to it, adding, "Don't let being scared make the decision for you. The Ninety-first Psalm is a good one for that."

"You read the Bible?" she asked, the question important to her.

Not very often, but I attended church, which, under the circumstances, made it okay for me to reply, *"Yes I do."* Then I left her to deal with it while I hurried to the cruiser's starboard wall, slid open a window, and put an ear to the screen to listen. I heard insects . . . waves slapping the hull . . . but no whine of a distant outboard motor coming our way.

Or was there?

# Twenty-four

I was searching the cabin, looking for some kind of weapon, when Olivia appeared from the forward sleeping berth and told me, "They're coming! I saw a spotlight. Ricky and the other guy need a light to find markers at low tide. We've only been here three days, so it could be both of them."

The wind had kicked up, so I had yet to hear a motor, but I didn't doubt the woman's words. The church-minded heiress had not only changed clothes—jeans, running shoes, a plaid shirt—but her attitude had changed as well. She was still scared, so was I, but she'd gotten control of herself, and I was gaining confidence in Olivia's unexpected steadiness. Maybe it was the voice of a Key West Coast Guard radioman who had just told us, "We're scrambling a helicopter out of Saint Pete, plus local police, but my lieutenant advises that you leave the vessel immediately! Do you copy?"

*Yes*. Since I had reattached the antenna coupling, the boat's VHF radio received and transmitted just fine. A helicopter and police boats that might arrive in an hour, though, didn't solve our problem, as Olivia was aware. So I suspected the Bible verse I'd recommended had also played a role in her decision to leave Ricky Meeks behind.

Olivia was stowing the Bible in her pocket now as she exited the berth and asked, "Any luck?"

I shook my head, *Nope*. I had taken a quick look at the engine hoping to discover how Meeks had disabled the ignition system. Get the cruiser running and we could ram the little aluminum boat as it approached, shotgun blazing away or not. No luck, though, which is why I'd searched for weapons while waiting for Olivia to change.

315

And why my eyes had come to rest on the propane stove.

"Hannah, what are you staring at? They're *coming*."

I didn't respond. Through the open window, I still couldn't hear the sound of an outboard motor, so I remained focused on the stove and the propane cylinder beneath it. I was looking from the stove to a pair of miniature oil lamps, then back to the stove when Olivia broke into my thoughts, saying, "I know *exactly* how to do it. I've gone over it in my head too many times to count."

"Do what?" I asked, more puzzled by her tone than what she said. Confession mixed with conspiracy, but with a razor's edge. Like that.

"At first, commit suicide," Olivia replied, not blinking as she looked into my eyes. "Kill Ricky and myself. Because I never had a way to escape—until tonight. Or a reason . . . not after what he's done." Her strength wavered. "And after the things I let him do, maybe I should've gone through with it."

"That's a question you should take to church," I said, too impatient to debate. "Right now, I'm wondering if he'd smell the gas. And what if he's not smoking a cigar? Wait—I should've checked. Does this stove use a pilot light?" I hurried to peer beneath the burners, but then tilted my head to listen. Had I heard a motor? I went to the starboard window to check. Yes, a boat was coming, but still a long way off. I slammed the window closed, then hurried to the stove.

"Get going, I'll follow," I said, motioning to the door. "Be careful you don't twist an ankle or something when you drop off the railing. I'll close up the cabin."

I had no way to light a candle remotely or an oil lamp, but there was a chance that Ricky would be smoking when he came aboard—or Eugene if he had come to join in the fun. Open the stove's valves before we left, close the door behind us, and the cabin would fill with combustible propane within minutes. That's why Lawrence Seasons had replaced the galley in his yacht—gas was dangerous in a cabin boat. But whether I could actually do it—lay a trap that might kill two men—depended on the argument still going on in my mind. Was such a thing legal? Was it *right?*

Whatever I decided, I didn't want Olivia Seasons to have a hand in it. She had more than enough guilt to deal with as it was. We had talked while she changed clothes, me explaining why I'd come here, then listening to her hints about Meeks's drug use and cruelty.

Olivia heard what I'd said, but her attention had turned inward, the subject of why she hadn't killed herself and Ricky still important enough to discuss. "The only thing that stopped me from doing it was I couldn't find anything in here"—

she tapped the book in her pocket—"that forgives suicide. Punishing him, though, both those men, I've got some of those passages highlighted to prove—"

"*Olivia,*" I said, raising my voice. "Get out of here *now*. We've only got a few minutes!" I wasn't exaggerating by much. Maybe five minutes, possibly less, judging from the distant buzz of a boat that was getting louder by the second.

"No," the woman replied as if speaking to herself, but then said it again with more confidence. "No! You're leaving first. I'm going to do it." She nodded at the propane tank, which I was checking to confirm the valve was open. "Figuring it out will take you too long. You're right: what if Ricky's not smoking when he comes in? I've gone over this in my mind a thousand times, Hannah. I know how to work it. Go find your gun!"

I had been kneeling by the stove. Now I stood. Olivia didn't sound calm, exactly, but there was a sureness in her attitude that I had to take seriously.

"The first thing he'll do if he thinks I'm gone is open that"—she pointed at the little fridge—"to see if I robbed him. That's where he hides valuables—that container I opened while you were on the radio? He bought it at some novelty shop. Thinks it's too clever for me to understand."

I had seen Olivia close the refrigerator door after retrieving a manila envelope, which was odd, but I was too busy with Key West Coast Guard to ask questions that could wait until later.

"I know it makes no sense to you, which is why I have to be the last one to leave this boat. Besides, I have the *right*—you don't." Once again, Olivia touched a hand to her back pocket.

It was true I didn't understand how a refrigerator door could trigger an explosion, but she didn't give me a chance to ask. Instead, she silenced me by pointing to the cabin's only mirror. "You know why I covered that with a towel? Because I can't bear to see what he's done. Haven't had the courage to look at myself since our so-called honeymoon—a cruise to Key West that was so . . . *disgusting,* I can't believe it was me." Eyes closed, she shook her head.

*Sybarite.* I had been right, but took no pleasure in it now.

As if it were accidental, I had moved between Olivia and the mirror, afraid she would pull the towel away. Her appearance was better now, wearing clothes that reminded me of certain birdwatchers I'd met. The tall ones who prefer tartan plaids and move with the gawky grace of wading birds. But Olivia might be upset by her face, and this was no time for emotions or arguing. I had just made a decision of my own.

"Neither one of us is going to booby-trap this

319

boat," I said in a tone that refused questioning. "If Ricky's going to burn in Hell, let someone else be the judge. We're getting out of here right now!" I put my hands on the girl's shoulders, gave a reassuring squeeze, then steered her toward the door.

Olivia balked for an instant but didn't argue, which was a relief. What I didn't notice, though, was that she left behind a little beach bag she'd packed with mosquito spray, her purse, the manila envelope, and her sketchbook. Of all those items, as she'd already told me, her drawings were most important.

Later, that detail would prove Olivia Seasons still knew her own mind. She had left the bag on purpose.

We went out onto the stern, where mosquitoes were waiting beneath a sky blacker for all the stars. To the east, heat lightning sparked over the Everglades; to the north, my eyes struggled until I had matched the whine of an outboard motor with a gray shape that was gliding toward us fast, now only two or three hundred yards away. Closer than I'd expected due to a southeast wind that was blowing the sound away from my ears.

"My Lord," I said, "we cut this too close. Get going!" I urged Olivia toward the front of the boat, now wondering if I should risk even a minute or two feeling around in the water for the pistol. That the gun had belonged to my Uncle Jake made it more of a loss but didn't compare with the sudden panic I felt. I was desperate for a shield. Anything that would keep two hard men at a distance, whether my engine started or not. The thought of Ricky's hands on me again, or Schneider's rough features, was too loathsome for my imagination to allow. Yes—a small amount of time was worth risking even though the chances of me finding the pistol were slim. Nothing hides a small object so well as a few feet of black water, especially when it's near a boat that is shifting on its lines like the cruiser was doing now.

"Do you see them?" Olivia had some speed in her legs and was already on the front of the boat, me right behind her. To get a better look, she stepped up onto the hatch that opened to the v-berth below, then said, "There they are!"

"Don't use your flashlight," I warned, crossing to the rail. "That engine's so loud, they won't hear us once we're in the water. But if they see a light, they'll know it's us and might—" I caught myself before making it worse. *Start shooting,* is what I'd intended to say. Instead, I told her, "You get over the rail first. Then me."

"Aren't you going to look for your gun?" Olivia asked the question without turning. She appeared inches taller than me because the hatch was elevated, a lean exclamation point against the mangrove darkness.

"Not until we're in the water," I said, irritated because I was waiting, one leg over the safety rail. "Which is where you should be right now."

"I'm *coming!* But someone should keep watch while you're looking." Then Olivia's voice dropped to a hoarse whisper, saying, "Shit, it's Eugene *and* him!" The familiar profanity seemed an endearment when she added, "Don't panic. There's a bar too shallow to cross, so they'll have to wind through the channel." She turned and made a shooing motion with her hand. "Go! I'll be right there—promise!"

It did pop into my mind that, later, I didn't want to have to explain to Lawrence Seasons why I'd allowed myself to be separated from his niece. On the other hand, we needed that pistol. Olivia had meant what she said, and I believed her. So I lowered myself down the railing, then used a branch to balance myself in the tangle of roots. The outboard seemed louder for some reason, now I was near the water. It pierced my ears like the whine of a dentist's drill, boring deeper into my head as the boat flew closer.

I pulled off my shoes, as I knew I must, and waded along the edge of the cruiser, searching the bottom with my feet. The bottom was hard shell and marl, the water warm to my waist. Off to my right, from the shadows, boomed the baritone *Woof* of the alligator or croc I'd heard earlier. It was close now, somewhere at the edge of the mangroves. The croc I'd seen on Sanibel was over twelve feet long, four hundred pounds, but there wasn't enough room in my head for more fear. So I ignored it. Funneled all my concentration into my toes and continued searching. I'd been at it for less than a minute when a spotlight torched the mangroves to my right and caused me to duck. That's when Olivia's face appeared over the railing and she called, "I forgot my bag! Keep looking, Hannah."

If I could have reached up and snatched the girl into the water, I would have. "No!"

"Or . . . I'll meet you on the ridge, if you think that's safer."

"Don't you dare!"

"But I have to!" Olivia was already turning. Then, over her shoulder, she had to say it again.

*"I promise!"*

# Twenty-five

Now the little boat was close enough that I could hear fragments of what the men were saying. Eugene complaining to Ricky, ". . . damn light out of my eyes! How you expect me . . ." And Ricky slurring, "Son of a . . . you *want* me to bleed to death . . . !"

Then Eugene, his voice turning toward me as

the boat turned, saying, ". . . shotgun off the deck, it'll rust . . . awww, no more beer!" And Ricky answering, ". . . drive the damn boat," before raising his voice to warn, "To the right, the right! Missed the last marker . . . !"

From where I stood, having just climbed onto the cruiser's bow—for the second time that night—I couldn't see if the jon boat made the turn in time. I'd been squatting over the forward hatch, trying to open its corroded hinges, but now paused to listen. Obviously, Ricky felt confident he had reached his destination, because, after several seconds he switched off the spotlight and roared, "OLIVE OYL! SUGAR DADDY'S HOME!" The man sounded staggering drunk from beer—or loss of blood—his oily confidence gone.

Eugene's mistake at the steering wheel, Ricky's mistake with the spotlight, I had no way of knowing, but one of them had misjudged the channel because an instant later I heard the boat bang aground. An aluminum hull skipping across oysters makes a chalkboard screech, but it isn't as loud as an outboard motor grinding through shells. By the time Eugene surrendered to the noise, killing the engine, the jon boat was somewhere off the stern of the Skipjack, which had just begun to respond to the smaller boat's wake.

I hurried from the hatch, reluctant to believe our good fortune until I had seen it for myself. When

I got a look, though, I knew what had happened was bad luck, not good. Eugene was inspecting the damage, standing in water not deep enough to cover the oysters they'd hit, while Ricky blistered the smaller man with insults and held the spotlight. The light told me the jon boat had missed a switchback so sharp, it would have taken the men several more minutes to wind their way to us. Instead, the aluminum hull had skated across a mudflat onto an oyster bar and had stopped only three or four boat lengths from deeper water and the Skipjack cruiser.

On a tide this low, even a wounded man could wade to the boat we were on. Thirty paces to the boarding platform that hung off the stern, then step over the transom. And they soon would, which Ricky confirmed by growling to Eugene, "Hurry up, get inside there, see if she's got a visitor." Then he called toward the cruiser, "Olive! I'm comin' aboard, honey . . . your sugar's hurt!"

I took a step back and pressed my face against a cabin window, trying to peek between the curtains. Then rapped my knuckles against the glass, demanding a response from Olivia, while my eyes monitored the men. Ricky was having balance problems, struggling to stand upright beside the jon boat. Eugene, a pump-action shotgun in his hands, was wading toward us—but then stopped to light a cigarette. Ricky wasn't smoking, I had already noticed.

I sniffed the air. Remnants of outboard fumes, even the sulfur-dense mangroves, were masked by the bug repellent I had coated myself with. No propane smell that I noticed, though, so what had Olivia been doing? It had been three or four minutes since she'd gone to retrieve her bag but had yet to reappear. Now the reason seemed obvious: the forward hatch was corroded shut and she couldn't exit the cabin's main door without being seen. Eugene, shotgun ready, was waiting on Ricky, who was also wading toward the cruiser. He had a spotlight in one hand, the other using an oar as a crutch.

"*Olive Oyl.* I'll take the hide off you, you don't open that door!" Ricky swung the spotlight to probe the cabin while he confided to Eugene, "They might go out the front. You take this, go around the other side. I'll take the gun."

The men had similar accents, both Westerners, but Eugene's voice had a rougher edge, which was evident when he replied, "Shut up! Pay what you owe me, then you can give orders."

"You little runt! Can't drive a damn boat and now you—"

"I'm sick of your mouth! Hell"—Eugene turned to look at Ricky, the shotgun turning, too—"you're 'bout to fall down, you're so weak. So what you gonna do about it?"

Ricky started to say, "Give me the shotgun, you'll get your money," but stumbled midway because of the rough footing. Which gave Eugene a reason to grin into the spotlight and dismiss the big man with a wave.

"Me, I'm thirsty. I'll drink a beer and worry about witnesses later." But then Eugene hesitated, as if undecided, while Ricky leaned on the oar to catch his breath, the two of them only fifteen yards of water away from the boarding platform.

One or both men would be on the cruiser within minutes, so I didn't see what happened next. If Olivia wasn't coming out, I'd have to pry open the forward hatch and make her. Or . . . risk timing the spotlight just right and sneak in through the cabin door. The door was faster but too dangerous, so there was only one smart choice.

After avoiding another swing of the light, I crawled fast as I could go to the front of the boat. In my mind, I was picturing Olivia standing on the hatch door and wondered if her weight— which wasn't much—had somehow crimped the hinges. What I *hoped* was the girl hadn't locked the hatch from inside. That would have been suicide, and she had already spoken about her beliefs on the matter.

No . . . Olivia didn't want to die because, as I drew closer to the hatch, I could hear her thumping a wooden object against the thing, trying to force the lid open. My spirits brightened, but relief doesn't solve problems. What could I use to help her? To let Olivia know she wasn't

327

alone, I tapped the hatch three times, then my brain went to work after hearing three eager taps in reply. Fisherman's pliers wouldn't offer much leverage, the little flashlight in my pocket even less. I had to find another way.

Ricky—or whoever was now holding the spotlight—was painting the cabin again, wading to get a look at the cruiser from a different angle. The change put me in danger but also helped me to scan the deck for a tool. As I watched, the beam touched the bowsprit . . . a coil of rope where the seat of my jeans had landed earlier . . . an anchor with wide flukes . . . a stainless steel windlass that was used to winch the anchor off the bottom.

*The windlass!* I could use the crank handle as a lever. If that didn't work, I could clove-hitch a rope to the hatch and winch the stubborn thing out by the roots if needed.

A lever was a simpler solution, though. Quieter, too. First, though, I had to tell Olivia to stop making noise, which I did by conversing through a wind scoop:

"I'll get you out, don't make another sound. *Olivia . . . ?*"

"The damn thing's stuck!"

I hadn't put my face to a vent to test the air, but what I smelled was unmistakable. *"The propane!"* I hissed. "Turn off the gas, you're no killer!"

In reply, I heard, "He'll never stop looking for me!"

Knowing what I knew about Ricky Meeks, it was the sad, scary truth, and I was in no position to judge. My main worry was that the girl would kill herself, too, but there was no time for discussion. So I went after the winch handle, crawling on hands and knees toward the bowsprit. As I reached the coil of anchor line, though, the spotlight forced me to my belly by panning across the bow. Then Eugene's voice froze me, saying, "There's something ain't right about this. You sure that Smith girl fried her cooling system?"

The plodding rhythm of men walking in shallow water stopped abruptly. It seemed a long time before Ricky answered, "What'd you see?"

"I think your damn boat's empty, that's what I see so far! Did she kill her engine or not?"

I sensed the light pivoting toward me, one of the men curious about what he'd seen on the bow. I stopped breathing, alert to any nuance in the conversation that might signal I'd been spotted.

Ricky's voice: "You forget I took her boat keys? Just do what you're told to do before I pass out."

Eugene: "Smart-ass answer for everything, don't you? Die anytime you want—long as it's after I've got cash in my hand."

A white tube of light illuminated the deck around me, then hovered like a flare. I tried to melt my body into the fiberglass, my face in the doughnut of coiled rope. The light lingered for so long that the odor of salted nylon stayed in my nose for seconds after the light had pivoted away in search of a new interest. Nor did I immediately move. It was because of what my eyes had found inside the coil where I'd plopped down after the rotten branch had hit water. Even in darkness, beneath a nest of leaves and broken twigs, Uncle Jake's custom pistol glowed with silver residual light.

Behind me, there was another thump of wood hitting fiberglass, then the squeak of a corroded hinge. I looked and saw Olivia's hand feeling around for the lip of the hatch door. She'd broken the thing free! But the men were so close, they'd heard it, too.

Ricky: "Boat's empty, huh? Dumbass—get moving!" Then in a louder voice: "Hannah Smith! You'll get your head blown off, you try tricking me again! *Olive?* Help that bitch instead of helping your husband, I'll take me a new bride and make you watch!"

In fact, I was the one helping Olivia, after scampering to the broken hatch, the weight of a nine-millimeter pistol in my hand. I tried to lift the door, then put my shoulder against it while the girl pushed from below. Corroded aluminum becomes pliant as leather just before it snaps if you jimmy it back and forth enough. The hinges were gradually bending while the men continued to talk, their footsteps muted by deepening water where the cruiser floated.

Eugene: *"Somebody's* in there, the boat's rocking. Why you think she has all the lights on?"

Ricky: "Damn it all . . . mud just took my shoe. Don't *wait* on me!"

"Like bait, so I'm the first one she shoots. There better be some cold beer or—*Hey!* . . . You smell something?"

"Keep your paws outta that refrigerator! Olive's just happy her boyfriends are home, that's all. Goddamn mud . . . lose a shoe after everything else."

"*Propane.* Ricky, you don't smell that? Somebody left the . . . it's propane gas! Don't light a cigarette."

"Then get rid of the one in your mouth, buddy rough. I've had twelve-year-old girls weren't as nervous . . . OLIVE OYL! THIS THE LAST TIME I'M GONNA SAY IT!"

"You don't got to scream at a woman."

"The midget expert offering Big Ricky Meeks advice."

Which is when Eugene's voice called, *"Olivia?* It's me. We're coming aboard, Olivia darlin', so be sweet. Hear?"

I had both hands on the hatch when I felt the cruiser shift beneath a man's weight, then list again to port beneath more weight. It scared me

331

so badly, a charge of adrenaline provided extra strength, and the hinges snapped free with a gunshot *WHAP!* Instantly, Olivia's beach bag appeared on the deck, the girl right behind it, whispering, *"Run! They're coming through the door!"*

Not both men, though. Olivia had dropped over the safety railing to the ground first, and I had one leg over the rail when the spotlight flashed on, blinding me from twenty yards away. It was a man the size of Ricky Meeks behind the light, a shotgun in his hand—and probably wearing the shoe he'd lied about losing just to trick us.

"I warned you women!" Ricky screamed. "Freeze right there!"

Too late. The light knocked me backward off the boat, but I wouldn't have obeyed him anyway. When I landed hard on my shoulder at the water's edge, Olivia was there. She helped me to my feet, then tried to push me into the mangroves. I balked, though, because flashbulbs were going off behind my eyes, plus I had to make sure I hadn't lost the pistol again. I hadn't, but it gave Ricky the second he needed to find us with the spotlight and yell, "I'll shoot!"

Olivia hesitated, her face as pale as a flower in the harsh light, but then sprinted for the shadows. I tried to follow, even blind as I was, but smacked chest first into a tree and fell again.

Ricky pulled the trigger.

# Twenty-six

When I was middle school age, maybe twelve or fourteen, Loretta ordered me to set fire to the woodpile because bumblebees had built a nest in the ground beneath it. She was convinced it was true because bees had chased her from the chimney side of the house almost to the dock, and Loretta is not a woman who enjoys exercise, particularly running from bees.

"I had a Great-aunt Rosy—on my grandma's side—who was stung to death fetching firewood," she had explained. "So our smell might be something insects sense. You know—that runs in the family? I'm only thinking of your own good, Hannah, since the one in charge of wood, come winter, is the most likely to be killed. Plus, you're faster."

Not fast enough to outrun a tornado of bumblebees that came spinning out of the ground when I lit that fire. For protection, I'd worn socks as gloves, a hat with mosquito netting, and a U.S. Army jacket my father had left behind. The khaki weave had felt thick enough but wasn't, so I suffered four or five hot-poker stings before diving off the dock to safety.

*Bumblebee stings.* When Ricky Meeks fired the

shotgun, the pain was similar. Like a couple of hot needles had jabbed me. Not enough pain to keep me on the ground, though, especially with Olivia pulling me by the arm again, yelling, "Run!"

I did—but only after I'd grabbed the pistol.

With Olivia leading, we climbed over roots, crashed through limbs that tore at our clothing, putting all the distance we could between us and the next gunshot. It was too dark to see anything but ghostly shapes, even though my vision was improving. Every yard was painful. Olivia caught her ankle on a root and almost fell. A stub of broken limb pierced my jeans near the thigh, which hurt worse than the pellets that still stung my arm. Which is why we hadn't gotten far when Ricky yelled, "I see you!" and fired again —*BOOM!*

Shotgun pellets buzzed us, slowed by a flurry of mangrove confetti, leaves and twigs that rained down on our heads. The shot caused us to stop and crouch low, waiting for more. Instead, all we heard was the man's labored footsteps splashing near the front of the cruiser, and Eugene's voice from inside, calling, "What the hell's going on?"

Instead of answering, Meeks leaned his weight against the boat, waist-deep in water, and used the powerful beam to poke among the trees. If the man couldn't hear us, I realized, he might be unable to find us. Even if he'd lied about losing a shoe, he was still weak. He didn't want to risk such a wild thicket—not in pursuit of a woman who'd already shot him once. The same woman getting ready to shoot him again . . . and that's exactly what I had decided to do.

*No choice,* my mind was telling me, and I knew it was true. Which was why I had dropped to one knee, to steady myself, while using both hands to level the pistol. Dark as it was, Olivia knew what I was doing. She touched a shaking hand to my back, a silent question between two people with much in common: *Are you sure?*

I nodded yes, pleased when the girl removed her hand. Concentration was required.

Trouble was, I couldn't see Ricky any better than he could see us—even if he'd guessed right with the spotlight. We were separated by walls of vines and limbs a lot thicker than any Army jacket. The only space that appeared cleanly over the pistol's sights was the cruiser's prow, a few feet below the bowsprit. It was where Ricky's head would appear, I guessed, if he moved a few feet, so I held the pistol steady and waited.

From inside the cabin, Eugene yelled, "Goddamn it, answer me!"

"Get your ass out here and help search!" Meeks railed back and then turned to his right as if he'd heard something unexpected. When he did it, the left side of his face appeared briefly above the pistol . . . but I missed my chance because my finger wasn't on the trigger. It is a safety procedure I had been taught—the correct way, too—but kneeling in a swamp, waiting to shoot a man who has vowed to rape and kill you, is an unusual circumstance.

My trigger finger dropped to where it needed to be.

Ricky was still behaving as if he'd heard something, so I tilted my head to listen. It took a moment, but my ears found it: foliage rustling not far away, an animal with enough weight to crush branches as it pushed closer. Meeks, of course, suspected it was Olivia and me, sneaking away. Why two women would move toward a killer wielding a shotgun, was a question Ricky probably should have asked himself, but he didn't.

Instead, he swung the spotlight toward a patch of tree canopy that was moving and ignored Eugene, who yelled, "I want paid first! Go ahead and get yourself killed! Me, I'm gonna find a beer."

Ricky had no interest. From where I knelt, it appeared as if he shouldered the shotgun and waded a few steps toward the noise, but I couldn't be sure. The animal was bigger, moving faster than I'd realized, judging from the way trees parted as it advanced. Which, for the first time, caused me to remember that animals can wind-scent blood from miles away. Meat eaters, anyway. Sharks . . . vultures . . . saltwater crocs. And Ricky Meeks, waiting there, water up to his belly, in clothes brittle with his own blood—but the Texan didn't possess my local knowledge.

The temptation was to stand and get a better look, and I might have if I hadn't been waiting for a clean shot. And when the spotlight went out for some reason—maybe Meeks had dropped it in his excitement—there was an even better reason to stay put, so I did. In hindsight, it was a lucky decision because we heard Ricky holler, "Jesus Christ!" as if surprised by the sudden darkness. Then he fired the shotgun—*BOOM! . . . BOOM!* Two panicky shots spaced a moment apart before there was a third explosion—*kuh-WHUMPH!*—which wasn't a gunshot at all, although I didn't realize it at first. It was the sound of the cruiser blowing up, caused by propane gas, and something Eugene had done in the cabin—hunting for beer, my guess.

Either the shock wave or the heat blew me backward, along with a storm of foliage that had protected us from the blast. Before I could think about getting to my feet, I was already up and running, pursued by the screams of what might have been a man. I didn't want to risk what awaited my eyes if I turned, so I didn't. Even when I heard an animal crashing through the brush off to my right, I refused to look. Instead, I focused on Olivia's back and followed her as she snaked her way through the jungle. That girl could run!

There was no problem seeing now. Above us, the tree canopy was waxy with light from an inferno that consumed the Skipjack cruiser. Ahead, I could see an incline that told me the shell ridge was near. I had described the ridge to Olivia in case we got separated, but she didn't know the area as well as me so I yelled for her to stop and let me take the lead. The girl did, turning to look with a dazed expression, but then cringed. "You're bleeding!"

At first, I thought she meant my thigh, which was throbbing after being jabbed by a mangrove spike. "My best jeans, too," I replied, "but it doesn't hurt. Are *you* okay?"

Olivia was more concerned with a couple of bloody holes that dotted my Navaho shirt. "He shot you!" she said, using her fingers to explore my left shoulder.

I felt giddy for a moment, thinking, *Not as bad as I shot him,* but said nothing. The tiny pellets didn't hurt any worse than bee stings, a few drops of blood proved I was okay, plus I had noticed my friend's eyes widening at something she saw over my shoulder.

I turned to look, hearing, "Oh my God!" Then Olivia pointed, and asked, *"Hannah?"*

I had been wrong about a saltwater croc. What we'd heard crushing limbs was the two-hundred-pound boar hog that had threatened me earlier. The explosion had spooked it away, but now the

338

animal was returning to the fire, its sensitive snout held high, alert for the scent of a meal.

I knew where the hog was headed because of something else we could see: the blackened form of a man who had to be Ricky Meeks, stumbling through the mangroves, away from the blaze.

When she spotted him, Olivia almost backed a step, but then yelled, "I'm the one who did it, you bastard! *Me*. You stay away from us or . . . you'll be sorry!"

Ricky already was. I watched him drop to one knee . . . stagger forward . . . then clutch the trunk of a tree to rest, smoke rising from his shoulders. The man had lost the shotgun, along with most of his hair and clothes, which was obvious even from a distance. Even so, the girl waited, unconvinced, before repeating her question about pigs. "Hannah, you don't think . . . ?"

I nodded. "They'll eat anything. We can't let that happen . . ." I looked into Olivia's face. *"Can we?"*

In answer, she moved away so I could concentrate—once I had the pistol sights squared. My eyes tracking, the animal trotted like a Sunday horse, a profile of tusks with a spit curl tail, unaware it had been spared when Olivia amended, "No! Just scare the damn thing away!"

Two shots I fired, missing low and to the right. It would have been a disappointment to all of my great-aunts, particularly Hannah One. But it suited me.

# Twenty-seven

According to my mother, who is often wrong, the first full moon in July is called the Thunder Moon by modern Seminoles, a name passed down from pyramid builders who lived on our islands during the time of the Maya.

"Summer squalls!" she explained as if the reason was obvious. "If you expect to enjoy your date tonight, better wear something waterproof —*not* a cocktail dress that shows off what most respectable women keep covered. Including their bullet scars!"

Three dots beneath a Band-Aid did not constitute scars in my experience, so I continued to sip my coffee on this early Friday morning and pretended to listen.

"Who's the new suitor? That pretty lawyer woman who got you off the hook with the police, I bet. Shoot a man in his privates—even one from Ohio or Texas—most islanders would be on death row. I saw the way she looked at you the other night. Chumming up to me like it was my birthday, but it's you she wants to pull the straps and ribbons off of!"

Impressed by Loretta's witchy powers yet again, I raised my eyebrows, then repeated what

I'd said several times in the last three weeks. "Self-defense, Mamma. Instead of arresting me, a sheriff's captain even hinted around about offering me a job. So don't worry your head about death row. Same with Olivia Seasons. Didn't you think she was a sweet girl?"

I tried to keep my tone positive and airy. No need to provide the woman with ammunition by admitting it would be weeks before we were officially cleared—a worry that kept me awake nights—or that Olivia, after brightening enough to attend Chapel By The Sea and go shopping, had lapsed into a depression that required medical treatment. *"Guilt,"* the girl had admitted to me, even though it was her kidnappers—both still in critical condition at Tampa Burn Center—who had to worry about the electric chair.

Loretta had seen me pack the little black cocktail dress, though, and wouldn't drop the subject. "You're gunning for someone tonight," she accused, delighted by the double meaning. "Must be Jake's fishing client, Lawrence what's-his-name. I told you he made a pass at your own aunt, which, of course, didn't faze you. But did I mention he might have offered money? Your Aunt Hannah never traded her body for pay—far as I can *prove,* anyway. That's why I can't help noticing my own daughter, who was raised in the church, is suddenly rich as Croesus—"

I let the woman talk, numb to her tricky method

of asking how I could now afford full-time nursing, a hired van to take her to the Edison Mall once a week, plus a few improvements to the house and dock.

"It's called a bonus, Loretta," I interrupted finally. "It's what a professional investigator gets paid when she does a good job. You can thank me later for having the porch painted, the wiring fixed, and hiring Ralph Woodring to dredge the dock. Next Sunday, you can thank Olivia, too."

True, I'd had our dock basin deepened for my own benefit—and the benefit of the most beautiful boat I'd ever been granted the right to use, let alone live aboard. But the money was mine to spend as I saw fit, which included a nice bonus from Lawrence Seasons, plus an unexpected present from Olivia.

Her gift had come in the form of a manila envelope, which contained what remained of Olivia's private checking account. Even before the Coast Guard helicopter had arrived, she'd thrust it into my hands, insisting I keep the envelope but open it later. To me, thirteen thousand cash is a lot of money, although my millionaire friend would dismiss it as "nothing."

Soon, I would be asking myself why a wealthy heiress would kneel at a mini-fridge to retrieve an amount she considered insignificant. To make room for a device to detonate propane, was the obvious answer, even though police hadn't thought beyond a cigarette. Last night, Olivia had been strong enough for me to finally ask another question investigators had not:

*"What did Eugene see, Olivia, when he opened that door to get a beer?"*

It felt good when the girl entrusted me—only me—with the truth, although I was still surprised by her careful answer.

*"A candle will burn for more than twenty minutes in a sealed refrigerator. A friend of yours timed it."*

I was less surprised by the act itself. The Bible verse that had inspired Olivia wasn't the 91st Psalm, as I'd recommended. She had memorized a tougher verse from the Book of Kings and even recited it as we drifted in the Gulf, the lights of the Coast Guard helicopter finally in sight:

*"You have done more evil to your slaves than all who lived before . . . I, the LORD, will burn you up as one burns trash until it is gone . . . then you will be eaten by dogs, as those who die in the field will be eaten by vultures."*

Olivia and I were friends, good friends, and becoming closer, but it would be a while—after a mojito or two, perhaps—before I could allow myself the irreverence of suggesting that "dog" had been a misprint in the Holy Scripture.

As mother talked, she was lounging in her La-Z-Boy next to the fireplace where, even on a July morning, the owl andirons blinked at me as warmly as they had when I was a girl on winter nights. While I finished my coffee, she cranked the chair's handle, got to her feet, and marched to the window as if to prove something.

"No clouds yet. What time's your date? By six we'll have wind, she'll be pouring by seven— and don't say I didn't warn you!"

Loretta spoke in such a wistful way, I had to smile. "I hope it *does* rain!" I replied and meant it. The reason had to do with Marion Ford, who had invited me to look through his telescope after dinner. It was our third date in three weeks—if you counted an afternoon spent fly-casting for tarpon, another slogging through the mudflats. And I did even if he didn't. So far, the biologist had been fun, attentive, easy to be with, respectful, and *very* proper, but that's all.

I appreciate good manners in a man, but his passion for improper behavior had become a more interesting quality, which I could now admit. After three formal dates—*sort of*—and several phone conversations—brief as they were—we'd both proven our respectability. Now I was willing to risk Marion Ford's transgressions —*if* he could be maneuvered into trying.

The biologist had a way about him. His low voice vibrated through my rib cage when he spoke. The spark of our elbows bumping hummed in my abdomen for hours. Quiet as he was, Marion Ford had something boiling inside him.

Rage or passion, darkness or light, I had yet to find out, but my bawdy aunt's journal had hinted at both, as I'd discovered by rereading it the night before. I'd also learned from her writing that the biologist and his strange hippie friend both had a fondness for storms. Maybe a good soaking was just the thing to loosen Marion Ford's behavior.

That's why Loretta had failed to dampen my spirits on this summer morning by threatening my evening with a Thunder Moon that brought rain.

Instead of stumping her, though, my optimism about bad weather only provided another opening to show off the powers God has granted Loretta after damaging her brain with a stroke.

"I bet you do hope it storms!" she cackled. "A real frog choker. One of those Gulfstream thunder-boomers that causes men to puff up, throw the covers back, and a single woman to jump. A skimpy black dress and lightning. I'd call that an unfair way to trap an innocent man"—my mother turned to smile at me—"if I didn't know what a good girl my sweet Hannah is."

Because the last part sounded more like the mother who'd raised me, I had to clear my throat while I checked my watch. It was morning twilight, birds outside twittering, impatient for the heat of sunrise. I had a full day ahead of me. While Loretta continued to ramble, I stood and took my cup to the kitchen.

Lawrence Seasons and Martha Calder-Shaun

were expecting me by ten a.m. to sign insurance papers and to discuss an LLC for my investigation agency—a business I'd agreed to continue as long as I could still book charters on the side. Since having a private talk with Martha, I no longer felt uneasy around the woman. In fact, I liked her better. I had been right to suspect she knew more about *Sybarite* than she'd admitted but wrong about her knowing—or warning—Ricky Meeks.

"Sure, I considered doing the Key West cruise," Martha had explained. "Sounds like it could be a lot of fun—with the right people. But I had nothing to add *factually* when you brought it up. You disapprove on some kind of moral grounds? That's your problem, kiddo, not mine. But it's not illegal—and why risk pissing off Larry?"

The woman was plainspoken, a trait I admire, which is why I had offered to give her fly-casting lessons during her next visit to the islands. In return, she'd agreed to give up on seducing me.

"It would've turned into a brawl, anyway," the attorney had smiled, and then added something rude about both of us battling to be on top.

Something I still felt uneasy about, though, was posing in Darren's studio. Around one p.m., I would be having lunch with the photographer and Nathan to talk about scheduling what Darren referred to as "your first sitting." Whether there would be a second sitting, let alone a first, was something I didn't mind discussing if it made

Nathan happy. But there was too much happening in my life to make a decision today.

Plus, I didn't have time to pose. At five, I was supposed to be at Elka Whitney's house for drinks and a movie. An old one that the breakfast cereal heiress had selected after one of our nightly phone sessions: *Double Indemnity*, starring Fred MacMurray and Barbara Stanwyck. Elka had been uncommonly sweet to me after hearing some of what had happened on Drake Key, so we had shared movies and conversation often during the last three weeks. That would give me just enough time to shower and change before meeting the biologist at his lab. Sunset and moonrise are simultaneous, as they always are on a full moon, so Marion had told me to be at Dinkin's Bay, where his lab was located, around eight.

While I moved around the old house, collecting my things, Loretta remained at the window, a new subject on her mind.

"They still talk to me at night, you know. Mothers crying, a famous Indian king bawling for revenge. Who else they got to comfort them, now you've gotten rich?" She was referring to the centuries of people her new neighbors had displaced with a septic tank, so I listened more closely. After all, a smart man—strange as he was—had taken my mother's claims seriously. As a daughter, it would have been rude not to show similar respect.

"Have you taken a look at the Mausoleum lately?" Loretta asked me.

I stopped what I was doing and glanced over. Locals usually referred to the concrete structure as "the Walmart" or "The Bunker," as if Nazis had built the thing.

"Tomlinson called it that," I remembered, then walked to join my mother at the window. "He still stops by?"

"Tomlin-who? Oh . . . you mean *Tommy*. Tommy Scarecrow, that's his Indian name. Him, me, and Billie Egret, we've done three ceremonies to purify what those stupid fools have done. Build a big fire in the ceremonial plaza, chant, and smoke the pipe. Billie, he's teaching me the Green Corn Dance. In return, I tell him secrets the ancient king says in my ear at night. The king gives me orders sometimes."

*Smoke?* The news hit me harder than her claim of conversing with dead royalty. My mother had never smoked in her life. Could the contents of that ceremonial pipe explain why she had been so spunky of late? According to some things I'd heard about Tomlinson, it was possible. Before I could ask, though, she made enough room at the window for me to view the structure that had decapitated three thousand years of Florida history. The concrete walls had been too dark to see when I'd arrived that morning. Now I could.

"My Lord," I moaned. "Not again, Loretta!"

Instead of Day-Glo orange, she had used a brush and the same color of citrus yellow I had paid painters to use on the porch.

"You try refusing a dead Indian king!" the woman pouted, but then took the offensive. "Besides, Scarecrow held the ladder for me, so it was safe. Tommy's got backbone! He's the one you should be wearing skimpy dresses to impress. That man's as smart and sweet as they come—plus he's got ways of making a woman smile."

My bawdy Aunt Hannah had felt the same about Tomlinson, from what I'd read in her journal. But I'd also read interesting details about my date, Dr. Ford, that made me want to reply something tart.

So I did. But not before hugging my mother close and steering her to the porch to get a clear view of the dock. "I've stopped settling for second best," I explained, meaning Tomlinson, then nodded toward the water. "Why would I?"

Moored to the dock, the hull of my new home glowed midnight blue in the fresh sunlight, floating weightless as an orchid, as free as a swan.

# About the Author

Randy Wayne White is the author of nineteen Doc Ford novels—most recently *Deep Shadow*, *Night Vision*, and *Chasing Midnight*—and four nonfiction collections. A onetime veteran fishing guide, he lives in an old house on an Indian mound and spends much of his free time windsurfing, playing baseball, and hanging out at Doc Ford's Sanibel Rum Bar & Grille on Sanibel Island, Florida.

## Center Point Large Print
600 Brooks Road / PO Box 1
Thorndike ME 04986-0001 USA

(207) 568-3717

US & Canada:
1 800 929-9108
www.centerpointlargeprint.com